QUARTER SHARE

For more information or to leave a comment about this book,
please visit us on the web at:
www.solarclipper.com

To my wife, Kay

For twenty-seven years she put up with my wanting to be a writer.
For the last three, shes put up with my being a writer.

Now I have to put up a book shelf.

The Golden Age of the Solar Clipper

Quarter Share
Half Share
Full Share
Double Share
Captains Share
Owners Share

South Coast
Cape Grace*

Tanyth Fairport Adventures

Ravenwood
Zypherias Call
The Hermit Of Lammas Wood*

* Forthcoming

QUARTER SHARE

NATHAN LOWELL

Durandus

Chapter One
Neris: 2351-August-13

Call me Ishmael. Yeah, I know, but in this case it's really my name. Ishmael Horatio Wang. My parents had an unfortunate sense of humor. If they had known what I'd wind up doing with my life, they might have picked a different one—Richard Henry Dana, perhaps. Exactly why they picked Ishmael Horatio is a long, and not terribly interesting, story that starts with the fact that Mom was an ancient lit professor and ends with my being saddled with these non sequitur monikers.

That particular story was over eighteen stanyers before the two Neris Company security guards showed up at my door with long faces and low voices. Perhaps it was their expressions, or that they were looking for me and not Mom, but either way I knew their visit wasn't good. I didn't think they had come to drag me off to juvie or anything. I'd never been a troublemaker like some of the others in the university enclave. They had come for me though—to tell me she was dead.

"Flitter crash," the tall one said.

They're not very common but you do hear about them from time to time. You always expect it to happen to somebody else. It wasn't even her flitter. It belonged to Randy Lawrence, her boyfriend.

"He's dead too," the short one explained.

They spoke gently, their words washing past me. Nothing seemed to stick. The security people weren't going to put me in foster care or anything. Eighteen stanyers made me old enough to live by myself on Neris. Eventually they stopped talking, and I never even noticed when they left.

We had been on our own if you didn't count the Randys, the Davids, and the occasional Dorises for most of my life. Dad was somewhere in the Diurnia Quadrant. He'd never been a big influence and I didn't even know what system he was in.

With Mom gone, I was alone—really alone—for the first time in my life. It wasn't the standard, *I've got the apartment to myself for a couple of stans* kind of thing, but a deep and utter sense of loss. For a time I just walked from room to room in a kind of daze. I woke the next day sprawled across the couch but didn't remember even lying down. As bad as the night had been, morning brought something worse—lawyers.

First, the plantation attorney showed up and notified me that the Neris Company intended to sue for damages to the granapple vineyards where the flitter crashed. "We're sorry, Mr. Wang," she said although there was no hint of regret in her voice. "Mr. Lawrence had inadequate insurance to cover this kind of damage. In order to protect our client's investment, we have filed liens to appropriate compensation."

I glared at her. "So, what does this have to do with me?"

She examined her paperwork as she spoke, "We are in the unenviable position of placing liens against *both* estates since there is no way to determine who was piloting the craft. The flitter came apart in midair, you see. The falling debris and... er... remains damaged an estimated square kilometer of vines."

That was really more detail than I wanted.

As she was leaving another company lawyer arrived with an eviction notice. Mom was—had been—a Neris Company employee and a member of the faculty at the university for years. Since I was no longer a dependent, I had just ninety local-days to find employment or leave the planet. Survivor benefits would have applied if she'd been killed on the job. Dying on her day off didn't count.

In the middle of the afternoon, an email from Human Resources informed me there were no openings available for unskilled labor. As Neris was a company planet, the Neris Company was the only game in town, so I figured I'd be leaving.

The last piece of that day's bad news came from the family solicitor assigned by the company. He showed up wearing a rumpled suit and a tie that looked as tired as he did. "Mr. Wang," he began after we'd settled at the kitchen table. "I'm so sorry for your loss." Of all my visitors that day, he actually seemed to have meant it. "I don't want to take up more of your time than necessary, but you need to know where you stand with regard to your late mother's estate."

I nodded for him to go on.

"There isn't one." When he saw the look on my face, he shrugged. "I should say there's not much of one. As a faculty member, your mother didn't earn a great deal. It was enough for the two of you to live in relative comfort, but there wasn't much left over." He almost sounded apologetic.

I almost felt sorry for him.

He took out the paperwork then, her life insurance, will, and the settlement forms from the vineyard liens. We spent the next half-stan going through them in blur of sign here, and here, and here. Finally I had to sign the insurance forms to receive a check which was the payout amount adjusted for the plantation claim and cremation costs. The NerisCo people were efficient; I had to give them that. Barely a day had passed and my mother's remaining net worth was in my hands. It would be enough to cover my rent for the ninety days and I'd have a bit left over. I could accept it or fight and become tied up in probate with Neris Company arbitrators, and Neris Company lawyers, for the next Neris Company stanyear.

Company planets suck. I signed. What else could I do?

❀   ❀   ❀

Three days later, a courier delivered the urn containing my mother's ashes. I placed it on the coffee table. She'd liked coffee, and we'd spent a lot of time sitting there with our feet up, talking—mugs of fragrant brew in hand.

That was it. Nobody else showed up, not my mates from the enclave, not company people, not Mom's colleagues from the university—nobody.

To be fair, I didn't have a lot of friends to begin with. I'd read about best friends in novels and such, but I'd never actually had one. Angela Markova had been the closest thing when I was a kid, but she left Neris at the end of fifth form when her father took a job with another company. I'd never really found anyone to take her place.

Something about being booted off-planet made you an instant pariah—no need to add water. I'd seen it before when people ran afoul of the company. Within ninety planetary days, I'd have to be gone. Nobody would bother to reach out to me in the short time I had left.

For more than a week I went through the motions of what would be considered a normal life. Eventually, the voice in my head stopped saying, "I can't believe she's dead," and shifted to, "*Now* what am I going to do?"

In a month I was supposed to start at the university. Growing up with a professor, I really didn't have a choice. We'd had several long, and occasionally heated, discussions on the subject. I hadn't wanted to make a decision about what to do with the rest of my life with so much of it left ahead of me. Over time, I'd come to believe there might be some value in getting a degree in plant biology. If nothing else, signing up for college had gotten my mother to stop bugging me about it.

As a company planet, the University of Neris restricted enrollment to employees and their families, but even so it had a surprisingly good curriculum and one of the best biology departments in the quadrant. Its reputation was bolstered by being on a planet full of granapple vineyards. The university's standing, combined with the corporate incentive provided to dependents of university staff, made U of N a good option.

I just didn't know what to do with myself when that option expired.

❀   ❀   ❀

By the end of the second week, it became clear that I had a serious problem. Passage off-planet cost more than I had—a lot more—several kilocreds more. I couldn't afford to buy passage, and I couldn't stay. NerisCo would repatriate me to the nearest non-company system, Siren, but they would charge me for the ticket and I'd start my new life deep in debt.

I needed work that would pay to get me off-planet. Unfortunately, I could only see two options left: enlisting in the military, or signing on with one of the merchant vessels that visited periodically. The Galactic Marines recruited aggressively on Neris. There were always kids looking for any way to get out from underneath the company, but I knew I could never be a marine. I lacked the soldierly instinct and that whole killing and dying thing wasn't for me, so my only real choice was the Union Hall. I confess I really didn't want to go there either, but beggars have few choices.

The next morning, I gathered my courage and trammed over to Neris Port. It was one of those perfect, bright, warm days when the soft breezes carried the spicy, tart smell of granapples out of the vineyards and into every corner of the town. The delicate bouquet covered even the hot-circuit board smell of the tram. It made everything seem too cheerful and pleasant. I hated it.

The Union Hall occupied a refurbished hangar at the edge of the shuttle port. When I stepped in out of the sun, the cavernous hall felt cool and smelled faintly of an institutional-grade floor wax. My footfalls echoed from the far wall as I walked past a row of data terminals and a long counter with five workstations, only one of which seemed to be in use. Aside from the functionary behind the counter, a slightly scary looking older fem with an artificial left arm, I was the only person there. It took my eyes a few seconds to adjust to the light level, and by then I had reached her station.

"Whaddya want, kid?" Her voice bounced off the ceiling.

I crossed to her position at the counter, noted her nametag said "O'Rourke." I smiled tentatively at her and said, "I need to get off-planet."

"Son, this is the hirin' hall. The ticket office is down thata way. Just keep goin'. Ya can't miss it." She smiled a bit nastily I thought and pointed with an artificial finger.

"I can't afford a ticket. I need to get a job that will give me transport."

O'Rourke looked hard at me. "Ya need a lot more'n that, I'd wager. Ya lookin' to hire onto a ship?"

I nodded dumbly.

"Ya ever sign The Articles before, kid?"

I could hear the capital letters in *The Articles* as she spoke the words. I shook my head.

O'Rourke rubbed the back of her neck with her good hand and cast a why me look up at the ceiling. Finally, she sighed. "Okay, kid, everybody has a story. What's yours?"

I didn't know how much to tell her, so I gave her the rough outline. "I was supposed to start at the university next month. My mom is—was—a professor there, but she died in a flitter crash. Now the company says I have to get off-planet because she's no longer employed, and I'm no longer a dependent."

O'Rourke stared for a moment but then something changed in her expression. "Good story. Where's yer card?"

I pulled out my identification and slotted it into her reader. My particulars popped up on the display. O'Rourke examined it, scrolling and *tsk'ing* as she scrolled. She'd only checked through date of birth, and education level, before starting to shake her head. "Forget it." Her voice was not unkind but she also didn't look at me. "No specialty and you're just barely eighteen. Technically, I could offer The Articles, but we got no open berths for quarter shares just now."

I wondered what language she was speaking for a half dozen heartbeats before she noticed my complete lack of comprehension. She explained again, slowly, "You're old enough to be contracted, but ya need to have a ship willin' to hire ya—give ya a berth—before ya can get a job. With this skill level, that means somethin' entry-level, what we call a quarter share, and nobody's got an open one on file." She pointed at the data screens mounted on the wall. "We have three ships in port now, and two inbound over the next week or so. Only one with a postin' is the *Cleveland Maru* but that's a full share berth and you're not qualified."

I examined the scrolling display carefully and it seemed to confirm what she had said. The listing showing CleveMar had an AG2 position, whatever that was.

"What's all this stuff mean?" I pointed at the display. My brain had already shut down, although I hadn't realized it, and my mouth engaged without conscious control.

She considered me for a tick, and then shrugged. "Sit down, kid. I'll show ya a few things." She took me to one of the dataport alcoves and demonstrated the use of the terminal. It allowed spacers to scroll through the various jobs, ships, and companies. I'd seen help wanted posts on NerisNet before, but this was a whole different bag of granapples. The display showed ship names, company affiliations, size, cargo capacity, propulsion systems, and even a list of the berths. The default setting showed only the openings, but with a little manipulation, I could find out how many positions of each kind were on every ship.

After a few ticks of walking me through the controls, O'Rourke went back to her place at the counter. I could see what she meant about the open slots. I went through each ship's particulars. Her summary of the situation seemed to be depressingly accurate. As large as the ships were, they didn't need a lot of crew. Out of that small number, the entry-level quarter share ones accounted for only a tiny fraction.

"What's a share?" I asked, calling to her from where I sat.

"A share is extra pay ya get if the voyage is profitable. Owners, captains, and the other officers get the most, but everybody gets somethin'," she called back.

"So in an entry-level position, I'd get a quarter of a share?"

"Yeah, but don't be plannin' to retire on it. It's not much. Better than a spanner to the cranium, but it isn't all that many creds."

As I looked through each quarter share listing: engine wiper, mess deck attendant, cargo loader, I realized these were the dirtiest tasks and probably boring to boot. I sighed. Beggars, as they say, can't be choosers. Unfortunately, even begging couldn't get me a job where none existed. I shut down the terminal and headed for the exit.

"Thank you, Ms. O'Rourke," I called over my shoulder, as I braced myself to step back into the midday glare.

"Hey, kid, if ya're serious about gettin' a berth, pack a bag and be ready to go."

I stopped with my hand on the door feeling like a big, cartoon question mark floated over my head.

O'Rourke beckoned me to the counter. "I like ya. Ya remind me of my nephew. Here's how this really works. No ship will pull in here with an open quarter share, but they often unload a troublemaker. Some idiot signs on but then doesn't pull his weight. He gets here, to the ass-end of nowhere, and put ashore with no income and no way home. A few days dirt-side gives him a bit of motivation, so to speak, to do better. Of course, that leaves the ship short-handed."

"And if I'm ready to ship out?"

"Well," she said slyly, "ya'd have to be ready to go on a few stans notice and can't take much with ya. Twenty kilos is the mass allotment for a quarter share. But ya don't need clothes and there's hygiene gear on the ship. Only thing ya really need to take is entertainment cubes and personal stuff."

"I don't need clothes?"

"Shipsuits, lad, shipsuits. They come with the berth. Ya pay for them out of yer first few chits. But they don't count against yer mass allotment. One change of civvies will get ya through, if ya're careful with 'em." She smiled at me, and I felt she'd just given me some valuable insight. I only had to figure out what it was.

"Thanks, Ms. O'Rourke. How will you contact me?"

She pointed to the display that still had my data on it. With a couple of keystrokes, she saved it and gave me a broad wink. "I think I'll be able to find ya, kid. If ya're serious, be ready. The *Lois McKendrick* is comin' in late next week. Rumor has it she's got some deadwood that needs seasonin' dirt-side. That gives ya about ten days to get ready." She pulled a data cube from a rack under the counter and tossed it to me. "Here, read up. It'll save ya some problems down the line."

I nodded with a smile of thanks, stuffed the cube in my pocket, and headed home to figure out what to take with me. How do you fit a whole life into twenty kilos?

It didn't take long to get back to the flat I'd shared with my mother. It still felt weird walking in and knowing she wasn't there— that I was really alone.

The hardest part was going through her personal things. It made me a bit queasy dealing with her underwear drawer. I felt silly for being so squeamish. I had folded her bras and panties hundreds of times while doing laundry, but this was different somehow. Finally, I took her suits and dresses to the local charity drop. I just emptied the rest into the refuse bin without really looking.

She had a ton of professional stuff like books and papers and such. Her peeda had been with her, and lost in the flitter, of course. She had left a portable computer though. I donated her books to the library, while her pictures, data cubes, and records went into storage boxes. I packed her diplomas on top. Altogether it didn't amount to much, maybe a hundred kilos in five boxes.

In contrast, looking around my own room, I realized I could walk away and probably wouldn't miss any of it. My peeda was already stocked and I had some spare storage cubes and my good boots. The problem was my bag. I only had a heavy suitcase. It massed three kilos empty and seemed kind of clunky.

❀　　❀　　❀

After three days of sorting, tossing, filing, and just generally working my way through the flat, I finally finished. I took out O'Rourke's data cube and slotted it into my peeda. The title was *The Spacer's Handbook* published by the Confederated Planets Joint Committee on Trade. The CPJCT, it turned out, was the arbiter of all things trading related. The cube reminded me of the scout manual I had as a kid. It had everything you needed to know about being a spacer: what to wear, how to wear it, and when and whom to salute. A little holo clip showed the proper technique for the last. The saluting part wasn't too difficult, and you only did that under special circumstances, and only to officers.

The manual listed the various ranks and shares: quarter share, half share, full share, and on up to owner's share. The thing was huge. I checked the size on the chip and gasped when I saw just how big it was. The Encyclopedia Galactica was smaller. I hoped I wouldn't need to read the whole thing.

The introductory chapter caught my eye with a small section titled: *Shipping Out*. It explained the mass allotment increased as you rose through the ranks. As O'Rourke had said, the shipsuits were provided and items like toothpaste, shampoo, and shaving gear were all standardized and available on board. *The Handbook* recommended that a new shipmate should report wearing decent civilian attire and not worry about a change of clothing. The illustration showed a somewhat dated picture of what a well-dressed person might wear to a casual dinner with a friend. The jackpot in this section was the recommendation of the duffel bag for loading your gear. The lightweight mono-mol bag encompassed almost a half-cubic meter of volume, but massed less than twenty grams and could be folded up to about the size of a handkerchief when empty. Spacers considered it a standard and, according to *The Handbook*, "could be purchased at a reasonable cost at any Union Hall." I smiled, thinking I should pay another visit to my friend O'Rourke. In the meantime, I started weighing out gear on the bathroom scale.

Twenty kilos turned out to be a lot.

Chapter Two
Neris: 2351-September-03

My peeda trilled sharply, jarring me awake. The display showed a simple text message from O'Rourke: Time to go! I was more than ready. I wanted to get on with it before the anticipation drove me crazy, or my money ran out. While the payout from the company had been enough to cover ninety days' rent, I had other expenses to cover and my funds evaporated at an alarming rate. The sooner I stopped paying to live on Neris, the better.

Shipping the personal artifacts turned out to be part of Mom's employment contract. A team from Neris showed up to take our stuff to a storage facility on Siren. Mom had designated it as origin-of-record on the employment forms but I didn't recall any connection we had there. I think she named it because it was the nearest Confederation planet. The storage company would keep our stuff as long as I made the payments. Pre-paying for a stanyear took a big hit to my cred reserve, but at least I wouldn't have to worry about it.

Between O'Rourke and *The Handbook*, I'd managed to get my duffel properly stenciled with my name and ID. In the end, I'd kept Mom's computer, a relatively new portable model. It had processing capabilities that my peeda didn't. Her computer credentials gave me almost unlimited access to the university and I used them until administration cut me off. I got quite a bit of stuff downloaded including materials on astrogation, environmental sciences, advanced math, accounting, materials sciences, and even some on plant biology. These were all subjects recommended as useful by *The Handbook*. They looked overwhelming, but I burned them onto cubes and stashed them in my duffel. Even with the holo and music cubage, I was way under my allotment and only had about eight kilos.

I tossed what few things remained into the disposer, and shouldered the nearly empty duffel bag. At the door, I stopped and looked back before flipping the light switch. I could feel a lump start to harden in my throat and my eyes water. This apartment had been home for most of my life and I was walking away forever—the connections severed cleanly, surgically. I looked around, smiling at the memories and listening for the echoes of our time in the flat. In the end, I heard nothing except the soft whooshing of the environmentals. I flipped off the lights and locked the door behind me for the last time.

When I got to the Union Hall, it was a madhouse. For the first time I saw somebody there besides O'Rourke or the Assistant Hall Manager, a mousy man named Fredericks who didn't talk much. People filled the hall. They queued up in lines to use the data ports or waited to see O'Rourke or Fredericks. All of them talked loudly to each other and their accumulated voices made the huge, echoing space almost unbearable.

Shrugging off the sensory assault, I got into O'Rourke's line and arrived at the counter in a surprisingly short time. She smiled when she saw me. "You ready to go, kid? There's no backin' out once yer under Articles."

I nodded. I knew the drill from *The Handbook*. Once I signed, I would be committing to serve for two stanyers. It wasn't quite the military, but it was close and I had no other options. This door opened on a new future. My tongue stuck to the inside of my mouth and my stomach cramped. "Yeah, I'm as sure as I can be. Thanks for everything, Ms. O'Rourke."

She smiled wider at that. "Good to go then, lad." She pressed the buzzer that opened the counter and nodded toward a door. "Through there. Captain Giggone will want to talk to ya. Pass the interview and we can get ya processed." She winked. "I put in a good word for ya so don't make me look bad."

Swallowing hard, I pushed through the gate and into the office. A harried-looking, gray-haired woman sat behind the desk. She appeared older than Mom but somehow more energetic. I stood at attention and waited for her to acknowledge my presence. The captain examined me for a few heartbeats while I did my best not to shake. "Sound off!" she barked.

"Wang, Ishmael. Unrated. Applying for an available quarter share berth, sar." O'Rourke had coached me in the appropriate responses. She had me practice the drill several times on my last visit so I knew what to do. *The Handbook* also provided instructions on how to address various officers under different circumstances. The book covered this precise scenario, complete with a sample script.

"Why do you want to ship out?" she asked.

"I need to leave before the Neris Company kicks me off-planet. I don't have enough creds to buy passage." Belatedly, I remembered to add, "Captain."

"You know this is going to be difficult, don't you, Wang?"

I nodded.

"Excuse me, Wang? Did you say something?" she barked.

"Um, yes, sar, that is, no, sar. That is. I know it's going to be difficult, Captain." Gods, I sounded like such a jerk.

She stood up and looked at me. "Ms. O'Rourke says you're good people. Why would she say that, Mr. Wang?" She asked the question with a softer tone to her voice.

The fact that she didn't follow the script caught me off guard and I blinked in confusion. "I—I don't know, Captain. I've only met her a couple times. She's been very helpful."

After a moment's pause she resumed her previous tone. "You need to know I run a tight ship and don't put up with crap. You'll be the lowest of the low, and work your backside off for the next two stanyers. The work will be boring, difficult, and unrelenting. Your shipmates will taunt you, and the living conditions will be challenging to somebody used to having his own room on a nice, quiet planet. In short, your ass is mine and will be until I say it's not, or your contract expires, whichever comes first. Can you deal with that, land rat?"

I paused for a second, or perhaps two, before answering her. She had summed it up succinctly and brutally. I had no idea which quarter share berth I might get. It really didn't matter. I needed to get off the rock and had few choices. "Honestly, I don't know, Captain. But I'd like to give it my best shot."

She smiled then. "Good answer, Mr. Wang. Welcome aboard." She stuck out her hand and I shook it. "You'll get a standard contract, steward attendant pay plus quarter share. Do well and I've always got a slot open. Now, go get your contract signed and your shipsuit on. Most of the little band we call crew will be off the ship, and we can get you settled in without a crowd of hecklers to help." She grinned and I saw a twinkle in her eye.

"Thank you, Captain," I told her and meant it.

Time shifted to an accelerated pace. I thumbed my contract and was officially under Articles, employed by Federated Freight, the *Lois McKendrick's* owner company. Fredericks, the Assistant Hall

Manager, punched through the paperwork, sending the notifications to Neris Company and snipping off the few dangling threads of my old life. He showed me to a changing room. O'Rourke had taken my measurements earlier and already selected the right sized shipsuit and boots in Federated Freight colors of green and gold. The suit fit my meter and a half perfectly and the shipboots molded to my size twelves as if they had grown there.

As I packed my shore leave clothes into the duffel, I caught movement out of the corner of my eye. A stranger stared back at me from what I realized was a mirror. He looked me over from the sandy mop on my head, down the tailored shipsuit, to my new boots. I was thin after three weeks of eating my own cooking but Mom had always said I was wiry. That was apparently a good thing. The stranger smiled and I found myself smiling back. He straightened up and shouldered his duffel. I gave him a kind of salute and headed out the "Crew Only" doors to find the shuttle.

The hallway beyond the doors led to a security checkpoint and an entry tube. Mom and I had taken trips up to the orbital before. It was a popular tourist destination for residents as it was technically Confederation space and not owned by NerisCo. The exotic shops and restaurants provided variety from the largely homogeneous life on a company planet. This trip, however, was much different. The stark behind-the-scenes entry had no decorative panels or padding. The floors, ceiling, and even the walls, had a certain gritty look—a kind of utilitarian plainness that felt disconcerting at first. Stenciled labels stood out on exposed pipes, electrical runs, and hydraulic lines. After the passenger port's careful, pastel decor, the crew tube felt strange but refreshingly more real.

All this splashed across my brain in a surreal time warp where everything progressed at light-speed around me, but where I moved in a kind of paradoxical slow motion. In the next blink, I stowed my duffel in the overhead and strapped down on a well-worn shuttle seat. Again, the shuttle felt at once familiar and strange, like the difference between a passenger flitter and a cargo crawler. Even the seat belts were unfamiliar, with a cross-the-chest X harness instead of the single shoulder strap I normally used. It was easy enough to figure out, just different. This was going to take some getting used to. My eyes kept trying to focus, but the starkness of my surroundings made everything blur together.

The shuttle pilot came through the cabin smiling and nodding as he examined the craft. "We'll be up to the station in just a few ticks," he said. "No time for beverage service and if you need to use the head, I'd do it now." This was apparently some kind of joke because he chuckled.

"Thanks," I answered, somewhat dazedly.

As he finished his inspection, half a dozen people wearing gray and blue shipsuits came into the cabin and strapped down. Small patches on their shoulders read *"Murmansk."* I assumed that was the name of another of the ships docked at the orbital. They nodded to me, but absorbed themselves in chatting up one of their group who apparently had engaged in some misadventure overnight. She seemed embarrassed by the attention but the group teased her in good-natured fun and she gave as good as she got.

My ears popped when the pressure doors closed and the locking rings thumped away from the hull. The speakers gave a ping-ping-pong sound and a woman's voice said, *"Secure for lift."* With no more ceremony than that, the shuttle got underway and boosted into the clear, golden afternoon light. I took one last look out the port at the rows of granapple vineyards arrayed across the land-scape as we spun upward crawling out of the gravity well. The acceleration pressure pinning me to my seat seemed incongruous with the perceived decrease in speed as we gained altitude. The shuttle rolled and I lost sight of the ground, just the darkening sky and a bit of the stubby wing, flashing red from the blinking navi-gational lights along the side of the ship. The engine noise ramped back as we climbed and the air outside became thinner. Soon, the only sound came from the airframe itself. I settled down and zoned out completely until the heavy clunks of the docking clamps shud-dered the craft. The trip had taken a full stan, but my warped time sense made it feel like a tick. The cabin speakers gave a pong-ping sound and the other passengers unbuckled even before the woman's voice said, *"Docking complete."* I let them clear out before I hit the releases and retrieved my duffel.

Outside the shuttle bay, a kid waited in a green and gold shipsuit like mine. I thought he might be older than I was, but his baby face made him look younger. He grinned when he saw me and held out his hand. "You must be Wang. I'm Philip Carstairs. Everybody calls me Pip." His green eyes had a laugh in them and I found myself grinning back.

"Hi," I replied. "Call me Ishmael."

He blinked a couple of times then looked at a note on his tablet before guffawing. "Oh my gods and garters—that's really your name?"

The familiar reaction usually grated on my nerves, but somehow coming from this guy it didn't seem so bad. "Yeah," I admitted a bit sheepishly. "My mother had a strange sense of humor."

He clapped me on the shoulder and motioned down the passage. "The first mate sent me over to collect you. Let's get you settled aboard and you can tell me all about it. By the way, you don't snore, do you?"

It seemed like a strange question and it caught me off guard. "Snore?"

"Yeah, Gilly, the guy whose berth you're getting, gods, but he made a racket. I don't think I've gotten a good night's sleep since we left Albert."

"I don't know," I replied. "I never noticed."

He laughed, again. "Well, then we'll let ya know."

Pip led me through the utility corridors halfway around the orbital. We left the shuttle bays and moved into the commercial docks. The decor didn't seem quite so spartan, or perhaps, I was growing used to the blatant utility exhibited at every turn. It somehow already began to feel right.

As we threaded our way through the station toward the ship's lock, I was conscious of my old life spooling out behind me. Each step took me further into an unknown world and I began to get a bit, not scared, exactly, but anxious. The what-have-I-done feeling had just settled around my lungs when my escort stopped at a lock. On the display above it read: *Lois McKendrick* 51-09-07 1600. Pip swiped his ID card and tapped a quick code on his tablet. The status light flipped to green and the lock cycled open. We stepped in and the lock cycled closed behind us. The inner lock revealed a crew member who looked up from her screen at a station just inside the hull.

"Hey, Pip. This the greenie?"

They butted knuckles and he answered, "Yup. Meet Ishmael Wang. Ish, Sandy Belterson."

Her dark brown hair and ice blue eyes were an odd combination. Added to the distinctly olive skin tones, she was an anomaly on two legs. She nodded with a friendly smile and said, "Welcome aboard, Ish."

I nodded a greeting and answered something I don't remember but it must have been adequate.

She turned to my escort. "Mr. Maxwell wants to meet with him in the office. He's there now."

"Yeah. He messaged me, too. Thanks."

Sandy waved and settled back to her reading. As I passed I noticed it was a lesson of some kind, charts rotated in simulated three-D while text scrolled rapidly across the bottom of the screen.

Seeing my glance Pip said, "She's studying for Spec II in Astrogation. Let's go see Mr. Maxwell before settling you in. We don't want to keep him waiting."

Aboard ship, the corridors—passages, I corrected myself—were barely wide enough for two people to pass. I followed Pip as he led me confidently through the maze. Every so often he'd comment on a space, "environmental section down there" or "officer country that way" but little of it meant anything to me. I hoped there wouldn't be a test later. He halted outside a door simply labeled: Office and knocked.

A rumbling voice behind the door said, "Come."

Pip opened the door, a real one with a knob and hinges and everything, not like the airtight hatches we had passed along our way. He led the way into a cramped room, and announced, "Attendant Carstairs reporting with Attendant Ishmael Wang, Mr. Maxwell, sar."

The man behind the desk didn't look up from his screen but just waved us in and wordlessly indicated we should wait. He was built like a knife with razor edges outlining his face and hardened steel in his bearing. A solid gray buzz-cut covered his scalp, not the white-gray the faculty members on Neris had, but a hard, dark gray. I didn't know if that reflected his age or just some genetic variation I hadn't seen before. Whatever the cause, it suited him. He wore the green and gold with collar pips and some discrete hashmarks around the sleeves that were pushed up to his elbows. He tapped a few keys and the document on his screen vanished.

"Mr. Wang." His head didn't just turn—it swiveled. His eyes tracked like the twin barrels of some odd gun, precise, mechanical, dead. The hair on the back of my neck stood up. "The captain sent me your file and I've assigned you to the open quarter share berth in the ship's mess. Mr. Carstairs will show you to the berthing area and introduce you to the rest of the mess crew."

It was as much instruction to Pip as it was a command to me and he responded with an, "Aye, sar."

Maxwell continued, "It should come as no surprise to you that you're taking the place of a crewman who failed to perform to our satisfaction, Mr. Wang. Please see to it that we don't have to provide the same courtesy to you in our next port of call."

"Aye, sar. I'll do my best," I replied in what I'd hoped was a steady voice.

"Dismissed, gentlemen." He swiveled back to his screen, bringing up the next document.

Pip stepped back into the passage and I followed as quickly as I could without making it seem like I was running. After we closed the door I started to speak, but a shake of Pip's head stopped me and we headed down the passage the way we'd come.

After we'd taken a couple of turns, Pip took a deep breath and said, "That went well."

I blinked at him. "Is he always like that?"

Pip shook his head. "Naw, he's usually not so friendly. You must have got him on a good day."

"Friendly? Are you crazy? That guy scared the crap out of me. Are all the officers like him?" I didn't remember being afraid of the captain—awed, maybe, but not afraid.

Pip chuckled. "No. Actually, Mr. Maxwell is pretty decent. With him, you never need to wonder where you stand."

"He was like some kind of robot," I exclaimed.

"Yeah, most people say that when they first meet him. But after you get to know him, you'll realize a robot is actually much warmer than he is." He lowered his voice. "Rumor is that he's ex-Spec Force. He moves like that because he doesn't want to kill anybody."

I gaped at him.

"Close your mouth, greenie," he snickered. "It may or may not be true, but either way he's the best first mate I've ever served under. He really knows how to keep the ship running efficiently."

"And that's a good thing?"

"You bet. The more efficiently we run, the larger our shares," Pip said as he headed down the corridor.

I started to wonder if I'd done the wrong thing by signing up, but I pushed that thought aside as soon as it entered my head. It was too late for second thoughts. I hurried down the hallway to catch up with Pip.

Chapter Three
Neris Orbital: 2351-September-03

Pip took me to the berthing area. I'd braced myself for some horror out of Hornblower with hammocks crammed together in dark squalor, but I found a large, airy room with ten pairs of bunks with corresponding full-length lockers. There was a table and chairs that were, of course, bolted to the deck, and a sanitary facility with more privacy than I had expected.

"There's another berthing area just like this across the passage for the Engineering Division. We don't have a full complement of crew so there are some spare bunks." He helped me pick one across from his, reset the palm-scan on my locker, and stow my gear. We drew linens from stores and he showed me how to make up a bed bordered by walls on three sides.

"Shipshape and Bristol fashion," I mumbled.

"What?" asked Pip.

"Nothing, just something my mother used to say." I smiled as I remembered my introduction to C. S. Forester.

After that he took me to the third mate, Mr. von Ickles, the systems and communications officer where I got my ShipNet credentials and tablet so I could access the ship's network and information stores.

Finally, he introduced me to my immediate boss, Specialist First Chef Ralf al-M'liki, a small, wiry guy with black hair and flashing eyes. He originally hailed from one of the M'bele planets and his galley was redolent of the spices and scents of his home world that were peppery, sweet, and sharp all at once.

We were on the mess deck. After brief introductions he walked me over to three twenty-liter coffee urns that gleamed atop a counter prominently mounted near the center of the mess deck. I'd never seen anything like them and I must admit I felt intimidated. They gleamed in polished copper and stainless steel and had built-in plumbing to serve each one. The fact that my new boss spoke of them with a kind of solemn reverence didn't help matters.

"These urns provide the life's blood of the ship," he explained. "The whole crew worship at this shrine to caffeine." The chef took a heavy mug from the rack, filled it from the valve at the base of the middle urn, and handed it to me. "What do you think, young Ishmael?"

I peered into the cup. A rainbow sheen floated on the oily sludge in the pristine white china. A burned, musty smell wafted up. An irreverent thought about burnt offerings drifted through my head but I had the good sense not to say anything about that. I took a tentative sip. It was better than it looked, even black. "Not bad, Mr. al-M'liki, but I think it could be improved."

He smiled. His shocking white teeth flashing against his olive skin. "Just call me Cookie, that's what everyone else does." He pointed to the urn on the near end of the counter. "Alright Mr. Wang, let's see what you've got. Use that pot. Do whatever you must to make me coffee to die for," he said before retreating to the galley.

When he was gone, Pip rushed over. "What in the name of anti and uncle matter do you think you're doing, Ish?" His eyes were wide in shock.

"Looks like I'm going to make some coffee. That's what Cookie asked for."

"Don't you think you're taking a hell of a risk being critical on your first day?"

I smiled. "I may be a greenie on the ship, but when it comes to coffee, I'm an expert. Even making it twenty liters at a time can't change that."

With a kind of focused detachment, I rolled up my sleeves and started in. First, I dragged over the stepstool, clambered up on the counter, and examined the container. Sure enough, a dark and peeling film coated the inside. A quick investigation showed the plumbing included both hot and cold feeds, and worse, lukewarm water filled the reservoir.

Nodding to myself, I clambered down, dragging the filter cone with me. I took it into the main galley and scrubbed it in the deep sink with a stiff brush and a mixture of hot water and white vinegar until it gleamed. I returned to the mess with a liter of vinegar and poured it into the urn. Cookie pretended not to watch, so I pretended not to notice, but I caught him glancing at me out of the corner of his eye.

Pip, however, rubbernecked with a red face and eyes bulging in alarm. "What are you doing? Good gods, man, do you know what it'll taste like if you use that?"

"I'm not making coffee with it." I clambered back up on the counter with my scrub brush. "I'm going to use it to scour the sludge out of this urn."

It took quite a while. I had to ask Cookie for a wrench and a bottlebrush and he showed me where to find them without comment. I took the level indicator tube off the front and scrubbed it as well. After more than a stan I finally got it sparkling inside and out to my satisfaction. I gave it a final rinse with scalding water and then shut off the hot water valve and cranked the cold tap all the way open.

Pip showed me where to find the supplies. The high quality paper filters fit the cone perfectly. The coffee, on the other hand, was another matter. When I popped the lid off the air-tight, I found some pathetic crud masquerading as coffee. I dumped it into the waste disposer, and dusted out the air-tight with a towel.

"This is too stale to brew properly. Where are the beans and grinder?"

Pip just blinked at me. "Beans? Grinder? We just put two scoops from the air-tight in the filter and let 'er rip."

"Who stocks the container?"

"Cookie."

I sighed and searched for my new boss. He smiled an odd little grin at my request and showed me where to find the beans, in vacuum sealed buckets stenciled with Djartmo Arabasti, and a Schmidt Coffee Mill that looked large enough to grind a whole bucket at a time. I pulled up the calculator function on my tablet.

Pip, who had followed me, gaped openly. "What are you doing? This is crazy!"

"I can't make anything worth drinking with that stuff." I concentrated on my measurements and my math. "This is going to be rough until I figure out the right combinations, but it takes from seven to fourteen grams per cup and there are about seven cups per liter. Based on that sample Cookie gave me, I should make a strong batch. So, I need about a hundred grams of coffee per liter. That urn is twenty liters but I'm only going to make a half pot, so I need about a kilo," I concluded, looking up from my calculations. "We'll see how well that works and then I can adjust the grind or the amount next time around."

I weighed out the beans into the empty air-tight and used a small brush clipped to the hopper to clear out the discharge chute. The unmarked grind scale didn't provide much information, so I just set the dial in the middle hoping for a medium grind and trusted the Schmidt. I dumped a tub of beans into the hopper and I carefully collected the ground remains as it spilled from the chute. I rubbed them between my fingers and brought the grinds to my nose. It looked good, had a nice texture, and a pleasant scent. I sifted the calculated amount into the filter and went back out to the mess. I watched the fill indicator carefully until I had exactly ten liters in the reservoir, then I scooped a bit of the cold water in a mug and used it to wet the grounds before locking down the lid and punching the brew button. While it dripped, I went back to clean up the grinder and put away the beans.

By the time I finished in the galley, the coffee was almost done. I noted the color in the level indicator, knowing it would appear weaker than it actually was. When the ready light came on, I pulled a fresh mug from the rack and poured it about half full.

Looking in, I saw a beautiful, rich brown brew without any hint of rainbow or oil on the surface. A satisfying aroma steamed out of the mouth of the mug. I took the brew to Cookie and offered it to him without a word. He tilted the cup and examined the color. He pushed his nose below the brim and inhaled deeply as a smile began to form. He took a slurping sip and then a deeper swallow, his eyes closed in concentration. Pip fidgeted beside me, but I waited patiently for Cookie's assessment.

He spoke without opening his eyes. "So, young Ishmael, is this the best you can do?"

Pip inhaled sharply in alarm, but I thought I knew Cookie's game at this point. "I don't know. It might be. There are just too many variables for me to know for sure."

His eyes snapped open and he peered at me, hawkishly. "Such as?"

"Mainly, I need to determine the correct brewing time. If the pot brews too fast, the grind needs to be finer. That's going to depend somewhat on the grav settings. I'm assuming we'll keep this general level of gravity all the time, or at least while we're making coffee. Then, I need to know more about the beans themselves. How fresh are they? How are they stored? What are the characteristics of this particular bean? Last, I need to know the crew's preferences." I ended with a smile. "Judging from the sample you gave me, they like it strong, dark, bitter, and oily. I prefer to skip the bitter and oily part but we must always consider the tastes of the drinker when brewing a perfect cup of coffee." My mother's voice echoed in my head as I said the last part. I remembered her saying those exact words as we explored the mysteries of bean and water together. I found it comforting as well as saddening.

"Pip," Cookie crowed. "You could learn from this one." He patted me on the shoulder. "You'll make an excellent cook. Now both of you drain and clean the other two urns." He filled his mug again before returning to the galley.

Pip grabbed china from the rack and drew off a mug of his own. He buried his muzzle into it and sucked down a swallow. His green eyes went wide as he dove for another drink. "Where'd you learn to do that?"

"My mom always said that coffee cost too much to make badly. She taught me how to brew at a young age."

"This might be the best this ship has ever had." Pip looked up to where I was working on the next urn with newfound appreciation. "And to think I knew ya when."

While we worked together on the remaining machines, Mr. Maxwell entered absorbed in reading something from a tablet. He didn't acknowledge our presence. I could feel Pip holding his breath while the first mate poured and then sipped. He kept right on moving back out of the mess, never looking up from his reading.

Pip and I exchanged glances and I'm sure he was wondering the same thing...did he even notice? My unasked question was answered when I heard his voice from the passage. "Good work, Mr. Wang. Carry on."

Pip's face split in a broad grin. "How do you suppose he knew it was you?"

Cookie strolled over to refill his mug. "Because, Mr. Carstairs, he's had your coffee." He gave me a wink and returned to the galley.

I had to chuckle at the look on Pip's face but I hid my grin by returning to scrub the urn.

❀   ❀   ❀

My duties, at least in those first couple of days, were pretty easy. Pip showed me where to find the duty roster and helped me learn how to find ingredients in the various storerooms and pantries. Mostly, my job consisted of ensuring there were plenty of sandwich fixings in the cooler and keeping the urns filled with fresh coffee.

I learned that there were three main seatings for meals: 0600, 1200, and 1800 ship standard time. Most of the crew went ashore when the ship docked so we only served watch standers and the few others who stayed aboard. Officers shared the mess with the crew, although they sat at one large table set aside for their exclusive use.

As the time for our departure approached, more and more people ate meals aboard. "Broke, most likely," Pip explained. Knowing the prices on the orbital, and the nature of Neris Port, I judged he was probably right. The pace in the mess picked up accordingly. Cookie took care of the menu planning, but he had Pip and me crawling through the storage spaces, pantries, coolers, and freezers to check the computer inventory against the actual stores. Where we were going, we couldn't just step out to buy a gallon of milk if we came up short.

"How much stuff is there?" I followed Pip to what felt like the tenth walk-in freezer of the morning.

"We carry stores for up to a hundred twenty days, but we're seldom underway for more than sixty at a stretch."

When he told me that, I got a strange feeling. "Sixty days? That's two months." During the short time I'd been aboard, I'd been too busy learning my new job and finding my way around to think much about being cooped up inside the ship for weeks at a time. What would it be like when I was trapped for two solid months?

Pip poked me. "Ish, It's okay."

I took a deep breath. "Sorry. It just hit me and I. . ."

"No worries. You'll be fine. Just keep working."

"I suppose, but the ship just seems so small."

He looked at me oddly. "Small?"

"Yeah, everything all packed together. The narrow passages. . . you know. . . small."

He paused and frowned at me for a moment. "You've never seen the ship, have you?"

"Of course, I have. I'm on it, aren't I?"

"No, I mean the *whole* ship."

He bipped Cookie on his tablet and asked, "Can I have permission to show Ish the way to the bridge?"

Cookie's response came right back. "As long as you don't get in the way up there, permission is granted. But don't take too long, the crew will be back aboard in three stans and we'll need more coffee."

Pip led me up a couple of levels and down a passage. At the foot of a stairway—they called them ladders on the ship I reminded myself—he paused. "Don't touch anything. Just look. Pay attention to any directions from the bridge crew," he said quietly to me before climbing the ladder. At the top, he used a formal sounding voice to announce us. "Request permission to enter the bridge."

"State your business." A woman at the top of the ladder spoke formally but smiled at him.

"Orientation for new crew member."

"Granted." She grinned at me as I stepped off the ladder.

Subdued lighting revealed a relatively large space with comfortable looking chairs bolted to the deck in key locations. A collection of nearly identical work stations formed a phalanx around the room. Panels and consoles flickered giving the area an odd radiance. I could see one screen that displayed what I took to be a Neris schematic with the orbital base and planetary surface plotted. A larger scale display showed the whole system with a blinking, blue path curving across it. It took me a few moments to register that there were actually ports facing forward and I could see that the ship nuzzled up against the outside of the orbital. I'd seen pictures of the station, of course, and watched it on shuttle approach, but I'd never been this close. It looked near enough to touch. I could see little scratches and blemishes in the surface finish and some kind of polarizing filter blocked the glare reflected off the orbital's skin. I turned slowly realizing that ports faced aft as well and I saw the rest of the *Lois McKendrick* stretching out into the star-spackled Deep Dark.

Leviathan never seemed so appropriate a term.

Gantry lights ran down the spine of the ship, illuminating the container tugs that wrestled the big, triangular cargo boxes ever-so-gently into place before locking them down. Twelve sections of containers extended into the distance. At the far end of the main spine, a small white light, two hundred meters out, marked the stern post. In one instant, I went from feeling like I was crammed in a shoe box to something akin to a flea on a pachyderm. It was staggering.

Pip was watching my face. "You'll get used to it. Do you still feel like the ship is small?"

I shook my head, unable to speak.

My tablet beeped. Cookie's voice came over the speaker. "Your presence is needed on the mess deck, Mr. Wang. Number two urn is out of coffee."

CHAPTER FOUR
NERIS ORBITAL: 2351-SEPTEMBER-07

The duty watch stander woke Pip and me, ending my long night of restlessness. I'd thrashed around the whole night unable to sleep knowing the ship would leave Neris Orbital and get underway for Darbat later that day. Pip slid out of his bunk and slipped past me heading for the san. I chided myself for being nervous as I straightened the blankets on my berth and secured my loose gear. I had already been confined for days but now it would be different. We'd be heading out into the Deep Dark and I would be locked in. I stretched to straighten my pillow when a voice startled me. "Nice package, sailor, but would you mind moving it out of my face?" The sound came from the approximate level of my knees.

The voice, a woman's voice, startled me so much that I fell into the empty lower berth under Pip's, banging my head on the upper rail. She lay in the bunk under mine. Even as I struggled to my feet, I noticed how attractive she was with her dark skin and hair. She wore just a ship's tee over an extensive collection of tattoos and blinking blearily she said, "You must be the new guy."

I tried to stammer something apologetic but didn't know what the appropriate comment might be. "C-c-c-call me Ishmael."

She propped herself on an elbow and squinted at me. "You're kidding, right?"

I shook my head, unable to think of anything else to say.

Pip, wet from the san and struggling into a fresh shipsuit, rescued me. "Beverly, stop scaring the help. Ish, get your butt in the san. We don't have much time to get to the mess deck."

The woman held up a slender hand to shake. "Beverly Arith,

pleased to meet ya. Wake me for afternoon watch?"

I shook the offered hand, mumbling, "Ishmael Wang," before retreating to the san.

Pip gave me grief all morning. "You've never seen a girl before, Ish?"

"She startled me. I didn't realize anybody was there until she spoke."

I'd known there were women in the berthing area. Tabitha Rondita slept on the other side of the partition from me, a nice woman and I didn't mind her little snorty-snores through the wall. We all shared the san and that didn't bother me. Bathing is bathing and everyone likes a little privacy when pooping. The shower and toilet stalls all had doors. I'd lived with my mom and she was not shy so seeing women in various states of undress was no big deal. All told, it felt like summer camp except we were adults and not giggly kids—supposedly.

When Beverly came through the serving line at lunch, Pip nudged me.

For her part, Bev just smiled, nodded, and moved on.

"NOW HEAR THIS. SECURE ALL LOCKS. STOW ALL GEAR FOR DEPARTURE. DEPARTMENT HEADS REPORT TO THE CAPTAIN'S READY ROOM." A countdown timer ticked on my tablet showing the time until we would get underway. Remembering the size, and assuming the mass of the ship, I found it difficult to believe that we'd be moving at all, let alone sailing out of the system on nothing more than pressure from the sun on an electronically generated field.

Cookie has served a particularly robust lunch that day and many people sat around afterward to catch up with each other. After the sparsely attended meals I'd grown accustomed to while docked, it seemed crowded and noisy. Even some of the officers stayed for a bit, chatting.

After the lunch cleanup, Cookie took Pip and me aside. "Gentlemen, we'll be doing dinner differently today because of departure. The captain has scheduled pull out at 1600 and we'll still be maneuvering at 1800. We'll be doing bento-boxes for the evening meal. Mr. Carstairs, you know the drill. Mr. Wang, it's important that we have plenty of coffee, but make certain the urns are secured. We may get bumped a bit and I want to keep things under control."

I nodded my understanding. Each of the urns had a lid that made them spill-proof once locked. A simple system of curved pipes kept the pressure normalized inside without violating liquid integrity. "Two urns or three, Cookie?"

He thought about it before replying. "Load and prep all three,

but only brew two. We can hit the button on the last when needed."
Obvious and logical, I should have thought of it myself and I made
a tally on my personal mental midget list.

All the preparation talk made me a bit nervous and Pip noticed.
"It'll be fine, Ish. We might get a little bump, but usually it's nothing. We just don't want hot stuff splattered around if we happen
to get a rough tug skipper. Once we get pulled back and the sails
are up, it'll be smooth again. You'll think we're docked."

There was nothing I could do about what was going to happen
to the ship. The professionals would be working that end of things.
To distract myself, I obsessed over the minutiae of keeping the urns
full. I ground enough coffee for six full batches, throwing the extra
into an air-tight and dropping it in a chiller to keep it as fresh as
possible. The trick was in the timing. With everybody on board
again, I assumed they would consume an amazing amount. *The
Handbook* told me that everybody should be at their duty stations
about a half-stan before the actual departure, so I figured we needed
to have the most brewed about a stan before. Accordingly, I timed
the urns to be full at 1500. I needn't have worried so much, but it
kept my mind occupied.

Bento-boxes turned out to be the shipboard equivalent of take-
out, finger food that wouldn't make a mess while eating. Cookie
drew on his ancestral heritage and made up a couple of variations of
spicy fillings. We spread the mixture over flat bread rounds, folded,
rolled, and then wrapped them in clingfilm. Pip, Cookie, and I set
up a production line. Forty-five crew needed a hundred and twenty
of these little buggers. I thought it would take a long time, but it
took less than a stan once we had a rhythm going. We'd done them
at a rate better than three a tick. I guess I shouldn't have been that
surprised considering Cookie did two for every one that Pip and I
completed. Spread, roll, wrap, stack—a mindless, but oddly social
task. The three of us gathered around the prep table and worked
side-by-side to prepare for the evening meal.

I thought we'd put them in paper bags for easy carrying but
Cookie had a better idea. He pulled out a stack of stamped, creased
cardboard sheets and quickly formed one into a box with a clever
folding lid. He repeated the action slowly for me to watch. I mim-
icked his moves and produced an identical box. It was as if I'd been
born folding them. Even Cookie seemed impressed by how rapidly
I caught on and he left the folding to me while he and Pip filled
the boxes: two rolls, one piece of fruit, a cookie, a package of sliced
vegetables, and small cups of dressing for dipping. The condiment
was the only thing that might have spilled, but each container held
only a few milliliters. With the lids closed, the boxes stacked on

each other and I noticed small indents that kept them from sliding apart—clever and then some.

"What about drinks?" I asked. "I assume people can't come down for coffee, can they?"

Cookie pointed to large insulated containers under one of the counters. "You'll be delivering. Fill one with black coffee and the other with light and take a pocket full of sweetener packets."

As the clock ticked down to pull out, the mess deck crowd thinned. I was able to prep and secure the urns with two fresh and full, and one on standby. We stacked the boxes on trays and placed them in the coolers. Cookie had it down to a science. While Pip certainly had been through it before, I marveled at Cookie's expertise.

"We run a restaurant, gentlemen," he reminded us regularly. "The customers don't have any other choice, but we owe them our best just the same." Finally, we completed the preparations and Cookie declared us ready. Pip and I collapsed into chairs at one of the mess tables to wait.

A few minutes later, the speakers announced, "*PULLOUT IN THIRTY TICKS. ALL CREW TO DUTY STATIONS. SET NAV-IGATION DETAIL. SECURE FOR PULLOUT. SET READINESS LEVEL YELLOW.*" For Pip, Cookie, and myself the mess deck and galley were our duty stations. We just sat and looked at each other.

"Do we need to strap in or anything?" I looked from one to the other.

Cookie smiled but Pip guffawed.

Our boss cuffed him playfully. "It is a fair question, jackanapes. Have you been around so long that you forgot your first pull back?"

Pip had the decency to look abashed. "Actually, no. My first time was on the *Marcel Duchamp*. I was a wiper in the environmental section and they strapped me into the scrubber." He looked both angry and embarrassed. "Bastards left me in there for three stans."

Cookie winked at me.

Pip just groaned. "It took me all trip to get the stench out of my hair. And I never did live it down. That's why I took the transfer to here."

This was the first time Pip had offered any information about himself. Thinking back, I realized I'd known him less than a week but it seemed like a lifetime. I already had trouble remembering what life had been like before the ship. "When was this?" I asked.

"Last stanyer. I'm into my second year at quarter share. Don't laugh."

"Why would I laugh? Isn't that good?"

Cookie chimed in, "Yes, it's very good, young Ishmael. Considering the alternative is to strand Mr. Carstairs on a company planet in the middle of nowhere."

I thought of the hapless attendant whose berth I'd taken on Neris and wondered if he had found another position.

"Well, I should have moved up to a half share by now." Pip's tone betrayed an undercurrent of bitterness.

Cookie tried to soothe his pique. "And you shall. But all in good time."

"ALL HANDS, BRACE FOR PULL BACK. ALL HANDS, BRACE FOR PULL BACK." The squawk box in the overhead made me jump with the sudden announcement.

Unconsciously I held my breath. My knuckles turned white as I gripped the edge of the table. Cookie smiled and Pip just lifted his coffee cup off the table. Somewhere I felt, rather than heard, a thump from the front of the ship, and my inner ear told me something had happened.

The speakers squawked again. "ALL HANDS, PULL BACK COMPLETE. TUGS CAST OFF IN THREE STANS."

"That's it?" I asked.

"We're underway, Mr. Wang," Cookie said with a smile. "Rather uninspiring, isn't it?"

It was definitely anticlimactic, but it cast a new light on Pip's story. Based on his reaction, he'd been quarter share for a long time and perhaps he had transferred out of embarrassment. I planned to have a heart-to-heart with my new friend because there was more there than he was saying. My speculation must have shown because he suddenly became very interested in examining his coffee mug.

Cookie told stories of pull backs where the tug captain hadn't had so deft a touch. He showed me a scar where he'd been thrown against a steam pipe stanyers before. "Usually, though, they're like this," he said.

Over the next three stans the speakers gave periodic status reports until finally all tugs released us and we were on course out of the system. As I had suspected, we had a lot of mass to get moving. The kicker engines, all the way aft, pushed us for only the first few klicks, and after that, they were secured. Once we'd gotten clear of the orbital, we ran up the field generators deploying the huge sails and the gravity keel. The ship picked up the solar winds which pulled us out of Neris' gravity well. The outbound leg was scheduled to last twenty-two days before we hit the gravity threshold and jumped into the Darbat system.

At 1800, the usual dinnertime, the captain called down and gave Cookie the go ahead to distribute dinner. A few crew, who had no navigational duties, came to the mess deck and sat together over their bento-boxes, talking quietly among themselves. Meanwhile, Cookie, Pip, and I set off to feed the other thirty odd people scattered around the ship. By 1830 we had completed our rounds and returned to the galley to clean up.

At 2000 the speakers came on one last time. *"SECURE FROM NAVIGATION DETAIL. SET THE WATCH FOR NORMAL OPERATIONS. SET CONDITION GREEN THROUGHOUT THE SHIP. SECOND SECTION HAS THE WATCH."*

I punched the button to start the last urn brewing and drained away the oldest pot. By the time the captain and bridge crew showed up, they had fresh coffee and Cookie had put out a tray of pastries.

Chapter Five
Neris System: 2351-September-15

Eight days out of Neris I began to synchronize with the rhythm of being underway. My days while in port had not prepared me for life with a full crew and the leisurely pace I had become accustomed to evaporated. Meals became more elaborate, serving lines grew, and cleanup took exponentially longer. In addition, sandwiches and snacks in the self-service coolers disappeared at an alarming rate now that more than just late watch standers came to the galley throughout the night.

Mornings were the hardest because we started early. Pip and I now woke at 0430 to prepare breakfast and help with bread preparations. We managed the biscuits and even did some of the batches of tortillas, pitas, and other flat breads for lunch. But Cookie was responsible for all the raised varieties. We had a wide selection, made fresh daily. We usually had rolls or crusty loaves for dinner and long, square loaves were required for sandwiches.

Breakfast cleanup often took until mid morning and segued smoothly into lunch. Most days, we got a couple of stans off in the afternoon before setting up for dinner. Pip and I alternated evening cleanup so every other night one of us had a short shift. I found myself looking forward to these quiet times when I had the galley to myself.

I learned a great deal from watching Cookie, and became fascinated with how he took the same basic ingredients and yet made something different time and time again. While Pip might have seen Cookie as a taskmaster, I began to admire him as an artist—the unquestioned maestro of the galley.

My own skill with the coffee turned me into a kind of celebrity. After seeing just how much of the brew the crew consumed when everyone was aboard, it made Cookie's words about it being the lifeblood of the ship make more sense. Still, I knew most people only from seeing them in serving lines. A mess deck attendant is not particularly high on anybody's radar—even ones who knew how to brew coffee. Bev, however, turned out to be a good bunkie. After recovering from my initial embarrassment, I discovered she had a wicked sense of humor, which I appreciated most when it wasn't directed at me.

The coffee urns were an albatross or, perhaps more appropriately, the stone of Sisyphus. Every other stan I had to make more. I learned to grind a full bucket of Arabasti at the start of the shift and measured it into air-tights. That gave me three full pots each morning and seven spares in the chiller. Most days I had to grind a second bucket in the afternoon. While it still wasn't up to the standard my mother would have insisted on, it was better than that first cup of bitter sludge that Cookie had given me. Just cleaning the containers had made a big difference and I devoted time each day to scrub one of the three urns.

I discovered techniques to minimize clean up time like keeping the steam tables at the right temperature or lining the serving trays with peel-away whenever we served something sticky. This last trick meant items could go right into the upright san unit without having to be scrubbed by hand. Pip and I alternated sweeping and mopping chores and worked together to clear the mess deck after each meal until we had it down to a science. He showed me how to use the protective gloves, first sprinkling a bit of talc in each, and leaving an inch or so of the cuff folded back to prevent water from running up my arms. The insulation saved my fingers from the scalding water we used for dish washing. Something I counted as a good thing.

As Cookie, Pip, and I began to mesh as a team. I found I could tell the time of day just by what the others were doing. Slowly, I found myself adjusting to the schedule and could stay awake for as much as two or three stans after work before nodding off.

Of course, that brought another problem. There didn't seem to be anywhere to go except my bunk, the galley, or the mess deck. I needed to find things to occupy my mind or I would begin wondering how soon before we got where we were going. With only a third of the passage to the jump behind us, I knew that dwelling on *are we there yet* would lead to no good end. Given that I had signed on for two stanyers, I really needed to find something to do with my time. Cookie found me in this mindset one evening after dinner.

I was wiping down the counter in the galley and he surprised me since he usually spent his evening playing cards with the other senior crew. "Mr. Wang," he started, but stopped and smiled at me. "Ishmael, you seem to be taking to life aboard very well."

I smiled back. "To tell the truth, Cookie, I'm not sure how well I'm really doing, but I'm trying. I really need to make this work. I don't have a lot of options."

"Yes, Captain Giggone spoke with me. You seem to be adapting to your recent loss."

His mention of my mother's death caught me out of the blue and I turned back to the pot I was scrubbing to give myself a tick to regain control. "Thanks. It's been..." I paused to think, "over a month now. I spent almost three weeks on Neris trying to figure out what to do."

He patted me on the back. "You've done well and landed on your feet after a terrible blow. I'm sure she'd be proud of you."

I nodded my thanks, not trusting my voice to remain steady. I worked silently for a time.

"What will you do now?"

"Now? I just got here. You're not planning to put me ashore in Darbat, are you?"

"No, young Ishmael. You misunderstand me. You're too good to stay at quarter share. I want you to think about going for half share as soon as you can."

"Will I be able to remain on the ship?"

He pursed his lips and cocked his head in consideration. "Well, you'd probably have to change vessels. The *Lois* isn't rated to carry a food handler, but you could switch to another division and stay aboard if a half share berth opens up." He folded his arms and leaned against the prep table. "I want you to start thinking about those kinds of possibilities."

"Wait a minute. I've been on this ship, what? Ten days?"

He smiled and nodded.

"Pip is in his second stanyer and he's still at quarter share."

"But you are not Mr. Carstairs. For you, staying at your current rating would be a waste. You have done more in your ten days than Pip has done in the seven months he's been aboard. I gave him the same test I gave you and he failed."

"You didn't give me a test—" I started to object, but then remembered. "The coffee?"

"Yes."

"But that's not fair. My mother was a snob when it came to coffee. She drilled that stuff into me. How was Pip supposed to know?"

"You continue to misunderstand me, Ishmael. It wasn't that you knew how to fix it. That, I confess, was a happy serendipity. What you did was take responsibility. You showed pride in a job well done and addressed the problems systematically. When you knew the solution, you acted. When you didn't, you sought help. Your contributions have made the ship a better place."

I'm pretty sure I blushed then. "But I don't know anything. Pip knows how everything works."

"And he proceeds on the basis that things must always work as they have, despite what his intelligence tells him." He raised an eyebrow. "Did Pip know the coffee was bad?"

I nodded in reluctant agreement.

"And his advice to you was to keep your head down and your mouth shut, was it not?"

Again, I nodded. "But—"

Cookie smiled and held up his hand to stop me. "But me no buts, Ishmael. Yes, you have knowledge he did not. And he knows things you don't. The difference is you use yours to help us all. That is what I look for in a shipmate."

"This is unfair. He's helped me so much and I don't want to come in here and leapfrog over him."

"Then perhaps you can help him in return. You could be a good influence."

I thought about that as I rinsed the pot. "I don't know that I can, but I'll try."

"Good. Now, what specialty do you think you'd like to pursue?"

"Specialty?"

"Ishmael, you could be an excellent cook, but I'm afraid if you took that path your talents would be wasted. You need to consider all possibilities. Engineering, perhaps? Environmental? Maybe you'd like to become a deck officer or cargo specialist?"

"Wait, Cookie, you're going too fast for me." I waved a soapy hand in the air to stop him. "Why would I want to do one of those things? Can't I just be a cook?"

Cookie smiled and gave a little shrug. "How you spend the time is, of course, up to you. As for cooking, it's my life and I love it. My pleasure comes from creating the best meals I can and making life more pleasant for the crew. You would make an excellent cook, Ishmael." He paused and considered me with pursed lips for a heartbeat. "But I suspect you would find that it loses its challenge rapidly."

"You might be right but I'm not even certain what the other choices are."

"Look in your handbook, young Ishmael, and consider that your feet are already on a path. It might be wiser to select a branch before one is thrust upon you by circumstance." With that, he strolled out of the galley.

I stood there considering his words and he startled me by poking his head back through the door. "And we're out of coffee out here. Please brew a new pot before you go." With a playful grin and a wink he left once more.

CHAPTER SIX
NERIS SYSTEM: 2351-SEPTEMBER-16

Pip was the closest thing to a friend I'd had since Angela Markova. It was weird. I'd only known him a couple of weeks. Granted, they were long weeks and we'd been working together almost non-stop every day. In many ways it felt like he'd taken me under his wing, but he also seemed—I don't know—adrift might be a good word. After Cookie's visit I had a hard time looking at Pip the same way. Of course that same conversation also made me look at Cookie differently. He was taking the role of a wise uncle. I shied away from the notion of father since I wasn't completely sure what that really meant. As for Pip, he became the rascally younger brother and Uncle Cookie had made him my problem.

Day nine out of Neris I stayed late to help Pip clean up and to talk. The galley was the only place we had that approached any level of privacy, and even there we were interrupted by people dropping in at odd hours to grab a cookie, make a sandwich, or ask me to brew another urn of coffee. Cookie's discussion weighed on me all day. Pip must have noticed because he started in on me as soon as Cookie left for his card game.

"Okay, Ish. What gives?"

I knew better than to play dumb, but I didn't want to confront that particular problem head on. "The walls are really starting to close in. There's no privacy. We work, sleep, work, sleep, work, sleep. It never ends. Not to mention that every time I turn around somebody's looking for more coffee."

Pip grinned. "I warned ya about that. You're the caffeine god now and it comes with a terrible price."

I knew he was teasing, sort of. "I know, but you're in your second stanyear. I'm barely into my second week. How do you cope?"

"Ishmael, my boy, it's all about the journey. In this business, you never get there, wherever *there* is, so you better enjoy the trip. As an allegory for life, I kinda like it."

I looked at him, perhaps a bit strangely. It was so unlike Pip, I wondered who he was channeling.

He looked a bit embarrassed and gave a half shrug. "I got that from the second mate on the *Duchamp*. Just before she threatened to put me ashore on Arghon."

I laughed. "So you were a troublemaker."

"Let's just say, I got off on the wrong foot with that crew. The *Duchamp* had just put into Arghon and the *Lois* came in right behind it. Word got around the docks that there was a woman on the *Lois* who wanted to get into environmental but there weren't any openings. By that time I had a miserable reputation and I really was afraid they were going to strand me. Alvarez, she was the second mate on the *Duchamp*, talked to Mr. Maxwell, and I gladly traded my space there for the opening in the mess here."

"Wow, luck was in your pocket that day, huh?"

He chuckled. "So it would seem. I never did find out why Mr. Maxwell was willing to take the trade, but that enjoy-the-ride speech was the last thing Alvarez told me before she kicked me out of the lock. It stuck with me. I've fit in better here, certainly. It feels more like I belong. I think part of it is because I've taken a different approach and I'm enjoying the ride, as it were."

I nodded and we worked on the pans in comfortable silence for a time.

"Cookie was here last night." I glanced at him out of the corner of my eye.

"That's odd. What'd he want?"

"Odd isn't the half of it. He wanted me to select a specialty to pursue."

Pip snickered. "Great gods and small piscatorials, you haven't been here a month and he's already planning your future?"

I shrugged and handed him a pot to dry and stow. "More like, he's afraid I'm gonna get bored as a cook and I need to be working on my next step now so I'll be ready when the opportunity comes."

Pip nodded and gave me a rueful grin. "Yeah, he's always after me to pursue something, too."

"So. . . ?"

"So, what?" He looked at me blankly.

"What are you pursuing?"

He looked a little sheepish. "Promise you won't laugh?"

I crossed my heart, leaving wet, soapy smears on my shipsuit.

He glanced over his shoulder before lowering his voice to a whisper. "Trade."

"What's that mean? You're going for cargo master?"

"Shh, keep it down. No, I'm running some smaller deals of my own."

"You're what?"

He looked over his shoulder at the door before continuing. "I'm picking up goods in one port and selling them at the next. Private cargo. Everybody's allowed to do it. It's in *The Handbook*, section fourteen. So long as you stay within your mass quota and don't break any Confederation regulations, you can bring almost anything you want aboard including trade goods."

I looked at him, dumbfounded.

"It's true. You can look it up."

"I believe you. It just never occurred to me."

He grinned. "Almost everybody does it to some degree. I'm just a little more serious about it than most."

"Then why the big secret?" He had me glancing over my shoulder as well.

He looked at me exasperated. "What do you think got me off on the wrong foot on the *Duchamp?*"

I shrugged. "I figured it was the scrubber incident."

He shook his head. "No, that was just the set up. When they found out I was serious about private trading, they started making fun of me. They teased me because I kept bragging about making a killing with private trade with just a quarter share's mass allotment. I think they figured if I was too green to know about pull out I must be clueless about trade as well. It didn't take long before I was a laughing stock." He stowed a tray under the counter. "The more I tried to explain, the worse it got."

I stacked the last pot in the drying rack and rinsed out the deep sink. "Yeah, I guess I can see that."

Pip looked miserable. "It made my life difficult. Somebody was always ragging on me about what I had for trade goods and laughing at the things I brought aboard." He sighed and looked a bit sheepish. "It sounds pretty petty now, but it was miserable to live through."

"So, you're still trading, but you're keeping it quiet."

He nodded with a little shrug.

We finished the cleanup, and I went to prep for more coffee. I called back over my shoulder as I measured grounds into the filter.

"So, how's it working out?"

He grinned wolfishly. "Well, I've only made a few hundred creds, but I haven't lost any yet."

"Did you pick up something on Neris?"

He looked at me like I was much stupider than I usually felt. "What do you think?"

"Come on, tell me."

He lowered his voice. "Granapple brandy."

"What?" I tried not to laugh. I didn't want to be like those on the *Duchamp* but granapple brandy wasn't exactly a luxury good.

"Grishom's, thirty-years-old and aged in the cask. I have four, one-liter bottles."

I practically choked. "But that's a hundred creds a bottle," I said in shock.

He nodded.

I just stared at him but then I made the connection. "That's why you weren't on liberty when I came aboard?"

He nodded again. "It took all my creds to buy them. I made one trip down when we made port to pick them up from my Aunt Annie. She'd found and held them for me."

"Aunt Annie?"

"Anne O'Rourke. She's the Union Hall Manager. You met her, didn't you?"

"Small galaxy...hey, wait. How'd you get them under your mass limit? You must have almost nothing on board."

He laughed. "Probably more than you. Four liters is only a bit over four kilos. Even with the glass bottles and presentation cases, it was under eight. How much mass did you bring up?"

He was right. "Less than ten kilos."

I realized I could have done the same thing, except I didn't know anything about private trading and didn't have four hundred creds to spare.

"What will they bring you on Darbat?" I found the whole thing fascinating.

He shrugged. "I don't know for sure. It depends on the market. Last one sold there went for two hundred creds, but a lot could have changed between now and then. I have a restaurant connection. He'll give me a hundred and a quarter a piece. That's my fallback."

"Nice margin."

Pip gave a self-deprecating shrug. "I doubled my money going into Neris."

"Wow! Really? What'd you carry?"

"Computer memory chips."

My eyebrows shot up. "Is there that much market for them?"

"You wouldn't think so, but yeah. I was able to buy a case back on Gugara for almost nothing. Neris Company controls all the cargo coming into the stores there and they apply a hefty tariff. It means company people pay much higher prices there than anywhere else. It really makes it hard to live there and difficult to save enough to buy a ticket off-planet."

"I noticed."

"It also means that a case of memory chips, without the tariff, can be turned around with a pretty good margin. It's lightweight, high demand, and practically liquid."

"How do you know all this stuff?"

"I'm from a trader family. It's in my blood." He grinned.

"You're full of surprises tonight." I raised an eye brow at him. "But what's a trader family?"

"Well, Aunt Annie has been a trader for going on forty stanyers. She's been taking a little down time at the Union Hall, but I suspect she'll be back on a ship within a few months. My father owns two ships now. I grew up analyzing trade and traffic patterns on the galley table on his first ship."

I knew I was gaping, but I couldn't stop myself. "You *grew up* on a ship?" I tried to picture kids on the *Lois*. "How'd you get aboard?"

He smacked me playfully. "Not all ships are like this one, buffoon. Dad and Mom are the owner-operators of a small hauler over in the Sargass Sector. It's small, just a few hundred tons. They run light freight out to the hydrogen miners and asteroid prospectors. We kept up on the trade data from the surrounding area because sometimes it was actually cheaper to take a jump over to Deeb to pick up something the clients wanted than to go all the way in-system to trade on Sargass Orbital. Depending on the orbits, it could be as much as three weeks into Sargass, but only four days out to the jump. Deeb maintained an orbital that was usually only eight days in on the other side. We could get to Deeb, do the trade, and be almost all the way back before we could have made it to the Sargass Orbital."

"So, what are you doing here? Why aren't you still working with your father?"

Pip didn't answer right away and when he did, he sighed first. "He casts a big shadow. I wanted to get out from under it. Aunt Annie is my mother's sister and helped me get onto the *Duchamp*."

"But if you grew up on ships, how could you have been fooled into the scrubber?"

Pip looked embarrassed. "I was playing the part of a wide-eyed innocent. I didn't want them to know I was an indie brat; so I pretended I'd never been on a ship before. The scrubber thing got out of hand, but I couldn't get out of it without letting on that I was playing with them."

"What tangled webs we weave..." I quoted.

"Something like that."

"So being an indie brat isn't a good thing?"

"Not to professional spacers. There's a bias and it can get pretty ugly, so don't bring it up, okay?"

"But you're a professional spacer now."

"Right. Some professional. I'm still on quarter share after more than a full stanyer."

"Well, if you picked a specialty..."

"But which one? I really don't like environmental, and I just don't have the chops for engineering. I'm an analyst, not an engineer. I've tried the cargo exam, but I just can't seem to pass it."

"Why not cook? You seem to do well with the inventory and accounting."

"True."

"I'm pretty sure Cookie would help. He likes ya and the two of you seem to work well in the galley."

He nodded. "But I don't know much about cooking. I didn't even know how to make decent coffee." He cast me an evil glance out of the corner of his eye.

"Bah, just look at it like a trade problem. Recipes are easy to come by and cooking is just imagination and technique. You've got plenty of imagination and the technique will come if you practice. Running the mess is more about getting the best food for the budget and that's what trading is, isn't it?"

I saw in his eyes that something clicked. I could practically hear the gears turning. "You know? That might work." He smiled at me. "For a greenie, you're darn clever."

I smiled back. "Just trying to do what I can. You've been helping me so much the least I can do is repay the favor."

"Well, this might be the answer I needed, Ish, thanks again." He paused for a moment. "Dangle's knees, I need to unwind a bit. Maybe get in a little workout and then have a nice sauna before sack time. Let's head down to the gym."

"The gym?" I didn't know whether to hug him or hit him. "Are you telling me that after all this time, you didn't tell me this ship has a gym?"

You would think that I'd be observant enough to realize that all the passages I walked past, through, and around each day on my way to and from the mess deck should lead somewhere. Truthfully, I always felt just a bit lost on the ship. When I didn't have a guide like Pip, I stayed on the paths I knew.

The gym occupied most of the deck directly under the crew berthing. Compared to the areas of the ship I'd seen, it was huge. The overhead was twice as high, and my spatial sense told me that we occupied an area almost as large as the galley, mess deck, and berthing areas combined. I looked at Pip incredulously. "Is this normal?"

"What?"

"This!" I waved my hands. "All this space. Man, I thought we used every cubic meter for cargo. We're living in a cracker box up there but down here, it's so spacious. What gives?"

Pip chuckled. "Oh, not all the ships have a gym this big, but Federated freighters over forty kilotons do. We're lucky that way. Even the smaller ships have some kind of exercise facility. It helps if the crew can blow of excess energy on long trips. Otherwise the walls really start to close in."

"Ya think?" I punched him in the arm. "What else haven't you told me?"

"I know what you're talking about." He laughed while rubbing his shoulder.

"Oh yes, you do. What else about this ship don't I know about? First, it was the view from the bridge, Now this. What else is there?

A holo theater and a zoo maybe?"

"I'm sorry. I just thought you'd figure it out with your tablet."

"What's that supposed to mean?"

"Pull up the ship's menu, doofus. Look at the schematic."

It took a heartbeat for me to realize what he was saying. My brain kept arguing with itself. One side said, *Oh for crying out loud. How could I be so stupid?* Then the other side took over. *How should I have known? It's only been two weeks and I've been busy.* I did what he suggested and blinked dumbly at the detailed map of the ship that appeared. I could rotate it around, zoom in and out, and even isolate systems like water, air, electrical, and data.

The ship consisted of a long, hollow spine with cylindrical structures on each end. The wedge-shaped cargo containers locked onto the spine and each other, six per section and twelve of those ran the length of the ship. The aft housed the main boat deck, along with some reactor/generators and the kicker engines. The schematic even labeled them as "Dynamars Auxiliaries" with an energy output rating that didn't mean anything to me, and the fuel requirements to run them. It showed we were at eighty-five percent capacity.

The forward cylinder was a bit larger than the aft. The bridge perched on the highest level. Under that were the officer's quarters, then the crew's deck, including places I was already familiar with along with areas I hadn't seen before like storage areas and various operational closets. I already knew the galley's pantries and coolers were extensive, but the schematic detailed every one of them, including some I hadn't even seen yet.

The gym level took up almost the entire width and length of the middle of the bow section except for the very front of the ship where the locks were. A row of lifeboat pods ran along either side. Looking around to compare my surroundings with what I saw on the schematic I realized that there was a catwalk running around the perimeter above the pods and I could see a couple of the crew running laps.

Below us were some more engineering spaces, including environmental, more power generation, and the field generators that created the solar sails and gravity keel that provided our main propulsion.

"Man, I feel like an idiot," I mumbled out loud as I kept discovering new ways to look at the ship.

Pip clapped me on the shoulder. "No, I'm sorry. I forget you're so green. I should have given you a real tour, but come on. *Tempus* is *fugiting* all over the place and I need to work out a little and get a sauna."

He led me to the changing room and showed me where to get a towel and work out gear. I was even able to buy some running shoes that were better than anything I'd had on Neris.

"They'll bill you for it, but they're yours to keep. Just grab an empty locker and palm it. You can store all that stuff down here."

I was a runner, but Pip liked the exotic weight machines and motorized devices. Personally, I thought he was just a gadget head, but endorphin junkies can't afford to be too judgmental. We split up and I climbed the short ladder to the track while he went to the workout equipment. He moved from one to another in some pattern that must have made sense to him. I lost track of Pip after I finished my stretching and dropped into a running trance. I knew I would probably regret pushing so hard, but it just felt so good. I could only go about eight laps before a lack of wind and an excess of lactic acid pulled me to a stop. I met up with Pip again and he led me through the changing room into a shower where we sluiced off the worst of the sweat, and then into the sauna for a luxurious steam.

I confess that I was a bit nonplussed when I sat down next to Pip on the smooth wooden bench and realized the older woman across from us was the captain. I started to get up again when she spoke. "Mr. Maxwell tells me you're fitting in nicely, Mr. Wang."

"Yes, sar. Thank you, sar," I mumbled, embarrassed to be caught in a towel.

She gave me a gentle smile. "Well, keep up the good work. I need to get out of here before I melt and I have a lot left to do tonight." She rose, then and spoke in a voice that carried through the steam, "Good night, crew."

A chorus of "G'night, Captain" came from around us in the steamy depths. She strolled out toward the showers and I couldn't help but admire her legs.

Pip elbowed me sharply. "She's old enough to be your grand-mother."

I blushed and hoped that the steamy air and the heat hid it but I heard a low chuckle from somebody just out of sight around the corner and blushed even more.

The gym, or at least the sauna, turned out to be the social hub of the ship. Even during the afternoon, I'd find deck, engineering, and other watch standers taking advantage of the facility. Evenings were more crowded and I was as likely to see the captain or Mr. Maxwell there as anyone else. At first, I was a little nervous about seeing the captain nearly naked, not because she was a woman, but because she was the captain. It didn't matter what she was, or wasn't, wearing, the mantle of her office stayed with her wherever she went, so I got used to it pretty quickly.

From that night on, my daily routine included a work out at the gym followed by a sauna. Most days we took our midafternoon break there and I found it refreshing to go back to the galley after a bit of exercise, a nice sauna, and a cool shower. We also adjusted our day to include some kind of intellectual stimulation. Between Pip's knowledge of ships and trade, and what I was learning about cooking, we had quite a lot of expertise between us. I even got Pip to tell Cookie about his background.

Pip was full of ideas for trading and broached one with Cookie during one of our sessions. "Trading ship's stores? Mr. Carstairs, you shock me." He frowned at Pip but turned his back, hiding the wink and the discreet thumbs up he gave me. "I wouldn't dream of using inferior ingredients."

"No, I didn't mean that. I have to eat here, too. I'm just thinking we could afford better stuff on the same budget if we get a bit creative about what we buy and where."

After that, Cookie and Pip spent at least a stan every day going over the inventory and budget. They were hatching something, but I didn't know what, and Pip refused to discuss it with me. Cookie treated my friend with new respect and I found myself smiling whenever I saw them with their heads together over their tablets.

That left me with my own problem. What specialty did I want to pursue?

It was odd, really. My classmates back on Neris had all played the what-do-I-want-to-be-when-I-grow-up game with themselves and each other. I'd watched them find and explore what they thought might be their particular callings: music, art, even business, and education. Personally, I just never felt the need. Mom had insisted that I take advantage of her position and the university—for all the good that did. I'd agreed to study something, just for the sake of going, because it would buy me some time to figure out what I wanted to do, but I'd never found the thing that made me say, "Yes. This is why I'm here."

Aboard the *Lois*, for the first time in my life, I felt the need to make some decisions. Life on a freighter was just unusual enough to have an appeal. The very idea of traveling through the Deep Dark intrigued me. Besides, with my food and living expenses covered, I could probably make a pretty good living. I hadn't seen a pay chit yet, so I wasn't sure. The company typically disbursed pay just before docking, and I had no need for creds aboard the ship. I knew there would be taxes and union dues deducted, along with a mandatory retirement contribution, but there would also be a share of the profit from the trip, a small share, but the potential for a little something extra. Somehow the pay didn't seem to matter. Lying in my bunk, listening to the low voices of my shipmates around me, I could begin to envision what it might be like to do this awhile, and it didn't seem half-bad after all. I fell asleep without getting closer to a decision about my specialty, but after my earlier disquiet, feeling much better about being aboard.

❀   ❀   ❀

It took me about a week of evenings to make it through the various specialties listed in *The Handbook*. I didn't want to leave the ship, but I discovered some interesting things about ratings and slots. For example, you could take any job listed at your rating or lower. I didn't know how that played out in practice, but I could see where, in a pinch, you might want to take an ordinary spacer slot in order to get off-planet when an able spacer berth wasn't available. Some ideas were self-evident. The more ratings you had, the more possibilities for employment. Despite that, most people specialized in one area and concentrated their efforts to get the largest share ranking possible in that division. That piqued my interest and I ran some questions by Pip the day before we hit the jump point.

"Why do people work up through a specialty?" I asked.

"Why not? The higher you go, the better the pay."

"Well, yes, and no. Within some narrow range, your pay is largely determined by your share and not by your specialty, right?"

We were swabbing down the mess tables and he stopped to look at me. "Sorta. Your salary goes up based on rank even after your share maxes out. The difference in base pay between able spacer and spec one is pretty large but they're both full share berths."

"Okay, but the key to earning is being on a ship, isn't it?"

We had finished with the tables and moved on to sweeping the floor. "I'm not following where you're going with this, Ish."

"Suppose something happens here and I get put ashore. As a quarter share, I don't have much to draw on for a new berth."

"I'm with you so far." Pip rinsed out his rag in a bucket and nodded for me to go on.

"Now, if I qualify as a half share in, say, cargo, then my options begin to open up. I'm eligible to take any quarter share berth that comes along or a half share cargo slot."

"But why would you want to do that?" he asked. "Take the quarter share berth, I mean."

"Well, maybe the next ship in port doesn't have a cargo slot open. It would be a cut in pay for me to take the quarter share, but it's still more than I'd make planet-side earning nothing and paying for everything."

"True enough."

"Now, what if I qualify as half share in cargo and engineering? Or cargo and deck?"

"Why wouldn't you go for full share in cargo?" he asked.

"Well, the qualifying exam for full share is roughly twice as hard as for half share, isn't it?"

Pip considered this and shrugged to grant me the point. "Yeah, I suppose that's one perspective."

"So, for the same amount of effort for full share cargo, I could get two half share ratings in other divisions. And if my goal is the best possible chance of staying employed, wouldn't it make sense to get a second and third half share rating in order to diversify my options?"

He stopped dead in his tracks and stared at me, his head tilted a little sideways. "That's an odd way to look at it."

"Yeah, but play the game with me. Take the long view. Where are the most jobs?"

"Full share berths are the most common."

"So if I want to be guaranteed, as much as possible, that under any given circumstances I can get a position on the next ship, what do I need to have?"

His response came instantly. "A full share rating in a division. You can take any lower position and the majority of them are full share to begin with."

"Close. What I really need is a full share rating in *every* division."

"Goldilocks and all three bears, man. That would take forever!"

"Not so long as you might think. A university degree can take four or five stanyers. Advanced degrees even longer."

"True."

"It's much better, from an economic stand point, to be out in the Deep Dark. When I'm planet-side I'm burning creds. So long as I have a berth, I'm making money. So, what I need is the ability to maximize my time on board, and that means being able to take whatever job is open as soon as I need one. Most are full share and, while a lot of those are specialized, my best bet would be getting rated in every division."

I could almost see his mental gears clicking that idea around. After nearly a full tick, he frowned at me. "True. But what if you like one kind better than another? Doesn't that factor in?"

"Yeah, but not to the extent that I'm willing to go broke waiting for that slot to open up.

He grimaced but nodded slowly. "You've got a point, but how long will it take you to make half share?"

"I don't know, but we're still twenty-five days out of Darbat. I bet I can accomplish a lot in that amount of time."

We finished sweeping and stowed our cleaning gear. Pip turned to me with a thoughtful nod of his head. "If the last three weeks are any indication, my friend, I suspect you're right."

Chapter Eight
Neris System: 2351-September-21

A loud electronic horn woke me out of a deep sleep and practically gave me a heart attack. Even before the klaxon had stopped, I heard people moving about in the berthing area, pulling on shipsuits and boots. When the noise stopped, it was followed by the announcement. *"NOW THIS IS A DRILL. THIS IS A DRILL. FIRE, FIRE, FIRE. THERE IS A FIRE IN THE PORT-SIDE ENGINE COMPARTMENT. ALL HANDS TO FIRE AND DAMAGE CONTROL STATIONS. THERE IS A FIRE IN THE PORT-SIDE ENGINE COMPARTMENT. ALL HANDS TO FIRE AND DAMAGE CONTROL STATIONS. THIS IS A DRILL. THIS IS A DRILL."*

Pip slapped me on the leg and grinned. "Come on, greenie. Move it!" Beverly was already out of her bunk and zipping a shipsuit. I grabbed mine and followed her and Pip into the berthing area where everybody grumbled but moved sharply. I dressed quickly still pretty disoriented from the sudden arousal. When we exited, Bev peeled off at the passage that led aft and I followed Pip to the galley where we found Cookie waiting for us.

"Such excitement, eh, gentlemen." His cheerful smile seemed out of place.

I managed a look at the chronometer and saw 0116. "Do we always do this in the middle of the night?"

Cookie shook his head. "No, young Ishmael, we do it at all times of day."

Pip snorted a laugh. "Last time was in the middle of lunch service. Trust me, this is easier to deal with."

I yawned and considered a cup of coffee. "What do we do, and for how long do we do it?"

Pip shrugged. "It depends on the fire and damage teams. They have to make their way aft, assess the situation, and pretend to get the fire under control. While they do that we just have to sit around and wait."

"If we don't have to do anything, then why did we have to get up?"

Cookie smiled. "Well, if it were a real fire and the ship was in danger, would you prefer to be asleep in your bunk? In an actual emergency, we would support those doing the real work by supplying food or beverages, helping to tend the injured, or otherwise lending a hand."

I nodded blearily. "Okay, makes sense. I can deal with that. How often do we have these drills?"

Pip snickered. "Only once a quarter for fire drills but we have suit and lifeboat drills as well. We get about a drill a month."

"Consider it a down payment on learning how to stay alive in case anything really bad happens, young Ishmael." Cookie smiled and patted my shoulder.

I chuckled and nodded. "Good point." I went out and started up a fresh urn of coffee.

After about ten ticks the announcement came over the ship's speakers. *"ALL HANDS STAND DOWN FROM FIRE AND DAMAGE CONTROL STATIONS. THE DRILL IS COMPLETE. THE DRILL IS COMPLETE. SET NORMAL WATCH."*

A tick later, the speakers crackled again. *"This is the captain speaking. Excellent work, people. Very fast response times and outstanding performance by the damage control teams in assessing the situation. My congratulations to you all."*

Cookie pulled a tray of pastries from one of the coolers and set it out just in time for about a dozen people who burst onto the mess deck. I was glad I had already started the brewing. The official exercise might be over, but the after drill action had only just begun. Cookie waved over his shoulder as he left, but we stayed around. It didn't last that long, really. Within half a stan most people had wandered back to their bunks and the ship quieted down once more. Pip and I stacked the dirty mugs in the washer and made a quick pass wiping down the tables to make sure we'd be ready for breakfast before leaving ourselves.

As I crawled into my rack I noted the time, 0221, and hoped that Pip and Cookie were right about not always having drills at night.

❀　　❀　　❀

As I was prepping for dinner, I was still pondering how best to approach my academic pursuits. Between *The Handbook* and the ship's tablet, I held all the answers to the normal kinds of questions in the palm of my hands. My problem was I did't think what I was considering was normal. I needed somebody who was actively engaged in moving up, someone who could help me plot a path to advancement. I'd already gotten Pip's perspective, and he was only a step further ahead than I was. Then I remembered that when I came aboard Sandy Belterson had been studying for Spec II in Astrogation. I made a mental note to catch her when she came through the serving line.

"Hey, Sandy," I smiled at her as I dished up her plate. "Would you have time to talk with me after dinner?"

"Probably. What about?"

"I'm thinking about my specialty and I want to find out more about the process. I know you're studying, so perhaps you have some pointers?"

She nodded. "Sure. Running track? Twenty thirty?" She took her tray and went to find a seat. Pip elbowed me and waggled his eyebrows. I just kicked him.

When I got to the gym at 2030, Sandy was already on the track. I changed my clothes and caught up with her.

She nodded in greeting. "Hi Ish. What's up?"

We paced ourselves so we could run and talk. "I'm considering going to half share. What's the process like?"

"It's in *The Handbook.*"

"Yeah, I read about it, but you're the only person I know who's actively working through it. Are there any tricks? Tips for getting through?"

She laughed. "I think half the crew is working on the next pay grade. And, no, it's just what you see. *The Handbook* has the curriculum and some practice tests. For half share, it's almost all book learning. As you move up you have to demonstrate skills so there's some hands-on stuff. Every quarter, the Training Officer administers the exams and, if you pass he adds the rating to your personnel jacket. You can also take them whenever you want at any Union Hall."

"Okay, I was just checking. It seems a lot like earning scout badges."

She laughed again. "I suppose it is, but as a system, it seems to work."

We reached the end of a lap and paused at the top of the ladder. "One last question. Who's the Training Officer?"

"The third mate, Mr. von Ickles. It's in your tablet."

"Thanks, Sandy. I appreciate it."

Chuckling, she headed down the ladder with a *you're welcome* wave over her shoulder. "Good luck," she called from below.

I took a couple more laps before heading for the showers and the sauna.

❋   ❋   ❋

The next day I experienced my first transition. I'd been through a jump before, but I didn't remember much about it as I was pretty young when Mom and I arrived on Neris. According to the count-down timer on my tablet, transition would occur sometime in the middle of the afternoon watch. We had already furled the sails and retracted the gravity keel. The kickers, the auxiliary engines in the stern, were on something called *hot standby* according to what I'd overheard from the engineering crew. Presently, we were lined up on the jump trajectory and just coasting into the correct position.

Sure enough, about 1400, as Pip and I were finishing cleanup, the announcement came. *"ALL HANDS, SECURE FOR TRAN-SITION. TRANSITION IN TEN TICKS, MARK."*

I looked at Pip. He shrugged. We stowed the cleaning gear and settled at one of the mess tables.

"It's no big deal," Pip said conversationally, apropos of nothing.

"It can't be too traumatic, I did it as a toddler, and I don't remember a thing."

"ALL HANDS, TRANSITION IN TEN, NINE, EIGHT, SEVEN..." the announcer counted down and I couldn't help but brace myself. *"...THREE, TWO, ONE, ZERO. TRANSITION COMPLETED. WELCOME TO DARBAT. ESTIMATED ARRIVAL AT DAR-BAT ORBITAL IN TWENTY-FOUR DAYS. SECURE FROM NAV-IGATION STATIONS. FIRST SECTION HAS THE WATCH."*

I don't know what I expected—some kind of sensation at least, perhaps a flicker of the lights, or some kind of trilling in my brain. Pip shrugged with a grin. "Told ya," was all he said as Cookie called to him from the galley.

"Mr. Carstairs, I have those figures we needed..."

He waved and I pulled out my tablet to message Mr. von Ickles for an appointment to talk about my education. I knew him, at least by sight, of course. Everybody comes through the mess line. It seemed like I'd no sooner hit send, when Mr. von Ickles walked into the mess deck. He nodded to me, grabbed a mug of coffee, and sat down at my table.

"How can I help you, Mr. Wang?" I didn't know how he'd even had time to read the message, but I plowed ahead.

"I'm interested in moving up to half share, sar. Is there anything I need to do? File an application? Notify you?"

He sipped his coffee. "Not really. It's just like *The Handbook* says. Half share is pretty straightforward. Study until you're ready and then just show up and give it a shot. I'll be administering the next round in about a month. Just after we leave Darbat." He paused. "You realize that passing the test doesn't give you the pay bump?"

"Oh yes, sar. I'm just thinking ahead. I don't plan on leaving the galley anytime soon. I just want to expand my options."

"That's good to know. This is the best coffee this ship has ever had." He grinned at me and then focused back on my question. "What test will you be taking?"

"Engineman, sar," I told him and I felt compelled to add, "First."

"First?" he raised an eyebrow.

"Yes, sar. I'm...uh...planning to pursue all four of the half share ranks."

He blinked. "Really?"

"I'm not sure what I want to do for the rest of my life, sar. About the only thing I know is I like life in the Deep Dark, and I want to do what I can to stay out here."

He pursed his lips and nodded. "Why not pick a specialty and take it up to full share? It's more money."

"Well, eventually, I will, but like I said, I don't know which division I'll like the most and until I figure it out I want to maximize my employability. If something should happen, and I find myself ashore for some reason, I want to be able to get back on a ship as quickly as possible, and not have to wait for a berth. In the amount of time it would take me to get up to full share, I could have at least two half share ratings."

"Makes a certain amount of sense." He sipped his coffee thoughtfully.

"For me, I'd rather be underway, even if it's not my favorite position, then to wait planet-side for a preferred one."

"True enough. But would you be able to do a job you hate for weeks at a time?"

"Sar, I have no idea which ones I might like more than any other. Until I get to actually do them, there's no way I can tell."

He nodded.

"That's another reason I want to diversify. So I can try them out. Once I'm rated in each, I should have a pretty good idea what the jobs are like and then I can pick. If I don't like something I'll know enough not to pursue it. Going through the test should give me some indication, won't it, sar?"

He leaned back in his chair and tapped the tabletop with a fingertip while he considered. "Yes, Mr. Wang. It probably will. It's certainly an interesting approach."

"Do you foresee any kind of difficulty, sar?"

He shook his head. "Only the time it'll take to get through all four exams. We only offer the tests once a quarter."

"Is there any limit on the number of tests I can take in a single period?"

He looked startled. "Could you be ready for more than one at a time?"

I shrugged. "I don't know, sar, but three months is a long time, and I've seen the half share curriculum. It doesn't seem like it would be that much compared to, say, a university program."

He smiled and gave a short laugh. "No, I suppose not, but at the university, you're not working ten stans a day in addition to going to school."

"True enough, but here I'm not drinking my nights and weekends away," I countered with a laugh of my own.

Mr. von Ickles grinned at that. "True enough, Mr. Wang. True enough."

He stood and headed out into the passage. At the hatch he paused for a tick and looked back at me. "Engineering is a good place to start but look at cargo as well. There's a lot of turnover with cargo handlers. The work is a bit boring and relies more on muscle than mind at the lower ratings. If you're trying to maximize employability, then having your cargo rating is a good step."

"Thank you, sar. I appreciate the tip."

He nodded and left me to ponder. I was still sitting there when Pip came out of the galley. "Problems? I heard you talking with Mr. von Ickles."

I shook my head. "Actually, no. He wasn't exactly supportive, but he didn't try to talk me out of it. What's up with Cookie?"

Pip ran a hand through his cropped dark hair. "We're good, but I need to find a computer. I don't want to run my sims on the ship's system just yet. The equations are getting complicated enough that I need to get some substantial computing cycles."

"You wanna borrow mine?"

"You have a computer? You brought one aboard?" He gaped at me with his mouth half open.

I looked up at him with a shrug. "Yeah. Is there a rule against it?"

He shook his head. "It's just that they mass so much and most people don't want to burn quota on something they can get using the ship's."

"Oh well, see, I didn't know that was available here, and it was my mom's. I thought it might be useful for studying and stuff and it has more processing power than my peeda."

"Studying what?"

"I downloaded several dozen courses from the University of Neris before they shut off Mom's access. Did I tell you she was a professor there?"

"You'd mentioned it, but I didn't think you'd have brought the university with you."

"Why not? Your aunt told me that all I really needed was entertainment cubage."

"And you put university classes in the category of entertainment?"

I shrugged and nodded.

"Amazing. What courses?"

"I don't remember. Plant sciences, astrophysics, advanced mathematics. I was just grabbing all kinds of stuff. It was right after they told me..." I choked up and looked down.

"Hey, no problem. I understand. We're clear until 1530. Can we go look?"

"Sure, let's go."

Down in the berthing area, we spread my stuff out on the table. Midafternoon was quiet since a third of the crew were on day watch and those who weren't were either sleeping or engaged in their own pursuits.

Pip whistled when I brought out the computer. "Nice machine. It doesn't mass anything like I would have expected it to."

I shrugged. "Mom used it for her work, although I stripped her stuff off and sent it all to storage. It's pretty empty now except for basic software and the courses."

We started cataloging the courses I'd brought from Neris: astrophysics, plant sciences, ecological studies, accounting, advanced mathematics, and at least ten others. We didn't get through the list because we kept getting side tracked by things we found and had to head back to the galley before we got through all the storage cubes. Pip kept exclaiming, "I can't believe this." Before we left I gave him the computer and credentials so he could use it.

"Thanks, Ish. This is going to make things much easier."

"What simulations are you running?"

"Oh, just some trading sims."

"Uh, huh." I looked at him out of the corner of my eye, but I let him off the hook as we shifted into the evening routine.

CHAPTER NINE
DARBAT SYSTEM: 2351-SEPTEMBER-28

The run into Darbat Orbital wasn't terribly different then leaving Neris. The daily mess cycle gave all of us a structure to our day that became second nature. Cookie and Pip closeted themselves with the computer and whatever simulations they were running during the afternoon break. I took that opportunity to load up engineering training, intending to take the engineman exam after Darbat. I flashed through the instructional component in about a week and started taking the practice tests. I didn't do too badly, but I couldn't get a passing grade.

The cargo materials were pretty straight forward: container types, cargo handling procedures, various techniques for securing containers and the proper way to use cargo manipulation tools like grav pallets and hoists. There was not a lot of meat to it, and I saw how somebody might get a bit bored.

Cargo handlers packed it in, made sure it didn't move while we were underway, and unpacked it on the other end. I vowed never to complain about mess duty again as I tried to envision forty days in a row of: yup, it's still there. The other side of that coin would be that you'd have a lot of time to study for another rating. Looking ahead to cargoman, I saw the program got into various cargo types, trade rules, and some other more interesting stuff about the classifications of stores. The study guide contained lessons on margin, profit, and more safety regulations. Mr. von Ickles' comment about turnover at the cargo handler level made a lot more sense once I saw what the job was, at least on the tablet.

I ran through the cargo handler instructional materials in one evening and took the practice exam just for fun. I aced it. Thinking it was a fluke, I tried another test the next afternoon and passed with flying colors again. Smiling, I sent a calendar note to Mr. von Ickles to reserve a seat at the cargo handler rating exams when they came up.

❀ ❀ ❀

Midmorning, about a week after jumping into Darbat, we had a suit drill. Pip and I had almost finished the breakfast cleanup when the klaxon started doing a whoop-whoop sound at about a billion decibels. My coworkers dropped everything and ran to a panel at the back of the galley. By the time the klaxon stopped and the announcement came, they'd already pulled out three lightweight suits with helmets attached and tossed one at me. *"THIS IS A DRILL. THIS IS A DRILL. ENVIRONMENTAL INTEGRITY HAS BEEN BREACHED. ALL HANDS DON PROTECTIVE GEAR. ALL HANDS DON PROTECTIVE GEAR. THIS IS A DRILL. THIS IS A DRILL."*

The sudden silence came as a blessed relief as I struggled to get into my suit. I had one leg in, and was working on the other, when I noticed my two co-workers looking down at me through their clear helmets.

Pip looked at Cookie for permission before speaking. "This," he said, indicating me sitting on the deck, "is why we drill."

Cookie spoke inside his suit, but I couldn't make out the words. It sounded like a short report made in a formal tone. I continued to struggle into my suit, but before I got the second leg fully in, the announcement came, *"ALL HANDS SECURE FROM DRILL. ALL HANDS SECURE FROM DRILL."*

The captain's follow-up announcement came immediately after, *"This is the captain speaking. Very good work people. At the end of three minutes only one person was listed as dead. Carry on."*

"Dead?" I asked.

Cookie took off his suit and nodded. "You have three minutes to get into a suit when the alarm sounds, young Ishmael. If you don't make it, your department head lists you as dead." I saw the disappointment in his face.

Pip and Cookie stripped off their suits, marked them as used by pulling a red tab on the hanger, and racked them back in the locker. Afterward Pip helped me, and we practiced with the suit for a stan before we had to set it aside and help Cookie with lunch. During the mess line, nobody mentioned it, but I could feel my ears burning and I knew everybody figured out I was the deader.

After lunch and the subsequent cleanup, Pip continued to drill me. Two stans later, I still couldn't get the suit on in under three minutes. My feet kept getting tangled in the legs no matter what I did. The longer it took, the more frustrated I became. For his part, Pip was right there encouraging me with, "Just once more. You'll get it this time."

Eventually, Cookie came over and watched me struggle under my friend's direction for about three ticks, before he interrupted. "Very funny, Mr. Carstairs. Now would you care to show young Ishmael how to do it correctly?"

Pip had the decency to look abashed as he had me turn the suit around.

"You had me trying to put it on backward for the last two stans?"

He nodded. "Yeah. Sorry. Entertainment is in short supply out in the Deep Dark."

"Jackanapes," Cookie cuffed him on the back of the skull with the tips of his fingers. "What if he'd needed to get into that suit in a real emergency?"

I was having trouble not laughing myself even as the butt of his joke.

Cookie took the suit, folded it up so it looked like it came from the locker, and showed me where to grab it. A quick flick of the wrists and I stepped in, pulled it up, and shrugged into it in almost one smooth movement. A quick toss of my head and the helmet slid into place and I locked it down on the first try.

They took turns showing me things like the radio, patch kit, and the instrument panel mounted on the sleeve.

Cookie pointed to the air supply timer. "This is for emergency use only as it has just one stan of air. Use it just to get to a soft-suit or a lifeboat. You cannot survive long in it so you must be sure you know what's going on around you if you ever have to put it on."

Pip patted me on the back. "Next time you won't be the dead one."

"How often do we have these drills?"

"At least once every nincty days. Sometimes more."

I took off the suit, folded it in the approved manner, and put the used indicator across the top before hanging it with Pip and Cookie's. Several more were in the locker.

I pointed to the hangers with red tags. "What happens to the used ones?"

Cookie answered, "Someone from engineering will collect and reset them for use. Never take a used emergency suit because you won't know how much air is left in it. You can't change out of them in a vacuum and it would cost your life if you needed forty-five ticks and only had thirty."

It was a sobering thought and I took it to heart.

As I closed the panel, I reached for my tablet. The ship's schematic had an overlay showing all the emergency suit lockers. I made a mental note of the one nearest my bunk.

Cookie in the meantime turned to Pip. "You will be doing evening cleanup alone for the next week, Mr. Carstairs."

Pip nodded. "Aye aye, Cookie." He may have tried to look contrite but he still had a big grin on his face. So did I for that matter. It wasn't something to joke about, but still, it struck me as funny. Personally, I think Cookie left the galley then so he could have a good laugh, too.

Funny as it was, I was getting a little tired of being in the dark so I went to Beverly after dinner cleanup. I found her reading in her bunk.

"Bev? Can you help me?"

She looked at me over the top of her tablet. "Dunno. Whatcha need?"

"What's the story with these drills? I'm getting tired of being caught off guard by them."

She chuckled. "Well, they're supposed to be a surprise, but if you've never been through them, I can see why you'd be frustrated."

"It's making me a bit crazy. I'm okay with fire and suit drills now, but are there others coming up that I should know about?"

"It's in your tablet under ship emergency procedures but I think the only one you haven't been through is lifeboat drill. Do you know what your boat assignment is?"

I shook my head.

"Look up your record. It's down near the bottom."

I pulled out my tablet and found the notation. "It says boat four."

"Odd to port, even to starboard," she said. "Four should be the second boat back from the bow. You know where the boat deck is, right?"

I nodded. "I've seen the hatches under the track, but I didn't look too closely at them."

"Next time you're in the gym take a look. Make sure you know where boat four is."

"That's it?"

She thought for a moment before saying, "There are some specialized drills, damage control and battle stations and such, but we only do those once in forever. Fire, suit, and lifeboat are the big three and we're required to do each of them once a quarter, so get used to 'em."

"Thanks, Bev. I'll remember."

I climbed up into my bunk and, on a hunch, I went through *The Handbook* and found a section on klaxon calls. The raspy buzz of fire, the whoop-whoop of hull breach, and the pingity-pingity-pingity of abandon ship were all there along with battle stations, general quarters, and a dozen others that I didn't recognize. Even mealtimes had special tones that announced each one.

We were still a week out of Darbat Orbital when I arranged to visit environmental during the afternoon break. I'd been working through all the instructional materials on engineering, but I hadn't been able to score a passing grade on the practice tests. There wasn't any one thing I was missing, but rather a kind of diffuse inability to keep everything straight, particularly with the environmental stuff. All the scrubbers, filters, cleaners, and recyclers kept getting jumbled up in my head. I contacted the section chief on my tablet and made an appointment for a tour.

I knew the Environmental Section Chief, Spec One (Environmental) Brilliantine Smith, from seeing her in the mess line. She was easily the tallest person on the ship. I'd guess her height at something over two full meters. I'd also seen her in the gym and sauna. She didn't carry an extra gram of fat on her frame. The best description I could think of was willowy. She kept her chocolate-brown hair short like the rest of the crew and had a kind of generic, galactic citizen look, except that she had to duck to pass through every hatch on the ship. She walked with a kind of stoop, learned no doubt through hard experience.

Walking into environmental for the first time was like stepping into wet gauze. The smell was unmistakable, but I didn't really find it objectionable. It was kinda funky and green smelling. Not quite fishy, but there was a hint of that, too.

Smith watched me enter and nodded approvingly. "You're okay."

"Excuse me, sar?"

She grinned. "No, sar, for me, Ish. I'm no more officer than Cookie." She grinned even more. "Just taller. They call me Brill, among other less flattering appellations, I'm certain."

"I—see," I said, although I only got about half of what she was saying.

"You're okay because you didn't wrinkle your nose when you came in."

"That's good?"

She nodded with a wink. "Between the humidity and the smell, about half the people that come in here turn around and walk right back out. The humidity's from the matrices and the smell is from the algae."

"Okay, that much I understand. But there is still a lot I'm

confused by."

"How far have you gotten in the instructional material?"

"All of it, actually, but I can't seem to pass the practice test. Things I get right on one, I miss on the next and around and around. I can't seem to keep the scrubbers and the filters straight."

"Filter the water and scrub the air down, mix water and algae to make it all brown." She chanted it in sing-song with a smile.

"Wow, I actually understood that," I said with surprise as it slowly penetrated my brain.

"First practical piece of advice we give people. Water gets filtered and air is scrubbed. Then they get mixed together. It starts with running the water through a collection of different media to filter out finer and finer impurities. Eventually, it goes into the scrubbers where it keeps the algae matrices wet. That's probably where your brain gets confused because the scrubbers work on both air and water."

"Okay, that makes sense so far. So, the air doesn't get filtered?"

"Actually, it does, but we don't have a separate filtering system for it. Not like the water. There's a simple electrostatic field that the air is passed through when it first comes into the system. It snags all the dust and other particulates out of the air. Technically, that's not a filter because a filter is a physical barrier, like when you make coffee. The weave in the paper has holes that allow the infused water to pass without permitting the grounds themselves. It's the same idea with the water system although the chemical processing is a bit more complex."

I nodded. "And because the air is passed through a field, and not a physical barrier, you call it scrubbing instead of filtering?"

"Exactly." She nodded and smiled. "The scrubbers also grab any odd gases that make their way into the system. Those are usually byproducts from work on the ship like trace amounts of free esters, ozone, and so forth. The goal is to keep the proportions of oxygen, nitrogen, carbon dioxide, and trace gases consistent. The air coming into the system is high on carbon dioxide and low on oxygen so we feed it into the wet algae matrix where the algae absorb the carbon dioxide and produce oxygen. Have you ever noticed that the berthing areas don't smell like a locker room?"

I nodded.

"The algae loves the stuff that makes that smell. It would reek if not for that."

"Right, thanks, that helps."

"Come on." She turned and beckoned me to follow with a wave of her hand. "I'll give ya the half-cred tour."

For the next stan, she showed me the inner workings that kept our air and water clean. I expected to be disgusted by some of the processing. Sewage isn't exactly appealing, but I found myself fascinated by the way the air and water systems intertwined on the ship. There was a certain amount of unrecoverable waste, but almost ninety-eight percent of the air and water was recycled. At each port, we topped off the elements that got lost, used up, or destroyed. I even got a perverse bit of entertainment out of the notion that coffee was continually recycled through the crew's kidneys, down to environmental, and back to the mess deck where it started the cycle anew.

When we got to the algae matrices, the-makes-it-all-brown part of the doggerel became apparent. According to *The Handbook*, the algae were a blue-green variety but when they were wet, exposed to light, and healthy, it wasn't green at all, but a kind of reddish-brown. The matrix itself, was actually a synthetic film that held each little alga suspended to maximize its surface exposure. My preconceived notions about tanks of blue-green pond scum were blown away.

I laughed out loud and she turned a quizzical eye in my direction. "I don't know why, but I had this idea that I'd find big vats with bubbling slime."

She grinned. "That's a common misconception. The bacterial recovery tanks are the closest thing we have to fit that impression, but they don't bubble. We actually have to aerate them to keep the aerobic bacteria alive, not the other way around." She looked pensive. "Now if we could just find a use for the sludge. . ."

"Sludge? What do you do with it now?"

"We press it into blocks, freeze dry it, and give it away to planets that need terraforming material. It's not worth selling, and we're prohibited from jettisoning it."

That struck me so oddly that I laughed again. "Are they afraid the galaxy will fill up?"

She shook her head. "No, actually, back in the thirty's it was okay to just drop 'em out the airlock. The problem was that one wound up splattered across the main viewing port of a passenger liner." She did a good job of keeping a straight face, better than I could have. "Rumor is that several members of the CPJCT Steering Committee were aboard at the time and didn't fancy having their view ruined by streaks of spacer sludge."

"Thanks, Brill. This has helped a lot."

My break was over and I needed to head back to the mess deck so we said our goodbyes and she gave me a friendly wave as I headed out.

For the rest of the day I kept chanting, "Filter the water and scrub the air down, mix water and algae to make it all brown," over and over in my head. Two days later, I took another practice test and passed. Not perfect, but it was the first passing mark I received on the engineering materials. I felt jubilant.

Chapter Ten
Darbat Orbital: 2351-October-22

The final docking at Darbat Orbital was just as uneventful as leaving Neris. It felt rather strange that after spending practically my whole life on Neris I was going to visit a different planet—or at least its orbital. I confess I had a certain level of excitement at the prospect, although rationally I knew it couldn't be all that different.

We set navigation detail right after lunch. Everybody got a good meal into them before we started the process and we spent the afternoon watch doing the actual docking maneuvers. We didn't need bento-box lunches so there was no extra work. All Pip and I had to do was the normal post-lunch cleanup and hang out until the ship was secured. Cookie planned for a small meal at 1800 but he would need only one of us.

Cookie smiled when I asked about it. "If there are more than three people left aboard for dinner, besides the watch section and the first mate, I'll be very surprised. First night in port is usually the quietest. You gentlemen split it up. We've got a four day port stay. Work it out between you and post it on the duty roster so I know who to look for."

I was excited about docking, not because I planned to leave the ship, other than a stroll around to stretch my legs and see the sights a bit, but because it would feel good to have the relatively relaxed duty that came from having most of the crew ashore.

Finally, the announcement came, "*ALL HANDS, SECURE FROM NAVIGATION DETAIL. SECURE SHIP FOR PORT OPERATIONS. THIRD SECTION HAS THE WATCH.*" We looked at each other and Pip grinned. I knew he was thinking about the bottles of Grishom in his locker. Cookie waved us out and we headed for the berthing area just in time to hear, *"NOW, LIBERTY, LIBERTY, LIBERTY. HANDS NOT ON DUTY MAY LEAVE THE SHIP ACCORDING TO STANDING ORDERS AND ESTABLISHED PROCEDURES. NOW LIBERTY."*

A hooting cheer came from the berthing areas and we stumbled into a maelstrom of half clothed bodies, grinning faces, loud plans, brags, and general teasing. Pip and I jumped onto our respective bunks to free the floor space and plan.

"You go, Pip. I'll take the duty tonight so you can get your business taken care of."

"Thanks, Ish. I'll come back for dinner tomorrow and you can take the next twenty-four?"

I nodded. I was in no particular hurry and I knew he needed to finish this deal and line up the next one. Of course, I was pretty sure he had another deal already in mind, but I didn't pry.

I dug into my studies, but with so much noise in the berthing area, it was all but impossible to concentrate. I checked the cred balance on my tablet and saw that I'd been paid, and it looked like the right amount minus charges for dues, taxes, shipsuits and my running shoes. It didn't seem like a lot for almost seven weeks' work, but the share amount was half again more, so I couldn't really complain. The share amount offset the deductions with a bit to spare, but I could see where doing a bit of private trading might pay off.

At 1600 I went up to the mess deck to help Cookie with the evening meal. He really didn't need me, but it gave me something to do away from the still noisy berthing area. I took a certain satisfaction draining out the two partial coffee urns, leaving the full one for dinner. It would be great to have an urn last for more than three stans at a time. I remembered my trip down to engineering with a grin as I thought about the filters below processing the black liquid that I drained away. *Filter the water and scrub the air down...*

After almost seven weeks of serving a full crew, port-duty seemed easy. I had a pleasant evening working with Cookie, and he was kind enough to help me clean up afterward.

While I swept out the galley after dinner, I took the opportunity to ask him about the mysterious project he and Pip had been working on.

"Ah, Ishmael, I really should thank you for breaking through to Pip. He's a remarkable young man."

"He's something. I'm not exactly sure what."

Cookie chuckled. "He has a most unusual way of looking at things."

"So, what are these simulations you're running?"

"We are experimenting with options for acquiring the supplies we need for the ship in some rather innovative ways."

"Oh?" I asked with the rising inflection in what I hoped was an adequate imitation of my mother's tone used to evoke additional information.

"No, Ishmael, not yet. When the time is right, all will be clear. In the meantime..." He slid an index finger alongside his nose. "We'll just keep on as we are, eh?"

I have to confess that this intrigued me even more, but Cookie knew how to keep his own counsel and I was unlikely to get more out of him, at least directly. As it turned out, I didn't have to wait long for my first real clues. We filled the rest of our time with small talk about Darbat Orbital, its restaurants, dives, and even less savory attractions. Cookie was a compendium of information and I took as much care to note some of the more interesting items on his litany of places to stay away from as from his recommendations.

The evening cleanup took almost no time compared to an evening underway. By 1900 I was running laps and looking forward to the sauna. Sandy Belterson came up from behind me and started matching my strides. I smiled in greeting.

"Hey, Ish." We had run together several times since our first conversation. I found her to be a good, companionable running partner. Often we said nothing more than "hi" to each other. That night, she wanted to talk.

"Hey, Sandy, you're not on-station?"

"Nah, I've got first watch duty tomorrow. If I go out tonight it just wouldn't be as much fun. I'll get a night on the town before we leave." She smiled wolfishly. "I try to pace myself. You?"

"Pip and I split the stay. He got first night and we'll trade off. We can't go on-station together because one of us has to be on duty."

She nodded and we ran a lap in silence.

"What's he doing?"

"Who? Pip?"

"I saw him leaving the ship with a duffel. He's trading, isn't he?"

"Yeah." That was all I would commit to.

"I hope he does well. He's a nice guy."

"Why wouldn't he?" We paused at the head of the ladder. I was trying to decide if I wanted to run another lap or just head for the sauna.

"It's not an easy thing to succeed at, especially on quarter share. The mass allotment is okay for personal gear, but too small to make a decent profit at trading unless you know what you're doing. It's hard to diversify enough and one bad deal can break ya." Her words sent a chill up the back of my neck. Glass bottles were so fragile and I hoped he wasn't going to have any problems.

"Yeah, well, he's an interesting guy," I said. "I bet he has depths we haven't even seen yet."

"Yeah. True of all of us, eh?" She offered a rueful toss of her head.

I decided to make one more lap before calling it a night after all and started running again. Sandy fell into step with me. "So, how's the half share thing going?"

"Not bad. I'm already signed up for the next round of tests that are coming up."

She beamed. "That's great. Which one?"

"Engineering."

"Excellent."

"And cargo."

"What? Two?"

I shrugged and panted for a few steps. Our conversation suffered from running too fast. "Why not? What's the cost? I might pass one, or the other, or both. And if I don't pass either, I'll just try again next time."

She panted alongside me. "True. Are you ready?"

"I think so. Of course I won't know for sure until the tests, will I?"

She nodded, flicking a stream of sweat out of her eye with the side of her hand. "You're full of surprises."

We slowed the pace for the last half lap, cooling a bit, and both lost in our own thoughts. I was a bit worried about Pip and hoped he was okay. I should have been thinking about the probability that it would be just Sandy and me in the sauna together and how awkward that would be, but it never crossed my mind. I almost stumbled on the ladder as I was carefully not thinking about that possibility. Turns out she just showered and disappeared, so it wasn't an issue. The sauna wasn't empty though. Mr. Maxwell was there.

He acknowledged my entrance with a nod. "Mr. Wang."

"Mr. Maxwell, sar." I smiled in what I hoped was an acceptable manner and chose my seat carefully. Not to close in case he wanted to be alone, nor too far away to appear rude if he wanted to talk.

"Mr. von Ickles tells me you're considering going for all four ratings." He commented as if speaking to the steam, rather than to me.

"Ah, yes, sar. I am."

"Interesting approach. Why are you doing that?" His head swiveled to aim his eyes at me through the murk.

I was worried about what he might be thinking and wasn't sure how to explain to someone of his rank. I didn't know what was appropriate. "It's not exactly easy to explain, sar."

"Well, Mr. Wang, I'd like to hear your reasoning." When I looked over, I was shocked to see him smiling.

I was almost too surprised to answer. "Well, sar, I'm not sure what I want to do, but these last five weeks have been the most challenging and oddly enjoyable in my admittedly short life."

"Yes?" With that one word, I knew Mr. Maxwell was a master at prying more information out of people. My mother had the same skill.

"I can't explain it, but I suppose the best word I can come up with is therapeutic." I realized that therapeutic was exactly the word and if Mr. Maxwell wanted to talk to me, then by the holy I would talk back.

He chuckled softly and then added seriously, "I lost my parents only recently as well. I'm sure it was not as traumatic as it must have been for you."

"I'm sorry to hear that, sar."

"Thank you, Mr. Wang, but you were saying... about your choice in career advancement?"

"Well, sar, being stuck on Neris, needing to leave before the company deported me, and having no real idea of what to do or how to do it... made me feel helpless."

He grunted.

"I lucked out when Ms. O'Rourke helped me get on the *Lois*, but I can't count on, or trust to luck in the future. I don't ever want to be stranded like that again, so I'm trying to select a path that maximizes my options."

Mr. Maxwell smiled again—a thoroughly disconcerting expression. "So you're pursuing all four half share ratings just on the off chance that you might get stranded somewhere?"

"Yes, sar. Partly. The other thing is that I really never expected to be working on a freighter, not in my wildest dreams. I have no idea what rating I might like best because I know almost nothing about any of them. The only way to find out is to study and perhaps do some of them to see for myself."

He nodded. "Prudent." The way he said it made it feel like a compliment.

I felt the irrational need to respond. "Thank you, sar."

Mr. Maxwell stood then and headed out to the showers. "Carry on, Mr. Wang. You've set yourself an interesting task. Good luck with it." He disappeared out the door.

I basked in the heat for a few more minutes, still somewhat shaken by our conversation and not entirely trusting my legs. Truth be told, I also wanted to give Mr. Maxwell time to finish his shower and leave. Junior crew members don't associate with senior officers as a rule. One close encounter with him was enough for one night.

Later, on a whim, I checked my tablet. The ship's record showed everybody's ratings. Mr. Maxwell had held all four, as had the captain. None of the other officers held any crew ratings at all, although they did have the appropriate licenses for their jobs. I wondered at that as I drifted off to sleep in the nearly silent berthing area. Tabitha was staying on-station and I kinda missed her little snorty-snores from the other side of the partition.

Chapter Eleven
Darbat Orbital: 2351-October-23

The morning grind was not just slow, it was practically non-existent. As usual, the watch stander woke me, but when I got to the mess deck, Cookie and I were the only ones there. While underway, there were always at least a couple people lounging about for first dibs on fresh pastries and coffee, but not that day. I got the urns going and started setting up the steam table, when Cookie stopped me.

"I would be most surprised if we have more than five or six people for breakfast, young Ishmael. We'll just have omelets, I think. Would you like one?"

He was correct, of course, and his omelet was perfect. Mr. Maxwell and the captain each came down, collected some food, and left. A couple of the engineering crew came in at the watch change along with Brill Smith. None of them seemed very talkative although the two from engineering had a desultory, "Yes it is, no it's not," back and forth about something that neither of them elucidated.

Brill smiled and brought her coffee to sit with me. "Quiet, eh?"

I nodded. "Not much happening this morning."

"Rating exam in ten days. Are you ready?"

"I think so, but..." I shrugged.

She chuckled. "You'll do fine." She leaned in and lowered her voice. "Did I hear you're taking two tests?"

"Yeah, engineering and cargo. The cargo one looks pretty easy."

"Then what? You gonna look for another berth?"

"No, I'm happy here and I've got enough to figure out without trying to unravel transfers. I've been aboard for less than two months and I'm still getting lost on my way to the head." I was only half joking.

"What then? You're just going to sit on your ratings?"

"Um, actually..." I started, but was a bit reticent about continuing.

Brill gave me a kind of sideways nod as if to say, Yeah? *Actually...* what?

"I'm going to study for steward and deck after that."

Brill slapped the table, making the engineers jump but it didn't stop their bickering. "I knew it." She grinned fiercely at me. "I'm sure you can do it. Deck is the hardest because there's so many things you have to know. I could never pass that myself. I'm just not wired that way. You're already immersed in steward so that shouldn't be too difficult."

"You think so?" After weeks of studying the wide-ranging engineering material, I had a hard time imagining somebody who'd mastered them would believe that deck was hard.

"Yeah, I've got half share rating in steward myself, but environmental is my love. I never want to do anything else."

"Then why did you take the steward test?"

"I started with that. I made the shift to environmental about five stanyers ago and I never regretted the change. The steward rating was useful. It got me up and going, but I'd never go back."

Cookie brought her omelet and I went to the galley to help him set the bread for later. We didn't cook that many meals when docked, but we did go through a lot of sandwiches, so he baked extra loaves.

"You're getting to be well thought of, young Ishmael." he smiled and nodded out to where Brill sat with her omelet. "I had no doubts, myself."

The rest of the day was extremely low key. After we got the bread rising, I did the normal galley cleanup but so little needed doing that I was done by 0900. Cookie gave me the rest of the morning off. "Just be back by 11:00. We'll be doing soup and sandwiches for lunch. I'll have you lay out the meats and cheeses."

I returned to my studies and went over air scrubber protocols once more before reviewing the regulations on disposing of used engine oil in an environmentally safe manner. Since we used it as reaction mass in the vacuum of deep space, I wasn't sure what that was all about, but it was on the test so I studied it.

More than once I marveled at how differently I saw the ship then as compared to when it was docked at Neris. Before, I was overwhelmed by the blur of everything around me, but docked once again the ship seemed somnolent. The same level of activity happened around me but the experience of being underway tempered my own reaction to it. By comparison, being docked felt like a vacation.

Lunch was as quiet as breakfast. A few of the crew stumbled in, some still half drunk. Most just got coffee to take down to the berthing areas while they got cleaned up for the duty shift change. Pip hadn't returned over night, but he had mentioned relieving me for the dinner shift so I wasn't so concerned. I remembered Sandy saying she'd be on duty, but I hadn't seen her. With no serving line set up, she could have come in, eaten and left, and I might never have noticed.

After lunch, Cookie filled the void of activity by having me shift stores around. "Young Ishmael, I'm expecting some shipments and we need to rotate the stock." He loaded a list of stores he wanted moved from one place to another onto my tablet. When done, I had completely emptied three pantries and one whole freezer. I wondered what he expected in the way of supplies but didn't want to pry.

After the stock rotation, I mopped up and made coffee before going to berthing to get ready for my first trip to a new orbital. Pip would be back to help with supper and I'd be free to explore on my own for the first time. I looked forward to a meal in a real restaurant where somebody waited on me for a change. I didn't really care what I ate so long as I didn't have to serve it or clean up after.

Cookie bipped me on the tablet to return to the galley while I was brushing down my civilian boots. When I got there, Sandy's words from the previous evening came back to me. Three Darbati officials stood, and a rather battered Pip slouched, at one of the mess deck tables. His right eye was practically swollen shut and his face had a bandage taped across his left cheek. His shirt and pants looked like he'd been used to swab a muddy deck.

Cookie caught my attention when I entered. "Mr. Wang, please help Mr. Carstairs to his bunk, if you would."

I got him to his feet and we headed for the berthing area. He moved carefully, and winced with practically every step. He didn't speak and neither did I. As we left the mess deck, I heard Cookie thanking the officials for bringing Pip back to the ship.

When we got to the berthing area, I asked, "Can you make it up to your bunk?"

He shook his head slightly. "Ribs cracked."

I lowered him to Beverly's bed while I made up the empty one under his.

I helped him out of his filthy civvies and rolled him into the fresh sheets. He didn't say a word.

"Can I get you anything?"

He shook his head slowly. "Need sleep," he mumbled a few more unrecognizable words and I think he was actually out before he finished speaking.

When I got back to the mess, the Darbatis were gone. I found Cookie in the galley. "I am sorry, Ishmael, but I must cancel your liberty for the evening."

"Yeah, Cookie, of course. No problem. I didn't have any big plans."

I waited for him to say something more, but he drifted through the galley straightening and organizing. I went to the mess and got us both cups of coffee.

"Thank you," he said in a quiet tone.

"What did the Darbatis say?"

"He was found in a cul-de-sac, beaten and robbed. He had no wallet, no id. Only the clothes he wore ashore. He regained consciousness just long enough to give the name of the ship. Fortunately, his injuries are not serious: a few cracked ribs, black eye, and the laceration on his cheek. He also has a knot on the back of his head, but no concussion. Pip will be fine in a day or two, but right now, he's in rough shape."

I wondered if Cookie knew just how bad off Pip was. I'm sure the physical injuries were nothing compared to the loss of the Grishom.

He looked at me apologetically. "You'll have to cover his duty rotations, I'm afraid."

I grinned at him. "Well, the show must go on. What's on the menu for dinner?"

We each focused on setting up for dinner mess. Cookie had a pasta casserole baking in the oven. We pulled it out and set it up buffet-style with some of his crusty rolls. I put out a chafing dish with a green vegetable medley. There was pie and ice cream for dessert, but I left the ice cream in the freezer.

Word of Pip's injuries spread throughout the ship. The mood in the mess deck was even more subdued than what could be accounted for simply by being docked. Cookie baked bread earlier in the day, so I ran it through the slicer and bagged it. I prepared a meat and cheese tray for midwatch and placed it in the ready cooler. The familiar routine helped a little.

Cookie excused himself and disappeared for about ten ticks. When he returned, he gave me a quick report. "He is sleeping quietly. Beverly is there." We went back to dealing with dinner, such as it was.

I was surprised at the level of concern for a quarter share screw up. Of course I didn't think of him that way, but others on the ship might have, especially if his reputation had followed him from the *Duchamp*. I finished cleaning up and Cookie stayed to help.

Cookie and I were just about done for the evening when he broke what had been a nearly perfect silence. "He was lucky, for doing something so stupid."

I just looked at him.

"He was on a trade run, was he not?"

I nodded. "Yeah."

"It was a valuable cargo?"

I nodded again. "A lot for a quarter share. Five hundred creds."

Cookie nodded. "Let this be a lesson to you, too, young Ishmael. Never trade alone."

I thought about what Sandy had said and added, "And don't let your friends go by themselves either."

He smiled sadly at that, but nodded in agreement. We shut off the galley overheads and went our separate ways.

Back in the berthing area, Pip was still asleep but Beverly was watching him from her bunk. She gave a helpless little shrug and mimed sleep. I nodded but didn't speak. Whatever he'd been through in the last day, it had obviously drained him. I couldn't help thinking that the loss of the Grishom hurt as much as, if not more than, any of his physical injuries.

Back to square one. That was going to sting.

CHAPTER TWELVE
DARBAT ORBITAL: 2351-OCTOBER-24

Rhon Scham was the duty watch stander the next morning and woke me. "How is he?" she whispered.

Before I could answer, I heard a hoarse, quiet voice from the other bed. "He's awake, needs to pee, and is hoping somebody will help him get out of this rack."

I clicked on the light and saw Pip looking up at me, his good eye open and a lopsided smile on his face. "You're among the living then?"

He nodded and held up a hand to Rhon who helped him get untangled from the covers and clamber up. "I seem to be, but you'll excuse me if I don't stand around chatting?" He hobbled into the san leaving Rhon and I smiling and exchanging glances.

She waved and left me to get on with the day. Beverly kicked the bottom of my bunk. "If the family reunion is over, can I have a little peace?"

I turned out the light.

Bev said, "Thank you."

It took only a couple of minutes to get myself cleaned up and into a fresh shipsuit. I left Pip in the showers and reported to the galley. I grinned at Cookie and he looked relieved.

"Pip is better, I presume."

I nodded. "Yeah, he's hobbling about a bit and needed help getting out of the lower bunk. He must be hurting."

Cookie chuckled. "Some mornings, any of us can feel like you have to step up to get out of a lower bunk, young Ishmael."

Pip shuffled into the galley right on cue. "This morning was just such a time, Cookie." The bandage was gone from his face but his eye was still swollen shut. He moved tentatively with an arm held tight to his side. Pip lowered himself gingerly into a chair. "What's a guy gotta do to get a cuppa coffee around this joint?" He grinned.

I smiled back at him. "You want the old pot or can you wait five minutes for the new?"

We all had a little laugh, the tension broken and I went out to get the urn going. By the time I got back, Cookie had poured Pip some fruit juice and was just flipping an omelet out of the pan. I finished setting up for breakfast service and pulled the biscuits out of the bread oven. Nobody spoke as the morning prep spooled out like a well-oiled cable. In just a few ticks Cookie, Pip, and I were left waiting for the crew to show up and looking at each other.

"All right, Mr. Carstairs," Cookie prompted with a smile, "the time has come and you will tell us what happened or I will ask Mr. Wang to beat on your other eye."

Pip chuckled. "Okay, okay. I went to sell the Grishom. My contact at Chez Louis gave me a hundred thirty a bottle because they were in the presentation cases. I didn't think anything of it, but I guess carrying over five hundred creds in cash wasn't the smartest thing I ever did. I headed back right away so I could contact my next deal." He looked at me then and shrugged. "I had a line on some entertainment cubes, a lot of them in plain brown wrappers. We're heading back to Gugara and there's a good market for that there."

I shrugged. Porn was porn and everybody had a preferred flavor, even ancient lit professors. Mom had quite an interesting collection of samples from various time periods. It still stung when I remembered her, but I could tell I was healing.

"Anyway, I tried to get to a depository and transfer the creds, but these three thugs were waiting near the lift to the docks. They backed me into an alcove so fast, I never saw it coming. I gave them my wallet and told them I didn't have anything else. They were pissed that there were only a few creds."

"Where was the cash from the trade?" I interrupted him.

"In my money belt. I'm stupid, but not totally ignorant." He took a sip of coffee. "Unfortunately, they'd tagged me as I left the docks. One of the thugs had a digital of me leaving with the duffel. They didn't believe me when I told them it was laundry. So the next thing I know, I'm waking up, stretched out flat in the cul-de-sac, beat to a pulp, and my belt is gone. That was sometime around morning watch yesterday as far as I can tell. Darbati Orbital Security found me, saw that I wasn't drunk, and figured I'd been mugged. I was coherent enough by then to tell them I was from the *Lois* so they took me to the local medical station. The medics patched me up, filled me with painkillers, and security brought me back here."

Cookie seemed alarmed. "Did you file a report with the authorities?"

Pip shook his head. "No, they never asked for a statement and by the time the meds kicked in I was too out of it. I probably couldn't have made one."

"Could you recognize them, Mr. Carstairs?" Mr. Maxwell's sudden appearance startled all of us.

"I—I don't know, sar,"

"Would you like to try?" His lips curled in a wry smile.

Pip thought for a moment. "I'd be willing to give it a shot, sar."

Mr. Maxwell nodded. "Have you learned anything from this experience, Mr. Carstairs?"

"I was stupid and I was lucky." He unconsciously echoed what Cookie had said the night before. "I got cocky and didn't take a wingman. I figured I could handle it and..." He petered out a bit but stiffened up and finished, "and I didn't want to risk people making fun of me for trading."

Mr. Maxwell nodded once, crossed his arms, and leaned into the doorframe. "Anything else?"

"The *Lois* isn't the *Duchamp*."

"Very good, Mr. Carstairs." Mr. Maxwell swiveled his head to include Cookie and me in his consideration. "And since we're all here and among friends, perhaps one or more of you gentlemen would tell me what in the Deep Dark is going on with ship's stores?"

There was a heavy stillness in the galley for about three heartbeats.

Cookie spoke, "We're trying out something to reduce the cost of supplies, sar."

Mr. Maxwell nodded. "I presume that something explains the nearly full container of frozen food being delivered to the dock? And another one of canned vegetables?"

Cookie nodded. "Yes, sar."

Mr. Maxwell didn't speak for a while. "What if we were to change course and head back to Neris instead of Gugara?"

Pip stiffened and looked at Cookie. Cookie didn't even flinch. "Well, sar, I'd say that's good."

"Why's that?"

"Because the extra frozen food is cobia fillets. We got them to swap in Gugara for some beefalo. They'll be worth more in Neris. We can trade some of them for fresh produce which, on our budget, we couldn't otherwise afford."

Mr. Maxwell didn't say a word, but it looked to me like Pip was holding his breath. Cookie seemed calm and unperturbed. Finally, Mr. Maxwell spoke, "That's an interesting notion. Do you have the extra mass allotment to carry stores for trading purposes?" He asked in a way that made it sound like he was really interested.

Cookie nodded. "Yes, sar, we do. The ship's rated for a larger crew than we carry. By being a bit more careful in stowage, we can take on up to fifteen percent more mass in stores without sacrificing either ship performance or jeopardizing crew meals." He paused for a heartbeat. "I believe we can reduce the cost of feeding the crew by close to twenty percent which would add a nice bit to our profit margin overall."

"And the quality won't suffer? We eat well on this ship. It's a matter of pride."

"No, sar, of course not. The whole point is to procure foods that we wouldn't normally consider because of the expense. I have some projections if you'd like to see them."

Mr. Maxwell nodded. "Yes, Cookie, I would like a look, but only out of curiosity. It's your budget and you know what it takes to keep the crew well fed and satisfied. I trust your mass figures and if you say it's going to save us money, then that's your call."

"Thank you, sar. I'll have them in your in-box by mid day."

Mr. Maxwell nodded and turned his attention back to Pip. "If you could put together a description of the thugs, and the general location where they attacked you, Mr. Carstairs, I'll circulate it to the crew and to the Darbati authorities. We'll be pulling out in a few days, but if you're well enough for a short stroll later, we might be able to spot them."

Pip smiled. "Thank you, sar. I'd be happy to try to help nail them."

"You know the creds are probably gone, right?"

"Oh yes, sar," he nodded, "but if we can keep them from hijacking anybody else, that's a win as far as I'm concerned."

"Thank you, Mr. Carstairs. Your efforts here are noted and appreciated." Mr. Maxwell smiled—yes, smiled—and somewhat enigmatically, I thought. He turned and left the galley, but I heard him grab a mug from the rack and fill it with coffee on his way off the mess deck.

Nobody moved or said a word for a long time after we were sure he was gone. Cookie broke the silence. "I have known that man for over fifteen stanyers and it still makes me nervous when he smiles."

Chapter Thirteen
Darbat Orbital: 2351-October-24

The rest of our stay at Darbat Orbital was fairly quiet. Pip wrote up a description of the guys that jumped him, including the model number of the digital imager and a rough sketch of a tattoo one of them had on his arm. Mr. Maxwell sent a copy to station security, our crew, and the Union Hall Representative on Darbat. Pip, Mr. Maxwell, and a couple of the cargo gang strolled through the station a couple of times before we got underway, but they didn't find anything. Darbat is a busy station. The culprits were probably lying low until any recently docked ships headed out. Typical port time for a union trader was seldom more than five days. I couldn't help but wonder just how many people were involved. Pip had only seen three, but that didn't mean there weren't others covering the other hatches. We speculated on it endlessly during port-duty in the galley. For me, it underscored Sandy's prophetic words on the track that night.

Over the next couple of days, the new stores came aboard and Pip watched me stow them in the spaces I'd emptied while he was busy getting mugged. I teased him about people who were willing to do anything to get out of shifting stores around, but it was all in good fun. We didn't talk about the fact that he was back to zero on his private trading. The deal on entertainment cubes fell through because without the creds from the Grishom, he couldn't afford them.

We were down in the pantry, when I offered to bankroll him. "If you can get a line on something good, I got paid and still have the money. It's not much, but..."

"Thanks, Ish. I still have a bit of cash from the last run, but between us I doubt we have the five hundred and fifty creds to follow up on the cubes."

I agreed. My pay, even with the quarter share, only came to a little over two hundred and fifty creds. From one perspective that didn't seem like a lot, but if I added in what it would have cost me for food, housing, clothing, transportation, and all the other expenses of being planet-side, I was actually making out pretty well. I know our budget on Neris was tight even with Mom being a relatively senior professor. Of course, there had only been two of us, but we had to watch our spending.

"I've been looking for some kind of deal, but I haven't found anything worth pursuing. The turnaround is just too short. Sometimes you luck out, but..." He shrugged and only winced a little. The ready-knit had nearly repaired most of the rib damage, leaving only the residual muscle tissue trauma.

"Got a line on anything in Gugara? If we pool our resources that'll give us a bigger bankroll and more mass quota to work with."

He gaped at me. "After this, you'd be willing to team up?"

I nodded and shrugged. "Why wouldn't I? You've got the connections and the know-how. I still need to learn more about trading, frankly, I don't have a clue. I might as well learn from the master." I grinned at him.

He gave a winced chuckle. "Well, I don't know about being the master, but thanks. I'd be happy to show you what I know, and there was something interesting on Gugara..." His voice trailed off. He whipped out his tablet and pulled up a file. "Yes, I thought I remembered this. I gave it a pass originally. Price is right, good profit potential, but too much mass. I didn't have the quota to cover it."

I grinned. "I have about ten kilos, maybe eleven. Is that enough?"

He did some quick calculations and nodded slowly, looking at the tablet. "Yeah, It's plenty. The deal masses fifteen kilos. Cost would be two hundred creds." He consulted the ship's schedule. "We're going to Margary Station after that." He grinned broadly. "Excellent. We can sell almost anything there."

"Why's that?" I tossed the last case of canned banapod on the stack and strapped it down.

"Because, young Ishmael," he did a wicked impression of Cookie, "it's an isolated station. They support an asteroid mining operation and there's little in-system production, except for the refined metals and some large-scale fabrication." He consulted his tablet again before continuing, "Interesting. There's a Manchester yard there."

"That's significant?"

He shrugged. "Dunno, but the *Lois* is Manchester-built. I wonder..." he began punching up data on his tablet but refused to comment further, absorbed in his research. I left him sitting on a stack of creamed spinach and went back to the galley to get ready for the lunch service.

❀　❀　❀

The pull back went without incident and getting underway felt good. I don't know if it was Pip's getting beaten up, having the crew aboard again, or merely the resumption of the normal routine, but it felt like I was somehow coming home as we started the long crawl out of Darbat. This was *normal* compared to the less demanding and, by now, less familiar, time in port. It was comforting in an odd way. That night I started my last passes through the instructional materials for the half share tests. Mr. von Ickles would administer them in eight days. I had cargo nailed down, along with the power and propulsion sections of the engineman exam, but I thought I'd better spend some time with Brill down in environmental before the test.

Two days out of Darbat, right after lunch mess, Mr. Maxwell just happened to stop by the galley during cleaning up. Ominously, he was smiling. "Good afternoon, gentlemen. I've been going over those figures, Cookie. I wonder if you have a few moments to spare to discuss them?"

Cookie shrugged. "Of course, Mr. Maxwell. Here?"

He nodded and laid a tablet down on the work counter. "Mr. Carstairs and Mr. Wang should join us."

Pip looked a bit guilty to me, although it could have been a projection on my part. Mr. Maxwell was obviously enjoying himself, and I'd been aboard long enough to know that the next stan or so would be interesting although not necessarily in a good way.

When we gathered around, Mr. Maxwell indicated his tablet. "I've noticed some things on these tables. For example, this column labeled *demand probability* and this one marked *possible margin*. These don't appear to be based on anything I know about. How were they derived?"

Cookie looked over the columns in question. "Oh, those are estimates based on the port-of-call and the current galactic average wholesale price, sar. These are for Gugara, they would change if we were to go back to Neris. We run them based on a specific pair of ports."

"You *run them* where?"

"On Mr. Carstairs' portable."

Mr. Maxwell nodded. "I see. That would explain why I only found this data in my in-box." He swiveled his gaze to Pip. "And where did you get this portable, Mr. Carstairs?"

I broke in before he could answer, "From me, sar. It was my mother's and I brought it aboard in my quota. I was planning on using it to study, but I've been so busy, I haven't had time."

Mr. Maxwell nodded. "We'll come back to the question of your studies another day, but I surmised as much." He turned back to Cookie. "I think I know the answer to this next question as well, but humor me. Where did you get the simulations that produce this kind of information."

"We built them, sar," Cookie replied.

"*We?*" Mr. Maxwell did not look at Pip.

Cookie and Pip nodded. "Yes, sar. Mr. Carstairs and I created them. We've been refining them for a few weeks now."

"This implies that you have considerable knowledge of the market conditions for a lot of ports." He looked pointedly at Pip. "Care to tell me how this works?"

Pip pulled out his own tablet. "I have a database, sar. I started it some time back. It has been a kind of hobby of mine. I keep it on a personal data cube." Mr. Maxwell nodded for him to continue. "When we get the updated market reports from the jump point beacons and station data, I have a little routine that updates my galactic standard prices files. And I research ports on our projected flight path, plus level one alternatives."

Mr. Maxwell concentrated intently on what Pip was saying, his brow furrowed in concentration. "Level one alternatives being...?"

"Oh, that's what I call alternate ports on our flight plan. From Darbat, we're scheduled for Gugara, but there are two other ports in jump range. We could have gone back to Neris, or we could have gone to Albert. Since we came from Neris, doubling back on our course is unlikely. We only do that every once in forever. We might, however, change course for Albert. We have last minute course changes about once every five jumps. So, Albert becomes a level one alternative and I tried to find out as much about Albert as about Gugara."

Mr. Maxwell nodded. "But since we came from Gugara before Neris, you didn't have that much to look up?"

"Yes, sar. Some minor market updates, but I got a good profile going into Gugara before. That cuts down on the amount of work I needed to do to leave Darbat with high probability goods."

"And how did you determine that our route changes only once in five jumps?"

"Oh, that was easy, sar. The ship's log has a complete record of all courses filed along with the actual paths taken. I just tracked the flight plans we've filed over the last five stanyers. Confederation regulations require us to project out four jumps, but we're allowed to amend those plans based on—well, whatever we want, really. Every time we change one, it sets a flag in our records, sar. I just counted the numbers of flight plans with flags and compared that to the total number of flight plans filed. The tablet tracks that for me."

Mr. Maxwell looked thoughtful. "So you research out four jumps along with possible alternate routes for every port we go to?"

Pip nodded. "Yes, sar."

"Where are we going after Gugara?"

"Margary." I answered without thinking. "Sar."

Mr. Maxwell swiveled his gaze to me and said, "Et tu, Brute?"

I blushed. "Um, no, sar. We were just discussing it in the pantry this morning."

Mr. Maxwell swiveled back to Pip. "Your assessment of Margary, Mr. Carstairs?"

Pip got a faraway look and started reciting as if he were reading off the inside of his own forehead. "Margary Station supports asteroid mining and ore refining operations. Proximity to raw materials attracted a branch of the Manchester Yards. High demand goods include quality foodstuffs, particularly frozen fish and canned vegetables since none of the direct jumps to Margary led to ports that export those goods. Luxury liquors, and explicit entertainment are also in demand. The shipyard provides a ready market for electronics, astronics, and engineering control systems and components because, while the raw ship manufacturing components are readily available in-system, the specialized clean rooms required to fab the guts of their ships are not."

"What are we carrying to Margary, Mr. Carstairs?"

"We, sar? You mean the *Lois* or as part of the ship's stores scheme?"

"Both."

"Manifests for the *Lois* list four containers of machine parts, presumably for the new ship that Manchester is building, along with a container of paper goods and textiles. We're scheduled to pick up two containers of rare earths bound for the smelters in Margary." Pip rattled off the list without looking at his notes. "Stores trades are not final yet, but I think we'll hold about a third of the cobia fillets and half the banapods for downstream trading. We also are planning on trading some of the cobia for extra coffee. Sarabanda Dark's wholesale prices are low on Gugara right now. We don't normally stock that in stores because it's usually so expensive, but it would make an excellent trading stock and help break up the routine of only serving Djartmo Arabasti." He seemed to surface as if from a kind of trance and added, "Sar," to his recitation.

"I see." Mr. Maxwell swiveled his gaze to Cookie, who merely shrugged a what-can-I-say sort of shrug. He swiveled back to Pip. "And your assessment for private trading?"

"I'm trying to find something we can buy in Gugara for the inbound run. I've had to start from scratch there because of my recent setback."

Mr. Maxwell just nodded.

"The key to private trade on Margary is the uncut precious and semi-precious stones."

"Explain, Mr. Carstairs."

"The asteroid miners frequently come across deposits of stones while prospecting and extracting the raw ore. The deposits are too small and infrequent to make it worthwhile for any of the normal precious mineral cartels to set up there. So the miners collect and trade them for booze, porn, and other recreational goods. There's a lively market on Margary Station that the authorities ignore because it helps keep the miners occupied and happy. For us, it's a good place because we can buy as much or as little as we can afford. If we manage to find something to sell there while we're in Gugara, good. That gives us more capital for buying up stones in Margary. But even if we don't, we'll have cash to buy a small number of stones which will serve to re-stock our trade goods for when we go to St. Cloud Orbital after that."

"I see. It's too bad you haven't given this much thought." A wry smile accompanied Mr. Maxwell's comments. "This *we* you keep referring to is. . . ?"

Pip didn't respond immediately so I raised my hand. "That would be me, sar. Pip's going to help me get started. With our pooled resources for cash and mass we have more options and I get to learn the ropes."

Mr. Maxwell nodded once as if in confirmation. Obviously, he'd worked that much out for himself. He turned back to our boss. "Are you in on this unbridled capitalism, Cookie?"

"No, sar. I don't trade anymore. My creds are invested with a broker on Stamar, and that's good enough for me. Cooking takes up too much time."

Mr. Maxwell turned to stare silently at Pip for almost a full tick. "Mr. Carstairs, would you consider playing a game with me?"

"A game, sar?"

"A game, Mr. Carstairs. Use your research database and propose for me one container's worth of mixed cargo. Assuming an empty container is available in Gugara, what would you put in it to take to Margary?"

Pip slid into his calculating mode. "Budget parameters, sar?"

Mr. Maxwell considered for a moment. "Give me minimum required investment and maximum potential profit."

"So cheapest full container and maximum probable return, sar?"

"Precisely, Mr. Carstairs."

"Aye, aye, sar. Let me see what I can do. I'll have a preliminary by midwatch. But our best information will be at the jump point beacon. We can adjust at that point, if that would be acceptable, sar?"

"Quite acceptable, Mr. Carstairs. Thank you. One more thing, gentlemen." Mr. Maxwell swiveled his steely gaze in my direction. "Mr. Wang, please see to it that Mr. Carstairs passes the cargo handler exam in six days."

"Aye, aye, sar," I answered briskly. There didn't seem to be an option.

Cookie had that funny look on his face. The one he gets when he's trying not to laugh. Pip just looked like he was choking on something.

Mr. Maxwell nodded one last time and left the galley.

I turned to Cookie. "Is it just me or does he seem to be spending a lot of time here lately?"

CHAPTER FOURTEEN
DARBAT SYSTEM: 2351-OCTOBER-26

After Mr. Maxwell's little visit, we finished cleaning up the lunch service. Pip started the cargo analysis and I went back to studying for my engineman exam. I knew when he finished his empty-container exercise for Mr. Maxwell, he'd be leaning on me to get him ready for the cargo test. Having been through that material several times, the cargo exam didn't worry me, but the engineering test did. I'd spent so much time with the instructional materials, I found I could practically recreate them from memory. The practice exams went pretty well, but I still missed about five percent of the answers. I hoped that would be good enough.

At 1600 I headed back to the galley to help set up the dinner service. Pip and Cookie looked up from the portable when I came in, and stowed it when they realized the time. Dinner included some of the new stores and it went pretty well. The crew appreciated the variety in the menu and it didn't hurt that Cookie had a great granapple crisp with vanilla ice cream for dessert.

While we were serving, I nudged Pip. "So? How's it going?"

He shrugged. "Okay, I think. I should be done with another stan's work, but I'll be ready for a work out and a sauna."

"Oh yeah, I'm with ya there. Tell you what. You finish your container and I'll clean up tonight. With any luck, we'll be done at the same time and we can hit the gym."

He shot me a grateful look. "Thanks, Ish. That'll help. I was a bit ambitious when I promised the results by midwatch. That's a lot of mass. And there's one other little distraction."

"What's that?"

"The manifest shows an empty container on the Gugara to Margary run."

I froze in place for a moment and shot him a quick look. "Will he...?"

Pip shrugged. "Dunno."

When we secured the dinner mess, I shooed Pip off to the computer and started tearing down the serving line and making the galley shipshape. The process was so familiar by then that I could do it on autopilot. I found my mind wandering back to the cargo and engineering exams. I'm a good test-taker, but this new context gave me more than a few butterflies. Before long I found myself chanting, "Filter the water and scrub the air down," under my breath. It was one of those things that once you get it in your head, you can't get it out. I found myself sweeping to the rhythm. It drove me crazy but I couldn't shake it.

"There!" Pip's sudden outburst from his corner of the galley startled me.

"Done?" I stowed the broom and looked in his direction.

Pip nodded. "Yup. Now, I need to go work out." He downloaded his planning files and sent them off to Mr. Maxwell. "Only a twenty percent best case margin projection, but we typically run a twelve to fifteen percent margin. And that's the least cost filled scenario. The gross margin goes down in the maximum probable return, but the actual profit triples."

"How does that work?" I asked as he stowed the portable and we headed out of the galley. "How can we make more profit with a lower margin?"

"Easy. Which would you rather have? Ten percent of a hundred creds or one percent of a million?"

I sighed. "Of course. Sometimes my own stupidity astonishes me."

"Yeah, well, you haven't failed the cargo handler test twice, either." He sounded miserable.

"What? You failed the test?"

He nodded, his mouth screwed into a grimace. "Twice."

"But the content isn't that hard."

"For you. I'm not good at tests."

His bitter words caused a sinking feeling in my stomach, but I didn't say anything while we changed up and went out into the gym. My mind had finally stopped repeating the doggerel about the filters and scrubbers but had gained a new chant, perhaps better suited to the situation. "I'm in trouble. I'm in trouble. I'm in trouble..."

Later that evening we got together on the mess deck with our tablets, and I walked him through the cargo handler instructional materials. "But I've been through all this." He pushed the tablet away.

"I know, but you've also failed the test."

"Twice." He reminded me.

"Okay, twice. So you're going to go over it again, then take the sample test and we'll keep doing that until you get it right."

It took less than two stans to get through the material together. "You don't seem to be having any trouble with this."

He shrugged. "It's not the information. I practically grew up on a cargo deck."

"Okay, well, let's do the practice exam and see how it comes out."

We settled in and I breezed through the test in a few ticks. I'd done them so often, they began to look familiar to me. It approached the level of silliness. When I got to the end, I'd gotten a perfect score again.

Pip, on the other hand, dithered over his tablet, checking, un-checking, and re-checking responses. He appeared to have no idea what he was doing. He finally finished and sighed. He turned his tablet so I could see his score: thirty-five percent.

"But you know this stuff," I said with dismay.

He nodded miserably. "I just can't take tests. Something in my brain shuts off as soon as I start anything remotely like a quiz or examination."

The chronometer clicked over to 2300 so we headed back to the berthing area and bunked down. The chanting in my head got louder. "I'm in trouble. I'm in trouble. I'm in *trouble*..." I kinda wished the filter and scrubber thing would come back. It didn't seem so ominous.

The next day went by in a blur. Time was getting short. During our afternoon break, I sat Pip down and watched him take the test again. Once more, he picked, un-picked, and re-picked his responses. There didn't seem to be any kind of pattern to it. It was almost like he chose them at random. He did better, forty percent, but still not good enough to pass. I thought he might actually have scored better using a random number generator. We both sighed and headed back to the galley to set up for dinner.

After cleanup, Pip started to pull out his tablet again, but I stopped him. "Come on, Pip. You need a work out more than you need to beat yourself with that tablet again."

"But the test is just a few days away."

I sighed. "I know, but that's not helping. You know the stuff. It's the testing itself that's killing you. More studying won't fix that."

"So what are we going to do?" He didn't seem like the same cocky spacer I'd come to know. There was something desperate and sad about him.

"I don't know, but there has to be something. Lemme think on it."

We changed up and I headed up to the track and started pounding out my frustration. The I'm-in-trouble mantra beat in time with my foot falls. Four laps later, Rhon Scham caught up with me and nodded a silent greeting. We ran together for three more laps before she spoke. "Wanna talk about it?"

I looked over at her, startled. "About what?"

"Whatever has you so distracted."

"What makes you think I'm distracted?"

She nodded downward. "You're not wearing running shoes. You're either really distracted or just felt the need to tenderize your feet up here."

I barked a single laugh and realized that she was right. My feet were beginning to get a bit tender from the rough grit that made up the track's surface, but it wasn't really that bad. We approached the top of the ladder so I slowed and stopped.

Rhon stopped with me. "Well?"

"It's the ratings tests. Mr. Maxwell has ordered me to make sure Pip passes the cargo handler exam."

"Aren't you taking it, too?"

I nodded. "Yeah, and it doesn't seem like it's that hard. Not compared to the engineman one."

"So, what's the problem?"

"Pip's failed it twice."

"Third time's the charm."

I just looked at her. "Maybe, but, Rhon, the instructional materials for that test are dead simple. There's nothing tricky or difficult about it. If you can memorize a few facts, you should be able to pass it."

"I'd heard that. Food handler is the same way." After a tick she said, "Maybe he just has a poor memory?"

I shook my head. "No. Pip has a lot of issues, but memorization isn't one of them. We've been going over the material together and he hasn't been able to beat a score of forty percent. It's like he starts the test and his brain turns off."

She shrugged. "Maybe he can't read well. He could ask for an oral exam."

I blinked. "Oral exam?"

"Sure. It's an old tradition but it's still in *The Handbook*. Back in olden days, sailors weren't known for their academic prowess. The standard way to move up in rank was to demonstrate their knowledge by performing various tasks."

"That makes sense."

"There's a set of hands-on exercises that the Training Officer can do for each test instead of taking the tablet-and-stylus version. It's not common because the tablet-and-stylus is just so much easier to deal with, but it's still there."

"Thanks. That might just be the answer."

I headed down to the sauna where Pip found me a few minutes later. He still looked glum. The steam made the soles of my feet sting but I didn't say anything to Pip. I wanted to talk to Mr. von Ickles first.

For the next few days, Pip and I struggled with the testing materials, quizzing each other as we served on the mess line or cleaned up afterward. I began to be a bit more optimistic because he answered correctly almost all the time when we were drilling each other informally like that. My conversation with Mr. von Ickles had gone well and I felt considerably less panicked by the time test day rolled around.

It's a kind of misnomer to call it test day. They were really test days. Each division had its own. Some of the tests were rather lengthy, especially as you moved up the ranks. Traditionally the first one was engineering, then deck, steward, and cargo was last. Cookie and Pip shooed me out of the galley right after breakfast and I reported to the ship's office. I was the only one taking the engineman examination and Mr. von Ickles sat me right down to begin.

One of the reasons I'm so good at taking tests is that my brain goes into a kind of fast-motion and time slows around me. When I start any kind of formal test, the world fades away and I'm not really aware of anything except the flow of the test. I always thought it was kinda weird, but the results were usually good so I didn't complain.

The engineman test was no exception. When I put down the stylus, it had only seemed like a few ticks, but the chrono showed that almost a full stan had passed.

Mr. von Ickles shook my hand. "Congratulations, Mr. Wang. I'll add the engineman rating to your jacket this afternoon." He smiled and showed me the grade. Ninety-two percent. I'd only needed an eighty to pass.

"What about cargo, sar?"

He smiled and winked. "It's under control."

Cookie and Pip congratulated me when I returned to the galley to help set up for lunch, but I couldn't help think there was a certain desperate look in Pip's eye. The lunch activities soon left no more time for worry and Pip and I both threw ourselves into the day's work as if it would erase our fears. I was cautiously optimistic based on my conversation with Mr. von Ickles, but I hadn't said anything to Pip about it. I didn't know how to broach the subject and I was still worried that it wasn't going to work and that I'd, somehow, let Pip down. After that I'd have to face Mr. Maxwell, but for some reason he didn't seem so bad when compared to failing my friend.

Inevitably, we got through the next couple of days. The night before the cargo exam Pip started to pull out his tablet, I stopped him.

"Not tonight. By now you either know the material or you don't—and you do. Beating yourself up won't change that."

"Easy for you to say."

"Not really, but it's still true. Let's get in a good workout, take a nice sauna and hit the bunk early. A good night's sleep will do as much for you as anything."

"Like I'll be able to sleep."

I tried to distract him. "Any feedback from Mr. Maxwell on your container load?"

He shook his head. "Naw, but I wouldn't really expect it. We'll need to revise it when we hit the jump point and grab the beacon data. That's still a couple of weeks out."

I nodded and we headed for the gym.

The morning mess went off like clockwork. Cookie planned an easy-to-clean-up-after menu for breakfast so we would make it to the test on time. Many people wished us luck on their way through the line. It surprised me how many knew and genuinely seemed to care. We finished serving, cleared away, and I even had time to make an extra urn of coffee. All the while, Pip seemed to get more and more agitated. He did his best to hide it, but he kept dropping things, like thirty-liter stainless steel pots. Cookie wished us luck and sent us off at the appointed time.

I felt really bad for Pip. As we made our way to the office, it felt like he was heading for the gallows. "Cheer up. If you don't pass, I'm the one in trouble with Mr. Maxwell."

He chuckled a bit at that and gave me a wry smile. "But I'm still the one who needs the rating," he pointed out.

"It'll be okay."

There must have been a hint in my voice, because he looked at me sharply. "What's going on?"

In all honesty, I had no idea myself. Mr. von Ickles handled the details and I really didn't know how this whole thing would play out. By then, we were at the office and I just went in without answering. Mr. von Ickles wasn't alone. Mr. Cotton, the head of the Cargo Division, stood beside him.

Pip glanced at me and I just shrugged.

Mr. von Ickles was all business, although I thought I caught a brief wink aimed in my direction. "Gentlemen, since there are two of you this morning, I've asked Mr. Cotton to administer the test for Mr. Carstairs. Mr. Wang, you're with me. Do either of you have any objections?"

We shrugged and just said, "No, sar," in unison. I struggled to suppress a smile. This was serious business, after all.

Mr. Cotton was a smallish man with huge shoulders, arms that looked as big around as my waist, no hair and a nose that looked like he'd run into a cargo container several times. He grinned. "Good. Mr. Carstairs, you will come with me please and we will commence, ya."

Pip cast one last look at me as he followed Mr. Cotton out. I gave him an encouraging smile and a thumbs up.

Mr. von Ickles cleared his throat. "If you're ready, Mr. Wang... ?"

"Oh sorry, sar. Yes, sar. And thank you, sar."

"Don't thank me yet, Ish. He still has to pass." He spoke quietly and sat me down with a tablet and stylus. "And so do you." He proceeded to give me the same instructions as the previous exam and as he did, my brain slipped into its hyper-test mode.

This test was actually a lot harder than I expected. The materials were largely the same as in *The Handbook*, but there were some interesting twists in the presentation of the problems. Working with Pip had given me a lot of practice. When I finished Mr. von Ickles was smiling.

"Nicely done, Mr. Wang." He pulled up the scoring display to show a perfect score.

"This wasn't as easy as I was led to believe."

He nodded and grinned. "Several people have said that."

"Pip's not back?"

Mr. von Ickles just shook his head. "No, I don't expect him for a bit yet. But you're free to go. I'll update your jacket this afternoon."

"Thanks again, sar—whatever happens."

He nodded and patted me on the shoulder. "You're a good shipmate, Mr. Wang. Don't worry. I think you'll be surprised by what Mr. Cotton and Mr. Carstairs are up to."

I headed back to the galley and helped Cookie get lunch going. It was almost a full stan later when Pip showed up, looking a bit bedraggled, but optimistic. Unfortunately, it was almost time for lunch service by then and we didn't get a chance to compare notes beyond a hurried, "How'd it go?"

I was surprised to learn that he wasn't sure. "Mr. Cotton said he had to report to Mr. von Ickles before he would release the results. I don't know." He shrugged.

He wasn't surprised to learn that I'd passed. "Brain boy," he teased.

Whatever the outcome, testing was all over for another quarter and we got on with the business at hand. Lunch went off without a hitch, as always. Cookie had gone overboard with the dessert course. Apparently being alone in the galley all morning had inspired him to bake cakes. If I hadn't known better, I'd have thought he was nervous for us. Suddenly, lunch and cleanup were over and we all just stood there for a tick, looking at each other, everybody carefully not saying, "Now what?" I half expected Mr. Maxwell to show up, but he didn't.

Finally, Cookie broke the silence. "You've both worked very hard, and I'm proud of you, no matter how it turns out for Pip. As for you, young Ishmael, congratulations, and I'm confident you'll be a credit to any department regardless of the ship."

It hadn't really sunk in that I'd actually passed two tests and that I was eligible to move up when a berth came available. I was so worried about Pip and the trading schemes that I hadn't really thought about it. I felt rather dazed, truth be told. "I'm not going anywhere right away, Cookie." I smiled at him.

He nodded and grinned back. "I know, but you've earned the ratings and that's an accomplishment to be proud of."

Pip just looked worried.

When we headed out for the afternoon break, I asked again, "So? How'd it go?"

"I told you. I don't know. Mr. Cotton didn't say anything at the end. Just told me he'd be reporting to Mr. von Ickles and then dismissed me."

"Well, that doesn't sound ominous." I tried to sound convincing, but I'm not that good a liar. "What did you do? You were gone a long time."

"Really? Just over two stans?"

I nodded. "I was done with my test in about half that time. Where were you?"

"Mr. Cotton took me out to the spine. We crawled in and out of containers. He kept asking me questions about this, that, and the other thing. I found one cargo strap that wasn't secured properly. We pottered about down there for quite a while talking about tankage, which we don't have much of here, and about the proper distribution of mass."

"You got into tankage and mass distribution?"

Pip nodded. "He's really easy to talk to. We talked about lots of stuff that wasn't on the practice exams. Actually, now that I think of it, very few of the questions he asked seemed to be from the handler practices that we did."

I chuckled. "As much trouble as you were having with those tests, I'd be surprised if you even knew what was in them."

He grinned ruefully. "There's that."

"Well, we can make ourselves miserable waiting or we can go see Mr. von Ickles and ask. All he can say is no, right?"

Pip didn't look terribly excited by the prospect but I dragged him down to the office. The door stood open and Mr. von Ickles sat at his desk tapping away on his tablet. He looked up as we entered.

"Gentlemen, how can I help you?"

Pip stepped forward. "Well, sar, I was wondering if Mr. Cotton had had a chance to talk to you yet, sar. About my test this morning?"

"Why, yes, Mr. Carstairs, he has."

Mr. von Ickles waited one long tick without saying anything else and I wondered if Pip would faint.

Finally, Pip started to speak, but had to stop and clear his throat. "Please tell me, Mr. von Ickles. How did I do?"

"I was just placing the notation in your jacket, Mr. Carstairs. Congratulations for passing the cargoman exam."

Pip gaped. "Thank you, sar. But, sar? I...um...you mean cargo handler, don't you?"

Mr. von Ickles made a great show of being confused but I could see the edges of his mouth turning up ever so slightly. "Well, let me double check. I have the report from Mr. Cotton here someplace." He muttered that last as if to himself but loud enough that we could both hear clearly.

Pip shot me a worried glance but I carefully kept my face blank.

Finally, Mr. von Ickles found what he was looking for and pulled up a report on the screen. "Yes, here it is. Oh, you're right. You were testing for cargo handler, weren't you?"

Pip nodded. "Yes, sar."

"Well, I'm sorry, Mr. Carstairs." Mr. von Ickles consulted the report again and I could feel Pip collapsing inside. "You seem to have skipped handler altogether and gone straight to cargoman. Mr. Cotton was quite explicit and very enthusiastic about your qualifications." He turned to Pip with a huge smile on his face. "Congratulations on your new rating, Mr. Carstairs. You seem to have qualified as cargoman."

I yelped and started pounding him on the back, laughing and shaking his hand. Mr. von Ickles held out his as well and Pip shook it dazedly. "But—"

"It's true." Mr. von Ickles smiled at him. "Sure, it's most common for ratings to work up from quarter, to half, to full share, but the reality is that you can try for any rating any time you think you can pass it. You don't have to take them in order. If you can pass the test, you can have the rating."

"And I passed?" he asked again, still dazed.

Mr. von Ickles chuckled. "Passed? You got full marks." He turned the screen so we could see. "Mr. Cotton is not an easy man to please, either, I can assure you. If he says you're rated as cargoman, I am not going to argue."

Behind us, I heard Mr. Maxwell's too familiar voice. "And neither am I."

We turned to see him leaning against the doorframe. "Nicely done, Mr. Carstairs. And thank you, Mr. Wang, well done."

"Thank you, sar," Pip and I spoke more or less in unison.

"Now, don't you gentlemen have anything better to do than clutter up the ship's office?"

We beat a hasty retreat, heading for the berthing area, both of us giddy with relief. Halfway there, Pip stopped and slugged me in the arm. "You knew!" he said while laughing.

"I didn't know. Although when you said you'd talked about tankage and mass distribution, I had a suspicion."

"Why?"

"Because that's not on the handler exam, it's on cargoman. When Mr. von Ickles started getting cute with the results, I got another little nudge. If you hadn't passed he'd have been a lot more...I don't know...straightforward about it. He's not the kind who'd torture you like that. If you'd failed, I suspect he'd have said something when we stepped into the office. It's not like a hundred people took the cargo exams today."

"But why did Mr. Cotton give me the test? Why didn't Mr. von Ickles just sit me down beside you?"

"Gee, I don't know." I never was that good a liar.

Chapter Fifteen
Darbat Jump: 2351-November-09

Two days later, just after lunch, we had another drill. This one was lifeboat but this time I was prepared. When the pingity-pingity-pingity alarm sounded, I knew where I was going and that I would be getting into a pod.

By the time the announcement came, "*THIS IS A DRILL. THIS IS A DRILL. ABANDON SHIP. ABANDON SHIP. ALL HANDS TO LIFEBOAT STATIONS. ALL HANDS TO LIFEBOAT STATIONS. THIS IS A DRILL. THIS IS A DRILL.*" I was halfway to the gym, which occupied the boat deck. I lined up with the other crew assigned to boat four, including Diane Ardele from the environmental section and Tabitha Rondita who had the bunk on the other side of the partition from mine. We spent about a tick getting everybody accounted for, before the boat supervisor, Second Mate Jillian Avril, opened the hatch and we all climbed aboard and strapped down. I had one bad moment when Ms. Avril closed the hatch, strapped down, and then punched the big red launch button. Nothing happened and I realized that the safety locks were still engaged and that she had only registered our readiness with the bridge crew supervising the exercise.

We sat there in the dimly lit boat for about five ticks and performed the required inventories of supplies and materials that we found listed on plastic covered cards. When we finished the inventory, Ms. Avril thumbed a communicator button on the bulkhead and reported, "Boat four, completed."

Two ticks later the communicator chimed and we all clambered out of the boats and lined back up on deck. With everybody out of the boats and the hatches secured, the announcement sounded, *"NOW SECURE FROM LIFEBOAT DRILL. SECURE FROM LIFEBOAT DRILL."*

The captain's announcement followed almost immediately, *"This is the captain speaking. Very well done, ladies and gentlemen. You set a new ship's record of under eight ticks to get the ship evacuated in good order. It's not something we ever want to do, but it's gratifying to know we could if we needed to. Thank you, all. Excellent work. Carry on."*

❀   ❀   ❀

We settled back into the familiar routine for the run to the jump point. I wouldn't have to worry about studying for a while. I knew I had to go back to it eventually, but the roller coaster of the previous couple of weeks left me a bit dazed. I could only imagine how Pip felt.

Twenty-six days out of Darbat we hit the jump point. For the three days leading up to it, Pip had been chewing on the bulkheads waiting for market data updates from the beacon. He'd no sooner siphoned the data dump off to the portable when we had to go to transition stations and deal with the jump. I thought he was going to come out of his skin in the ten ticks before we finally secured and he could fine-tune his stores deals and double check the data he'd used to fill up Mr. Maxwell's container. I don't think he'd been that keyed-up over taking the cargo exam. We still didn't know for sure whether Mr. Maxwell would really fill a container with Pip's manifest or not. The possibility that he might drove us mad.

Pip and Cookie fretted over the stores deals, endlessly debating how much of what to sell, and what to keep for Margary. They'd get into cyclical discussions where one would say something and the other would argue him around until they were both on opposite sides from their original positions, and still not in agreement. Whenever they got going, I went to the gym and ran a few laps. Eventually they hashed it out, but it took them almost a week after transition to reach a final agreement.

Of course, as soon as they got it settled, Mr. Maxwell came down to the galley.

"Mr. Carstairs, I have some new parameters for you. I assume you have the latest data from the jump point beacon?"

"Yes, sar, I've made some minor modifications to that manifest based on the current market situation. The problem is that our data on Margary is dated. A lot will have happened by the time we get there."

Mr. Maxwell twisted his mouth into a wry grin. "Still, we must do the best we can, eh? You have a budget of ten kilocreds. Give me maximum probable return."

Pip was already sliding away behind his eyes, already calculating. "Aye, aye, sar."

I shrugged and headed for the gym. Pip caught up with me before I'd gotten out of the changing room.

"What do you think, Ish? Is he going to fill a container?"

"I don't know. You're the cargo expert. Tell me this. If you give him a hypothetical load, how accurate are the projected outcomes?"

Pip shrugged. "Not certain at all. We can project until we're blue, but you only know for sure once you deliver the cargo. Until then, all you're doing is guessing."

I nodded. "That's what I thought. How often do we have empty containers?"

Pip considered the question for half a tick. "Most of the time there's at least one. Our cargo assignments come from home office and they're scheduling a lot of freight. With seventy-two containers to schedule, it's hard to get a full ship all the time, or even most of the time."

I nodded again. "Okay, so that leaves the creds. Where would Mr. Maxwell get ten kilocreds?"

He shrugged. "Dunno. Ship's discretionary funds probably."

"What about the captain?"

He looked surprised. "What about her?"

"Would she have the money?"

"Personally? Possibly, but she can't make that kind of deal. She's limited by mass just like everyone else. Captains have a large allotment but a container is six hundred metric tons. No captain has that much." Pip shook his head. "No, the only way we can do this without running up against company regs is if it is part of the regular cargo."

"Okay, so how does that work? You just got done saying cargo assignments come from the home office. And that the captain can't take on a container full of private trade goods."

"That's what I meant by *discretionary funds*. Each ship has the ability to obtain cargoes on the spot to maximize their own load. The ship has funds to permit the buying and selling of cargo on speculation in addition to the straight freight-for-hire contracts setup by headquarters. The ship's Cargo Division usually handles that. The share amount in our pay really comes mostly from that. The more speculation we do, and, of course, the more successful it is, the bigger the share becomes."

"And if we lose on the deals, the share shrinks?"

"A share is, technically, a share of the profit—no profit, no share. The company gets the owner's share on all freight. The skipper gets the captain's share. Those are standard percentages. In our case, Federated takes a twenty percent share. They have various contract arrangements with the captains but typically, they get a ten-percentage share. The rest is put into a pot, carved up, and allocated based on the number of crew and the total number of shares represented."

Pip was good at this math, but I fell far behind his explanation. "Wait. Give me an example."

Pip stopped and thought for a moment. "Okay, say, after this run into Gugara, the ship has a profit of a thousand credits. The company gets two hundred the captain gets one hundred. The remaining seven hundred is divided up by the crew shares. So, if you're full share, you get a full allocation of however much the crew share turns out to be."

"Yeah, but what's a crew share?"

"We have forty crew, if all of them are full share, then we divide the seven hundred by forty and everybody gets an extra seventeen creds or so."

"But we're not all full share."

"Yeah, but you can add up all the ratings and figure out how many full shares there are. In practice, all the officers and some of the department heads are double share. You and I are quarter share. So, you add up all the ratings for all the crew and say the total is fifty. Divide the seven hundred by fifty and a share is about twelve creds. You and I, at quarter share get three each. The half share people get six. The full share people get twelve. The double share people get twenty-four—"

"Okay, I get it. What about this stores scheme you have with Cookie? It's not part of the normal freight arrangement, is it?"

"Correct, but remember that share is from profit. The galley is an expense. If we can reduce that expense, then the profit gets bigger and there's more to share."

I finally began to get a glimmer of what he was talking about. "Got it. I think. But how much can you do really? Are ship's stores really that big a part of the expense?"

"Depreciation is probably the largest accounting item that comes out. These ships are expensive and their operational lifetime is relatively long, but they're depreciated over thirty stanyers. So, we basically have to cover about one thirtieth of the cost of a new ship every stanyer. The next largest is salary and benefits, followed by insurance. The ship's stores are next, I think. I can tell you we spend about five hundred creds a week on foodstuff."

The number surprised me, but I don't know why. Twenty-kilo buckets of coffee were expensive and we used a lot of them when we were underway. "So, how much will you be taking off the expenses?"

Pip shook his head. "I won't know until we get a final settlement, but we're shooting for a twenty percent reduction in costs over a stanyer. It's not a lot, on the grand scheme of things, but it would amount to something over five kilocreds added to the shared profit for the stanyer."

"That sounds like a lot to me."

"Well, the share pool for the last stanyer was about a hundred kilocreds, so we're talking about increasing it by about five percent. Nothing to sneeze at, certainly, but the real benefit is that we can get better meals out of it."

"How? I mean, I know Cookie explained it to Mr. Maxwell, sorta, but how does this work?"

Pip grinned. "We buy low and sell high."

I slugged him in the arm. "Try again."

"Okay, look, the most expensive foods are the fresh ones because they have a short shelf life. Typically we can't afford them, but they really make a difference in the quality of the meals. Frozen foods are cheap. Canned and processed foods are somewhere in the middle."

I nodded for him to continue.

"Look at coffee. We use the Arabasti because it's readily available, of a relatively good quality, and frankly, pretty cheap. Thanks to your magic touch, the crew has gotten to like it a lot better." He grinned at me to make sure I caught the teasing before he continued, "As a trade good it's not much use. Everybody has it and it's usually consistently priced from place to place. Sarabanda Dark, on the other hand, has a more volatile market price. It's limited in range because it's only grown on Gugara. The price fluctuates a lot based on availability and it is generally considered a better grade of coffee. Normally, it's too expensive and so we don't buy it."

"I suspect that's just snob appeal, but if it's more expensive won't that drive our operating costs up?"

"Yes, if we were planning on drinking it. But we're buying it to trade for things that are even more expensive."

"You are making my head hurt on purpose, aren't you?"

He laughed. "What we're doing is converting creds into trade goods that are worth more as goods than the creds would be. We're doing that two ways. First, a bumper crop of Sarabanda Dark is letting us buy it for fifteen creds. Normally, it would cost twenty. But more importantly, we're taking it someplace where that same bucket would normally be worth thirty creds. We've taken what is usually a ten cred profit and made it fifteen. That's a fifty percent increase because the price of Sarabanda happens to be low just now. It makes a good deal even better.

"If we buy a hundred buckets, it costs a kilocred and a half.

When we sell it for thirty creds it gives us three kilocreds. We get back the original kilocred and a half that we paid to begin with and an additional kilocred and a half. We can use that additional cred to reduce cost or we can buy something like fresh fruit for pies, or some other ingredients that our stores budget wouldn't usually allow. We've taken idle creds and made them work for the ship."

"Why isn't everybody doing this?"

"I'm sure many are. Sometimes it works. Sometimes it doesn't. For us, since we're going to Margary anyway, we get the transportation basically for nothing. We have the surplus capacity to carry the goods we need to trade and a limited number of creds to invest. What we need to do is build up our stock of trade goods so that wherever we go, we have something extra that's worth more to the people there than it was to the people we got it from. Almost everybody has something they don't want that we can buy cheap. In Gugara this trip, it's Sarabanda Dark. Next time, it might be beefalo steaks. Sarabanda Dark should be worth more on Margary, but not as much as it would be on St. Cloud because that is farther away. We'll need to sell some of it at Margary Station and use the creds we make to buy something that's cheap there but more expensive on St. Cloud."

"Margary has no planetary system. They import all their food."

"Actually, that's not true, but it's a commonly held belief."

"What? They have planets?"

"Well, yes, they have two gas giants, but that's not what I meant. They don't import all their food, most but not all. They do grow some."

"What?"

Pip just smiled. "Wait and see, Ishmael, old son. Wait and see."

CHAPTER SIXTEEN
GUGARA ORBITAL: 2351-DECEMBER-09

I finally got ashore on Gugara Orbital. After Pip's experience on Darbat, the more experienced crew adopted us. The problem was that he and I couldn't leave the ship at the same time. We were the only two mess crew so we were, by definition, in alternating watch sections. One of us had to remain aboard. It seemed a bit silly to me. We never did anything after the evening meal cleanup, but those were the rules. The upside was that I got to know some of the other crew members better.

Pip and I flipped a coin for first night liberty, and I suspect that he threw the call so I could go. I think he felt guilty because I'd missed Darbat entirely when he got mugged on the first night.

"You go and have a good time. I'll poke about the station net from here and see if I can find a deal we can go in on, okay?"

"But where's good? You know Gugara. Gimme some recommendations."

We sat on the mess deck and before I knew it, people surrounded us, all talking at once with advice on where to go.

Brill Smith took me by the arm and drew me out of the throng. "They're all crazy. Half of them will be broke by the time we leave. What do you want to do?"

"I have no idea. This is the first time that I've been off Neris since I was a toddler. I don't remember much about being out of the system. Come to think of it, it's been almost ninety days since I've been off the ship. Can that be right?" I started counting on my fingers. "I came aboard three days before we left Neris, and we were forty-five days to Darbat. Then four more there, and forty-four to here." I blinked in surprise.

"Oh, for crying out loud, Ishmael. And you're still sane?"

I grinned. "Well, that's open to debate, but I am shocked. It seems like yesterday, sorta. I can't really remember a time when I wasn't here, other than some fuzzy kind of idea that I used to live somewhere else."

"Wait 'til you've been doing this for ten stanyers. You really won't remember. You didn't get to go ashore at Darbat, did you?"

I shook my head. "I was just changing into my civvies when the Darbatis brought Pip back."

"What were you going to do there?"

I blushed and answered, "Eat."

"Seriously? You work in the galley and you wanted to get off the ship to eat?"

"Cookie is amazing. He's an artist in the kitchen." I shrugged. "But once in a while, I'd like to eat somebody else's cooking."

"Tell you what. In honor of your earning your engineman rating, let me take you out to dinner. A few of us were planning on going to a nice place we know up on level six. They have great steaks and good beer. You can get out and stretch your legs a bit. My treat for dinner. You're on your own after that."

"Okay, sounds like fun."

"Meet at the quarterdeck lock at 1700 ship time. That's only a stan from now so go put some party clothes on."

The throng was still gathered around the table talking about what they'd do on station, and didn't seem to notice that I wasn't even there anymore. I grinned. These people were nuts.

And I was one of them. It felt good.

It didn't take me that long to get ready to go. My civvies seemed oddly out of place on the ship, but my feet remembered my boots and it sure felt good to put them back on after so long in the standard issue ones. I made my way to the quarterdeck and met up with Brill and two of her people: Diane Ardele and Francis Gartner. Diane was a gamine with cropped red hair, a pixie face, and a wicked grin. Francis Gartner was a string bean of a guy, with long narrow hands and muddy brown hair. I knew them of course, from the mess line, but other than seeing the two occasionally in the gym, I'd never spent much time with them.

We checked out with the duty officer and left the ship. When I stepped out of the lock, I felt a momentary sense of disorientation. It looked just like Neris. I had the odd feeling that somebody was playing an elaborate trick on me. I froze after stepping onto the station deck plates and gazed around. Brill was in the lead and she didn't realize I'd stopped. Diane and Francis came up on either side of me and just stood there with me for a tick.

Brill noticed and turned to look back at us. "Are you coming? Or are you just gonna stand there rubbernecking all night. I'm hungry."

Diane answered her with a laugh, "Keep yer panties on. We'll be there when we're ready."

Francis, who really was almost as tall as Brill, leaned down to speak softly into my ear. "You okay, Ish?"

I nodded, looking around. The cold, sharp air smelled of hot hydraulic fluid from the station-side of the lock and some other indefinable station smell. It was a cross between iodine and mint, not unpleasant, but not the *Lois'* smell. I shook myself and started forward again. After three months in the *Lois'* cramped passageways and spaces, the orbital seemed airy and spacious.

Brill waited for us to catch up. "Feel a bit odd, Ishmael?"

"Yeah. For a second there I thought I was going nuts. I stepped out and it looked just like Neris."

They all laughed. Diane offered an explanation, "It's the law. The docks on all the orbitals are standardized from the size of the docks, to the spacing of the locks, to the height of the ceiling. It's the same everywhere right down to the padding on the deck and the colors of the walls."

I took a deep breath and let it out loudly. "Thank the gods. I thought I was going mad."

We all laughed and Brill led us up through the station to level six and into a restaurant named, Beef and Brew. The manager, a portly man with a florid complexion greeted us. "Brill, my dear, always good to see you again. You've made the loop finally?"

She nodded first shaking one of his big hands in both of hers and then hugging him warmly with a firm kiss on each cheek. "Maurice, you old charmer, you're only glad to see us because we spend so much money here."

"You wound me, my dear." He posed with an expression of mock horror, a hand held dramatically to his breast. "The money isn't the only reason."

Diane stepped up. "No, just the most important one." She smiled as she also greeted him with a handshake and a hug.

Francis smiled and shook his hand, but didn't offer to hug. "Good to see you again."

Brill introduced me, "Maurice, this is Ishmael Wang. He's a new crew member who joined us at Neris. This is the first time he's been off the ship in over ninety days so you must treat him well. He's feeling a bit exposed."

The manager beamed at me and I felt welcomed in a way that I couldn't remember ever experiencing. "Greetings, Mr. Wang, I'm delighted that you've chosen my humble establishment to break your long incarceration," he said enthusiastically.

"Thank you, I'm forward to a meal where somebody waits on me for a change."

Brill grinned at me before turning to our host. "Ishmael works in the galley on the *Lois*. He's been taking care of us for the last three months."

"Ah, you work with Cookie. How is he? And why has he not come with you tonight?"

"He's fine. His duties are keeping him aboard, I'm afraid."

"Well, let's not stand on ceremony here. Come this way, my old and new friends. I have a table which you should find acceptable." He scooped up a handful of menus and led us into the dimness of the restaurant.

I sighed happily as we settled at the large table with real chairs that slid on the floor. Maurice brought us a large pitcher of beer without asking and collected orders with joyous abandon. I had to admire his skill when the wait staff delivered all the meals perfectly to the correct person. The beefalo steak was superb and the greens were lovely and crunchy. They served the perfect baked potato with only a discrete dab of what looked and tasted like real butter. For the first time since NerisCo Security had showed up at my door that day, I felt myself begin to unwind.

Dinner was wonderful. I knew Brill was smart and funny. She really had helped me with the tour of the Environmental Section. Diane and Francis were likewise wonderful dinner companions. Being a professor's kid had two effects on me. First, I was surrounded by people who tended to lord their intelligence over anybody who didn't have at least two educational degrees and four decades of experience. Second, being surrounded by a lot of really smart people gave me a vocabulary and an appreciation for some of the larger ideas in human existence, unlike many of my peers. Because of that, I appreciated the dinner in a way that I seldom had experienced before. I felt like a grown up.

We lounged over dinner for at least three stans. Maurice occasionally stopped by the table to check up on us, but he never once made us feel unwelcome or that, we should move on. Finally, after we finished off our coffees, and a second round of desserts, we settled up and sauntered out onto level six. The four of us window-shopped and chatted, sharing stories of life planet-side, shipboard, and everything in between. I learned that Brill had a master's degree in environmental sciences while Francis held a doctorate in astrophysics. Diane had barely squeaked through secondary school.

She was just good with algae. They all three shared a passion for clean air and fresh water. I began to think of them as my friends. After a while we split up. Brill and I needed to get back to the ship, but Diane had other ideas. She stepped up and gave me a hug. "Good night, Ish. Francis and I are going down to the oh-two deck and dance the night away."

I hugged her back and shook Francis's hand. "Thanks for letting me tag along, guys. I had a great time. Funny how you can live so close together but not really cross paths."

They all chuckled knowingly. "Happens all the time." Francis winked at me.

Brill and I set out in one direction while Diane and Francis headed the opposite way.

We meandered from level to level, finally reaching the docks again. The cold air seemed refreshing, even if the smells of ships and machinery permeated everything. Eventually, we reached the *Lois* again. Walking up to the lock, with the visual image being overlaid in my head with the lock on Neris Orbital, I was suddenly smitten with the sense of coming home that I had only previously associated with returning to the flat in faculty housing I'd shared with my mother. I sighed contentedly.

Brill heard me and smiled. "You seem pleased."

I looked up at her with a smile. "Thank you for dinner. It was excellent and it felt really good to get off the ship."

"You're welcome, Ish. It was my pleasure. Next time, you can buy." She was only half teasing, I knew, and I considered the idea.

We stepped through the lock and checked in with the watch stander. I was shocked to see that it was almost midnight. We split up then, each headed for our berths. When I got to mine, Pip was still awake, reading something on his tablet.

He looked up. "Hi, there. How was dinner?"

"Great. Brill took us to the Beef and Brew and I met the owner. Fantastic meal. Lotta fun." I stripped out of my civvies and hung them in my locker, leaving on a ship-tee and boxers. I clambered up into my bunk, and was asleep before I knew I was lying down.

Chapter Seventeen
Gugara Orbital: 2351-December-10

I had the duty and Pip was off. He got up with me when the messenger of the watch came to wake me.

He sat at one of the tables and watched me prepare the urns. "So, what's the status?" I asked.

"I looked around for cargoes on the station net last night and I found some interesting things. I want to get over to the orbital as soon as I can and check them out."

He hung around long enough to get fresh coffee and one of Cookie's omelets before heading to the orbital. "No money this trip."

Cookie shouted after him. "You be careful just the same."

Cookie and I spent a pleasant morning with the duty crew who came in for breakfast. He showed me his tricks for making perfect omelets. The key was using the proper amount of water in the egg. He placed a great deal of emphasis on mixing the two until the result was a precise shade of yellow.

It took a while for me to learn the technique. "No, no, young Ishmael, use the fork like a whisk, not a bat. You need to mix the egg with air to get the correct color. You're not stirring porridge."

Eventually, I got the hang of it. "Very good, You could be an excellent cook if you applied yourself."

He entrusted the omelet making to me from then on and went off to set the yeast breads to rise.

Eventually curiosity got the better of me and I turned to Cookie. "How's the stores trading going?"

His smile gleamed in the galley's overheads. "Quite well, quite

113

well. Pip and I have placed our orders and we found several excellent deals."

"Did you get the Sarabanda Dark that you were hoping for?"

"Oh yes, and some lovely frozen beefalo at a very nice price. The profit from the frozen fish was not quite what we projected, but that's to be expected. All told, it was a good first trial."

"So, you're pleased?"

He smiled, and nodded, then waved me out of the galley. "Go. Scamper. I need some peace and quiet in which to make pie crusts."

I went back to the berthing area and crawled into my bunk. It was only midmorning, but I'd been up late the night before. I fell asleep almost instantly.

About a stan later, I awoke and Pip spoke from across the aisle, "You must have had a rough night."

"No, it was lovely, but it was later than I'm used to and I just felt like a nap. What's up? Did you see the cargoes you were looking for?"

"I did. I'm just trying to figure out what to do about them."

"Them?"

Pip nodded. "Rugs. Here on Gugara they have a small specialty market in the things you can make out of beefalo, besides meat. One thing is a heavy robe. Another is a decorative rug. I met a dealer and the stuff is beautiful. The robes are really nice, more like a long, leather coat with a dark fur trim. The rugs are roughly animal shaped but still well done. Personally I think they're kind of tacky, but who am I to say?" He held up his tablet and showed me some digitals. "I took these this morning."

"I see what you mean, but what makes you think these would sell in Margary?"

"Most of the people in the system live in hollow rocks. Over the stanyers they've carved out hundreds of them. If you're well off, you have your own. If not, or if you just don't care about that kind of thing, you live in one of the habitats. But they're all basically holes."

"You're painting a picture of cavemen in space."

Pip chuckled. "Well, it's not quite that bad. It's not like all these guys are crawling around low-grav or no-grav asteroids with EVA suits and pickaxes. They seal the tunnels against air and water seepage as they go. After the asteroid is exhausted, they strip out the gear and the company makes them available to the Margary Station Authority for disposition. MSA cleans them up, carves out apartments, and lays down a slightly better grade of sealant. They install ship-grade power plants, environmental processing, and gravity flooring. When done, MSA rents them out as flats to the miners, prospectors, foundry workers, and ship yard crew."

"Okay, I'm getting the picture, but beefalo robes?"

"I'm not too sure about the robes. Inside the units, it's like being aboard ship. Constant temperatures and all. I've visited there before and if you didn't know you were in a hole, you might think you were shipboard. That's why I'm considering the rugs."

I looked around the berthing area and tried to image a beefalo rug. "I still don't get it? Why would they be in demand?"

"Psychology. Everybody there knows they're actually living inside a rock. They are cold, hard, and sterile, at least in their minds. You said it yourself—cavemen in space. I'm looking for something that'll relieve that feeling. The rugs are soft, warm, and comforting."

"What's the problem?"

"Mass and expense. We can't afford them."

My tablet bipped then to remind me I needed to get up to the galley. "Back to work for me. Lemme know if you have any brain flashes."

Pip nodded distractedly and I got on with the lunch duty.

As usual for a port-side lunch mess, it was mostly soup and sandwiches set up buffet style. There weren't enough people to warrant setting up a serving line. The crew drifted in and out in doubles and triples. A lot of them loaded a tray and took it back to their stations. Brill came in and we sat together while she ate her soup.

"Thanks, again," I said. "Last night was so much fun. And Maurice knows how to make a guest feel welcome."

She laughed. "He's a dear. I met him stanyers ago." She dunked a chunk of bread in her soup and delicately nibbled off the wet edge. "Mmm, that's not terribly good manners, but it reminds me of home."

I chuckled. "No need to stand on ceremony here. We're all family."

"So, how's the trading going?"

"Which trading?"

She giggled a little. "You got more than one?"

I nodded. "There's the Pip and Ish pool. He's trying to show me how this works. So far, I'm mostly just holding his coat and watching from the sidelines."

She nodded sympathetically.

"Then there's the ship's stores deals."

"Yeah, I heard about those. All the extra supplies on the dock attracted a bit of attention in Darbat and that pallet of Sarabanda Dark waiting outside looks very interesting."

"Oh, good. It's here then?"

She nodded.

"Then there's the empty container problem."

"The what?"

"It's kind of a long story but the gist of it is that Mr. Maxwell assigned Pip an exercise in cargo trading by asking him to put together a manifest for the Gugara to Margary run to fill a hypothetical empty container. They've run the exercise with several permutations and the latest is a fixed budget starting point of ten kilocreds and he's looking for the maximum return on that budget."

"Sounds like an interesting story. Is there a punch line?"

"*Lois'* manifest list one empty container on the run to Margary." I offered the comment in what I hoped was a suitably offhanded manner.

Brill blinked for a tick. "Oh my."

"Indeed."

Her tablet bipped and she stood. "Time to get back to work. Gregor and I are swapping the sludge pools today. Wanna come help?"

"I would, but I'm on duty here."

She laughed. "Yeah, I can see where that would be a problem. You're so busy here in port." She cast a pointed gaze around the practically empty mess deck.

"Actually, I'd like to come down and see how it works. It was in the engineman exam but I've only got the theory, ya know?"

She nodded. "That'll change soon enough. Let me leave you with two words of advice for when you have to do sludge yourself..."

I looked up, interested.

"Mint soap."

We laughed and went about our respective duties.

While I was straightening up after lunch, Pip came slouching in and settled with the portable computer. He was frowning in concentration and seemed upset about something. "Problems?"

He shook his head. "Not really. I just cannot get a handle on a cargo for you and me. The stores trades for Margary are in good shape, although I still have some money and mass available on the empty container problem."

"Is it still empty?"

He nodded. "This looks like a dry run to me. No changes to manifest have been filed."

"That's kind of a relief, isn't it?"

He nodded distractedly. "Yeah." He didn't offer any more than that on the subject.

I served him a bowl of soup from the kettle before recycling the rest and threw a couple chunks of bread on the plate.

"Coffee?" he asked, distractedly.

"Anything else, sir?"

He shook his head and laughed at himself. "I'm sorry. I get so wrapped up, I forget."

I sat the mug beside his food and laughed with him. "It's okay. I was going that way."

I finished my cleanup and went for a run. I was the only one in the gym, and the sauna was empty too. As much as I liked the crew, having the place all to myself was strangely satisfying. I hadn't realized how tense I was until I started noticing an odd sensation at dinner with Brill, Diane, and Francis. It had continued throughout the day. Sitting in the sauna, feeling the long muscles in my back and legs begin to unwind, I finally recognized it. I was relaxed and it felt good.

Next day, Pip had the duty, but I felt a bit left out when Rhon Scham came down to wake him. So I got up and tagged along. The breakfast set up in the galley was probably my favorite time of the day. Everything was clean and fresh and the smells of coffee, yeast, bacon, and eggs hooked to something inside me that I couldn't really describe. The smell of coffee always said morning to me. Growing up, we'd not had a tradition of bacon and eggs in my house, but I could see myself getting used to it.

I kibitzed while Cookie and Pip played with omelets. I let Pip practice on me. Somehow I thought Cookie had taught him how to do them long ago, but apparently that was a mistaken assumption on my part. The omelet was good, filled with cheese and meat and thin slices of onion.

After I ate, Cookie frowned at me. "Are you going to spend your whole liberty here in the galley?"

I shook my head. "No, I'm heading out to do some sightseeing, but I'm feeling lazy and I'm in no hurry."

He smiled. "Young Ishmael, you are anything but lazy. You've earned your break. Go take it." Then he grinned. "Pip can make the coffee today."

We all had a laugh at that and I headed down to berthing to put on my civvies. As I was leaving the ship, I met up with Beverly at the lock.

"Hey, bunkie. Where you heading?"

She grinned at me. "I'm going shopping. You?"

I shrugged. "Dunno. Sightseeing mostly. My first time on an orbital other than Neris. I went out with some of the environmental crew for dinner last night but I thought I'd go for a stroll today."

She gave me a well, come on gesture. "I'm heading up to level nine to the flea market. Come with me." She lowered her voice a tad. "After Darbat, I'm not too keen on just wandering around alone, you know?"

She surprised me. Bev is about a meter and three quarters of menace. She keeps her hair cropped like most of us, but unlike other women aboard, hers was cut in a military crew cut and not one of the more feminine styles. She sported tattoos on most of her body and had piercings that made me wince just looking at them. In her shipsuit, she looked dangerous enough, but in her civvies: black leather pants and jacket, heavy boots and what looked like a pullover made of aluminum plates—I thought only an idiot would mess with her.

It wasn't all show either. In the gym I'd seen her working through some martial art drills and sparring with the crew. She even moved like she was dangerous, very smooth, aware, and centered. It was funny she wanted me, sixty kilos of coward, to watch her back. Go figure. They say there's safety in numbers and I felt safe with her.

"Sure, I've never been to the flea market."

As we left the ship she turned to me. "Never? There's a flea on every orbital."

"I always visited the Neris Orbital with my mother and she was more focused on the mainstream shops and the cube-sellers. It was a treat for us to go up to visit and we didn't do it that often. When we did, we spent a lot of time just gawking. She kinda looked down on the flea market."

Bev shrugged. "Everybody's allowed their own opinion, but if you're gonna be a trader, the flea market is your best friend."

"Really?" I was surprised. Pip had never mentioned the flea market. "Why?"

"You'll see," She just grinned, which was kind of a scary thing, but I forced myself to remember this was the woman who slept under me every night. I'm not sure that thought helped.

We didn't take the scenic route up through the various levels. Bev led me straight to the lift and we took it all the way up to level nine. When we stepped off the lift, I found myself in a maelstrom of sound and color. Almost the whole deck was one big open bay. It was carved up into aisles and each one was lined with stalls where people were buying and selling. The booths consisted of everything from prefab units with pseudo-walls and glazed displays, to a couple with stack upon stack of storage cubes, to a few people who had simply spread blankets on the deck and laid out hand crafted jewelry or clothing items. Ship and orbital time was almost in sync here, and even at this early hour the place was crawling with people. I was glad to be with Beverly. A space seemed to open before her as she moved through the throngs. I saw other people being jostled periodically, but nobody bumped into Beverly. I rode happily in her wake. If the Neris flea market was like this, I can see why my mother, fifty kilos and barely a meter and a quarter, would want to avoid it. I wasn't sure I'd want to come here alone.

Beverly happily wandered up one aisle and down another, occasionally exchanging words and sometimes good-natured insults with the vendors. I marveled at the array of goods and just tried to keep up. Clothing seemed to be a popular item. I saw obviously handcrafted garments that had been created from whole cloth, as it were, to obviously purchased articles embellished with punch work, or embroidery and even rivets. Beverly spent some time looking over a red leather jacket with an elaborate dragon outlined in what appeared to be black steel rivets across the back. The thing was stunning on her, but she put it back on the rack and we left.

"Nice work, but the red draws attention I don't want, and the rivets were stuck on with mastic, not punched through the fabric."

"You think the red draws attention?" I suppressed a certain level of amusement.

She nodded matter-of-factly as she sifted through a display of quilted, silk dresses.

"And the aluminum pullover and black leather doesn't?"

She grinned. "Well, yeah, probably, but when people see me in red, they think I'm... well, someone I'm not. When I'm in black, they leave me alone." She looked a little embarrassed, so I didn't push it.

At the next booth, I saw some of the beefalo rugs and robes that Pip had been talking about. The robes were nice and the rugs were quite soft. The short fur felt lush against my hand, but when I hefted one of the robes, I understood Pip's comment about the mass. It must have weighed ten kilos. The rugs were heavier.

Bev raised an eyebrow as she saw me examining the goods.

"Pip thought these might do well on Margary. Soft and warm in a cold, hard world."

She nodded. "Maybe yes, maybe no. Mass is the problem though, right?"

"Yup."

We continued our perambulations and at the next turn, a wizened, old woman sat behind a heavy bench and worked the most amazing patterns into a leather strap. Bev and I stood, along with several others, spellbound as she pierced, punched, pounded, and laced the lovely natural brown material. Her gnarled fingers moved with amazing speed and grace. In what seemed like only a few minutes, she lifted the leather from her work bench and displayed the finished belt to the crowd's appreciative applause before hanging it carefully on a long rack with several dozen others. She fished under the bench and brought out another length of supple, creamy brown strap. The scent of it cut through even the smell of the crowd. I was drawn to the rack of belts and began fingering through them.

Beverly stood close beside me and admired them as well. "This is spectacular work," she spoke softly. She took one from the rack and flexed it several times. "And this leather is amazing."

The lady behind the bench noticed us but didn't interrupt.

Beverly turned to her. "How much?"

The woman flickered a glance in our direction and smiled. "Are you serious, dearie, or just curious?" She spoke without looking up and I thought she had a pleasant lilt in her voice.

"Serious."

"Twenty creds each, fifty for three," the old woman said, working a spider web pattern into the surface of the new leather on her bench.

Bev grunted. "Interesting but not that interesting." She paused for about five heartbeats before making a counter offer. "Hundred creds for ten?"

The old woman grinned. "Child, my husband would beat me if I took so little. You cannot ask that of a frail old woman such as myself. But perhaps I could sell you seven..." She continued smoothly working the leather.

"Eight," Beverly answered after a single heartbeat.

"Sold," the woman replied as she put the finishing touches on the spider web. She finally looked up and gave a brief nod in my direction. "Your boy toy can have the same deal if he likes," she added, obviously talking to Bev and not me.

I blushed. Bev smirked. "How about it, Ish? Want to buy a new belt?"

In the end, Bev and I bought eight belts each. They were exquisite and weighed less than a kilo total.

As we left the booth, I murmured to Beverly, "I hope Pip wasn't counting on that mass."

She glanced my way. "You and Pip are working together?"

"He's trying to show me the ropes, but after Darbat, he's starting from scratch again."

"You mean along with the empty container and the ship's stores dealing, right?" She grinned at me.

"I know roughly what he's doing there, but this kind of thing..." I waved my hand around at the flea market, "is more what I thought the idea of private trading would be like."

She nodded, turning her head to scan the flea market. "Some of it. Pip seems to have good connections and he does his homework. I'm more spur of the moment. I'm also full share so I have more mass to spend and I can afford to carry stuff a bit before I unload it. Lemme know if you get into a bind, Ishmael. I can buy these from you if you need to recover the creds. The half-kilo isn't going to matter much in the long run, though."

"Thanks, that makes me feel a little better."

"No problem." She grinned, chucking me playfully under the chin. "Besides, I need to look out for my boy toy."

We continued our tour around the flea market, but we didn't buy anything else. Beverly spent most of her time looking at various crafted items like clothing, jewelry, and leather goods. She had me try on a leather coat that was to die for. It was a rich dark brown, smooth and supple, lined with black silk. It fastened with polished, stainless steel buckles that clipped together cleverly in a kind of loop and toggle arrangement. It fit like it was custom made for me.

Unfortunately, it also cost twice what I had and weighed almost three full kilos.

Bev shrugged. "Costs nothing to look. You'll be full share soon and you won't be worried about mass so much."

Eventually, we both got hungry, thirsty, and tired, so we sauntered down to a little bistro on level eight that catered to the flea market trade. They had some hearty sandwiches of thinly sliced and sautéed beefalo, onions, peppers and cheese on crusty rolls. We each got one and I couldn't resist sampling the coffee. Beverly bought a beer and we rested our tired feet for almost a whole stan before heading to the ship.

When we got back to berthing, I changed into a fresh shipsuit and hung the belts in my locker along with my civvies. Beverly stowed her purchases as well but went out with some of the bridge crew for what I suspected would be more of a pub-crawl than a shopping jaunt. I went up to the galley to see what was happening.

Cookie and Pip were stowing the buckets of Sarabanda Dark and I walked in just in time to help them lock down the last load. I whistled at the quantity. "That's a lot of coffee."

Pip wiped the sweat off his face with a towel. "You have no idea."

Cookie consulted his tablet. "That's the last of our trade stores." He looked up, smiling. "These should be very useful."

Pip looked it over and shook his head. "I hope so. If this doesn't work we're going to be drinking a lot of Sarabanda." He turned to me. "How was liberty?"

"Fun. I went shopping."

Cookie looked up. "Shopping? For what?"

"Well, nothing, really. I ran into Bev at the lock and she dragged me up to the flea market on level nine. We've been up there all day wandering from stall to stall."

"Bev? Our Big Bad Beverly goes to the flea market?"

"Hey, she's a good person to go with. Nobody messed with us."

Cookie chuckled. "I can see where Ms. Arith would be able to provide a security buffer."

"She dickers pretty well, too. At least I think it was good. I can't haggle for squat."

Pip looked interested. "What'd she buy?"

"Belts. Beautiful leather belts. I got some, too."

"Belts?"

I nodded. "There was this little old lady working them on a bench right there in the flea market. She had a big rack of them. She was asking twenty creds each, or three for fifty. Bev got her down to a hundred creds for eight."

Pip nodded appreciatively. "Not bad. Twelve and a half each, but that's a lot of cred for a belt."

I shrugged. "Maybe, but they are gorgeous."

Cookie broke in, "We're done here. Why don't you take your break?"

I took him down to my locker and took out the bundle of belts. I spread them out on my bunk so Pip could get a good look. He picked up each one, examining it, front and back, and running the lengths through his hands. He flexed them and even smelled them.

"If you start tasting it, I'm gonna make you buy it." I was only half joking.

He grinned. "This is excellent stuff. This is beefalo leather but it's been expertly tanned and the workmanship on these patterns— well, you just don't see that these days. Mostly it's punched out by machine. This is real hand tooled stuff, all of it."

I nodded. "She was doing the work right there on a bench in her booth."

"Yeah, but that's usually just the come-on. Typically, when you actually look at the goods on the racks, you find that those aren't any more hand-tooled than I am. These are the real thing."

I shrugged.

"You say she had a whole rack?"

"Yup. Probably had a hundred belts on it. All kinds of patterns. Bev and I commented that while some of them were similar, we never did find two alike."

"None of them had buckles?"

"No, they're all just like this with the snaps and punch work so you can add your own. Some were a bit longer, some a bit shorter, but all about the same width and every one of them was this gorgeous leather."

Pip just stroked the belts for a moment. "How much did the eight add to your mass?"

"Half a kilo."

He nodded. "Where was this booth?"

I told him and I could see him getting that look in his eye so I wasn't surprised when he asked, "How much mass are you willing to invest? How many creds you got?"

I checked my allotment accounts. "I've got about ten kilos and four hundred creds. I'm willing to throw half that into the pool."

"Me, too. Okay, we have more mass than money. Are you willing to invest some more in belts?"

"You think it's worth it? How many can we sell?"

He grinned. "I don't know. It's always a gamble. I don't wanna hurt Bev's market, but these..." he indicated the belts arrayed on my bunk, "are something special. If you were able to buy eight for a hundred in the middle of the trading day, she might be willing to give a better price near closing with more cash on the line. If we could buy eighty of them that would be five kilos, but at ten a piece, it'd be eight hundred creds and we don't have that kinda cash. I doubt that she'd be willing to go below ten creds, even on a bulk deal. Between us we've got about four hundred creds. If she'll go down to ten, that's forty belts and two and a half kilos."

I shrugged. I could follow his logic, but this was all new. It's one thing to speculate idly over what to buy and what to sell. This was actual creds and real risk. Then I remembered the pallets of Sarabanda Dark down in the pantry and realized that what had been idle speculation for me had real implications for Pip. I used my tablet to transfer two hundred creds to his account. "Go for it." That evening I went to the holos with Diane Ardele and Gregor Avery from the environmental section. Gregor was a skinny spec three who'd been with the ship for only a stanyer but was already looking for a new berth.

"Oh, I like the *Lois* well enough," he spoke with a kind of whispery voice. "But I'd really like to get on one of the big tankers. The crews are smaller and the shares are bigger."

We discussed the relative merits of various berths all the way to the theater and back. Well, I like the *Lois* because we don't have to worry about snakes in our bunks," Diane added her opinion to the mix.

Gregor laughed but I didn't get the joke.

I looked puzzled. "Snakes? I've not seen any animals creeping around the *Lois*, are there usually snakes and mice and such?"

Gregor roared and Diane blushed. "On most ships yes, but not the way you're thinking."

I was still completely confused. "Okay, I'm sure I'm missing something."

Gregor stepped closer to me before speaking quietly, "Some vessels have a liberal policy on fraternization."

I was puzzled for a moment then enlightenment hit me. "Oh, you mean. . . ?"

They nodded.

Diane shrugged. "I like men as well as the next girl, but engineering berthing isn't even my fifth choice for a romantic interlude."

Gregor nodded. "Those partitions are thin."

I blushed thinking about Tabitha and her little snorty-snores, grateful that there hadn't been the sounds of *fraternization* as well. I was also glad that we had made it back to the ship and we each went our separate ways before I had any more opportunity to think about fraternization and Diane.

Pip was reading in his bunk when I got there. "Hey, how was the show?"

I shrugged. "Nothing to write home about. Change of pace from you and Cookie, but let's just say, when they release it on holo-cube, it's not one I'll be buying."

He nodded and went back to his reading.

I was almost asleep when Bev came in from her pub-crawl. "Hey, boy toy." She greeted me playfully, but didn't say anything else before falling into her bunk still fully clothed and started snoring softly.

I could feel Pip looking at me. I glanced over and he mouthed "boy toy" with raised eyebrows. I just groaned, shut off my light, and rolled into my blankets.

Chapter Eighteen
Gugara Orbital: 2351-December-11

Having the duty was almost a relief. I admit I liked being able to come and go, and I enjoyed getting to know some of the people I'd only seen in the mess line. The only drawback was that I felt compelled to take advantage of being able to leave, even when I didn't have a good reason to go. Not that I hadn't enjoyed the day out and about on the station, but it still felt good to take a bit of refuge in the ship.

Pip joined us for breakfast, and other than a few waggled eyebrows in my direction, didn't mention the boy toy incident again. After he ate, he rushed out. "Gotta see a lady about a belt," he said waving as he left.

When he was gone, I settled into the comfortable routine of port-side mess deck duty. Cookie and I split the omelet duties and I helped him make the soup stock for lunch by peeling the onions and carrots. I hung around and he gave me pointers on making biscuits. By the time he was finished showing me his tricks we made too many for lunch, but he smiled and explained, "We'll have traditional biscuits and gravy for breakfast tomorrow. They'll be perfect for that."

After lunch, I settled into a chair on the mess deck with my tablet and a fresh cup of coffee. I started looking over the food handler information. It didn't look any more difficult than the cargo handler, but I remembered how the actual exam had taken some less than straightforward twists. I tried to think about what the steward exam might do along those lines. I hadn't realized before just how pleasant the mess was to relax in. The seats were unpadded but still comfortable, even though they were bolted to the tables. The coffee was close by, and Cookie's rummaging in the kitchen and occasional humming made it seem homey. Occasionally somebody would stop by for some coffee or one of the pastries that Cookie left out while we were in port. Sometimes they'd stop and talk, other times they just nodded and continue on their way. I found it an exceptionally pleasant way to spend the afternoon.

Dinnertime rolled around and Cookie put together a baked pasta dish with beefalo and a soft white cheese made locally on Gugara. I took a couple of loaves of Cookie's yeast bread and made garlic loaves, grilling them before chopping them into rough chunks and tumbling them into a towel-lined basket on the buffet-style serving line. Set up, service, and take down were easy. I finished cleanup by 1900, then ran a few laps in the gym before ducking into the sauna.

When I got back to the berthing area, Pip was waiting with a bundle of belts draped off the side of his bunk and a huge grin across his face. "My gods, how many did you buy?" I asked in amazement.

"Eighty." He beamed. "Well, eighty-one, actually."

"What? How'd you do that?"

"I found Drus right where you said."

"Drus?"

"Yeah, Drus Martin. That's the woman you met. You were right. That rack of belts was spectacular. I talked to her near closing and told her I wanted to buy a bunch to take off-planet for trade and asked for a wholesale price. We haggled for a while until the market closed. I helped her pack up and push her grav pallet while we continued to barter." Pip paused to chuckle. "She's a salty old bird, but I've gotta give ya credit, you know quality goods when you see them, Ishmael, old boy. At one point, I mentioned that you and Bev had bought eight each yesterday. I forget how it came up. Something about the price she could take before her husband would beat her or something."

I snorted. "She used that same line on us."

"Anyway, she stops and says, 'Butchy looking fem? Black leathers and an attitude with a skinny boy toy in tow?'"

I groaned because Pip was enjoying this way too much.

"I told her, 'Yeah, that's them.' By then we're at her storage locker on level five and she opens it up to move the bench in for the night. Gods, Ish, that place was stuffed with belts. She points out like three bales rolled up against the bulkhead. There had to be three or four hundred of them. She says, 'For the woman and her boy I will do this. Pick any eighty, and I'll let you have them for four hundred, final offer, but you have to take them off-station.' "

"Wow, that's incredible. But wait, I thought you said you got eighty-one?"

He nodded. "I did. While I was picking out the belts, and you probably know as well as I do that there wasn't a bad one in the bunch, she was busy at her bench. I didn't think too much about it. I was busy pulling out different versions and trying to keep track of how many I had selected. All the while I wished I had enough money to take them all, and the leather smell made my head spin. It was amazing." Pip talked so fast, I thought he might tangle his tongue and strangle himself.

"So anyway, after about a quarter stan, I gave up trying to pick and choose and just started adding at random until I had eighty and we signed the chits and transferred the funds. That was so much less nerve-wracking than dealing with cash. So, I'm bundling up the belts to bring back when she hands me the one that she had been working on. 'Your friend, he was a nice boy,' she says as she gives it to me. 'This is for him,' she says."

Pip pulled a single belt from the bunch and handed it to me. It was exquisite. Expertly crafted premium leather with an ivy vine pattern running the full length. I'd never seen anything quite so beautiful. Looking closer I could see some lettering in the middle of the vines in an ornate script that blended with the curves of the vines and leaves it read, "Boy Toy".

Pip was killing himself with laughter, but I didn't care. The belt was beautiful and she'd made it just for me.

"Wait," I said, "you got eighty belts for four hundred creds?"

He nodded.

"That's just five creds each!"

He nodded again. "Yup." He grinned obviously inordinately proud of himself.

"What if we can't sell 'em on Margary?"

He shrugged. "I hope we don't sell them all. We'll need to let a few go to get some capital, but these are going to be worth a fortune on St. Cloud."

I stood there dumbfounded while leaning on my bunk, turning the supple leather over and over in my hands. My fingers traced the textures that the old woman, Drus, had pressed into it.

After a few ticks I remembered something. "What about the rugs and robes idea? I saw some of those at the flea market and you're right about the mass, although they were nice. The fur was much softer than I'd expected."

"I added them to the list for the empty container. They took up the last of the cash and the final mass allotments almost perfectly.

I still believe they're the right cargo for Margary and thought the ship may as well get some advantage from them."

"You think he's actually going to do it?" He knew I referred to Mr. Maxwell.

Pip shook his head. "No, I doubt it. That's a lot of creds to gamble on the advice of someone of my rank."

I nodded. "Makes sense. Maybe it's a trial. See what you can come up with, but not actually follow through. As you said, that's a lot of creds."

"I'm relieved actually. If he'd done it and it went badly, I'd feel really guilty about reducing share."

"Yeah, but the flip side is that if it goes empty, it doesn't contribute anything."

Pip shrugged. "True, but we already have a lot riding on this leg, our belts, the extra stores, if there was also a container that I picked. Man, that's a lot for one lowly attendant to take responsibility for." He grinned but I thought his smile looked a little wistful at the edges.

Chapter Nineteen
Gugara Orbital: 2351-December-13

The next morning we left Gugara en route to Margary. To mark the occasion, Cookie brought out a bucket of the Sarabanda Dark and I made one urn with it when we set the normal watch. He even had those little signs on chains like you see in coffee bars, one read, "Djartmo Arabasti" and the other, "Sarabanda Dark." He laughed in delight when I hung them on the valves.

It was a short trip, twenty-one days out to the Burleson limit, but Margary Station was only seven more on the other side. Durations are dictated by the placement of the system's primary station in relation to the system's center of gravitational mass. We had to get far enough out of the system's gravity well to allow the jump drives to bend space. The calculations were complicated and based on the ship's mass, the system's mass, the power rating on the drives, the distance we planned to jump, and I wasn't sure what else. In effect, it meant we needed to sail right out to the edge of the Deep Dark.

Every system has a limited sphere where planets can support life. This habitable zone exists as a spherical shell around the primary star. Its location depends on the size and temperature of the star, but that area is usually deep in the system's gravity well where the jump drives can't operate. Normally, an orbital holds a geostationary orbit over a habitable planet, which means there is a long transit time between it and the jump point, twenty to thirty days was not uncommon.

Margary was an exception because there is no suitable planet in the habitable zone. Margary Station is out on the edge of the system because it orbits the star. The bulk of the population live in an asteroid belt just outside the orbit of the second of two gas giant planets and the station was positioned to serve them. We didn't have to claw all the way into the gravity well to get there or out again. As a result the run from Gugara to Margary was a short one.

We were all in good spirits on the way out of Gugara. I felt relaxed and refreshed after my short excursions on the orbital, and enjoyed the new tasks in the galley working with Cookie. I found myself excited to start the food handler exam and thought about trying the ordinary spacer test as well. Pip still celebrated his deal on the belts and occasionally ribbed me with comments about boy toy, although never when Beverly was around. The stores accounting hadn't been included on the trip into Gugara but the savings would be factored into the shares when we got to Margary. The total probably wouldn't amount to much, but every little bit helped.

The second day out of Gugara, Pip looked up the Sarabanda Dark prices in Margary, trying to get a feel for whether they were rising or falling. Coffee is one of those volatile markets that operates as much on emotion as fact and he worried that reports of the bumper crop might drive the price down in Margary. The short run between the two systems counted against us on that score because it meant that information and goods moved easily between them. I was sweeping out the galley when Pip gave a strangled cry, "Aphrodite's flimsy nighty!"

He startled me so much that I dropped the broom and turned. He was pointing at his tablet his mouth gaping in disbelief. I crossed to him so I could see what was wrong and saw that the spare container wasn't empty any longer. We pulled up its contents and found it filled with the exact list of items that Pip had given to Mr. Maxwell.

Cookie came to look over our shoulders and simply gave a little, "Hmm," before wandering off.

Pip looked up at me, the stricken expression still painted on his face. "I don't know whether I should cheer or cry."

I shrugged. "Well, your ideas are getting a good shake out, if nothing else."

"Yeah, but what if I'm wrong?"

"Look, the ship has seventy-one other containers, right?"

He nodded.

"If this one had stayed empty, how many creds would it earn?"

"None."

"Worst case is what?"

"None of this stuff sells in Margary and we need to dump it to take on scheduled cargo. That would be a ten kilocred loss."

"I doubt that. Is that really likely?"

He stopped to think for half a tick before speaking. "No. In fact. . ." he pulled up another manifest, "we're scheduled to have two more empty containers when we leave."

"See. Okay, so then, the worst case is we drag it to St. Cloud. What are your projections there? Will that stuff sell if it doesn't move on Margary?"

He tapped keys, first on his tablet and then on the portable. He was in zombie mode so I went back to sweeping. Finally he spoke, "Yeah, actually, the market is slightly better on St. Cloud."

"Okay, so you see, it should be fine, and it's not all riding on one throw of the dice, either."

Pip's color started returning and he stopped hyperventilating as he focused on refining the calculations for St. Cloud. "Okay, you're right. It's just that I'd made up my mind that Mr. Maxwell was just testing me and seeing that container showing up full surprised me."

I nodded in response. "You ready for another shock?"

He looked at me hesitantly. "What?"

"If I were you, I'd start planning what you'd put in those other empties once we land in Margary, because I'll bet Mr. Maxwell is down here the day after transition to give you that little assignment as well."

"He wouldn't," Pip said, but the color started draining from his face once more.

"Well, maybe not, but at least figure out what to reload your container with, assuming it gets emptied in Margary and earns a bit of profit."

Pip gulped and started hammering on the keys.

❀　　❀　　❀

Shipboard routine settled around us like an old sweater. The availability of the new stores worked wonders with the daily meals. For the first few days out of Gugara we had fresh greens and fruits. As they began to taper off, we still had an occasional urn of the nutty, rich Sarabanda to break up the monotony of the Arabasti. Cookie had ordered a bunch of canned fruit and he pulled a couple cases out of our trade goods to help me experiment with fruit crisps and cobblers. It was a lot of fun and livened up the luncheon preparation. The crew's sweet tooth seemed to appreciate the desserts.

I spent the evenings in the gym and sauna. I soon realized that I was in the best physical condition of my life. I spent my afternoon breaks alternating between studying for the steward exam and hanging out in environmental. I really wanted to get my hands dirty with some of the routine activities in that department to see if I'd like them.

One day, about a week out of Gugara, I went down to find them dredging out sludge. The process wasn't physically difficult. It smelled a bit funky, but nothing like you might expect. All in all it was just messy. The sludge that came from the water treatment plant had been biologically stabilized to the point where it was practically sterile.

As a normal part of processing, the sludge settled into the bottom of the water treatment ponds and even after the water had been pumped out, it was still wet, sticky, and slimy. We used mechanical scoops to load the sludge deposits into shallow metal containers, what the environmental gang called loaf pans. They were about a meter and a half long, a meter wide, and a half-meter deep. When full, we ran the pans through a combination freezer-vacuum compartment where the water sublimated out of it. After the loaves dried we knocked them out of the pans, wrapped each one in a sealant eerily similar to clingfilm, and stacked it in a storage space for disposition at the next port.

One pond yielded about five of these large loaves. The pans were incredibly heavy when wet, but once dry, the sludge cakes had about the same mass and consistency as polyfoam. One person could lift one, but handling it was awkward because of its size and shape. As we were finishing up, Diane told me they would do it one more time before hitting Margary, but on the other pond. I confess it wasn't as gross as I thought it would be, just grubby. I left them loading the last pans in the dryer when I went to clean up before heading to the galley for the dinner mess.

As I got into the shower, the raspy buzz of the fire alarm went off followed by, *"THIS IS A DRILL. THIS IS A DRILL. FIRE IN THE ENGINEERING BERTHING AREA. ALL HANDS TO FIRE AND DAMAGE CONTROL STATIONS. FIRE IN THE ENGINEERING BERTHING AREA. ALL HANDS TO FIRE AND DAMAGE CONTROL STATIONS. THIS IS A DRILL. THIS IS A DRILL."*

I played the shower quickly over my head and zipped into a fresh shipsuit in less than a tick. In under two, I was trotting into the galley where I found Pip and Cookie working on dinner. Cookie called in and we continued with the preparations. I finally felt like I was getting the hang of it.

❀   ❀   ❀

Nineteen days out of Gugara and two before the jump into Margary, Pip picked up the data beacon and downloaded the current market conditions. He spent almost the next whole day revising and refining his models. The longer he worked, the gloomier he seemed.

When we did the final jump prep, twenty-one days out of Gugara, he sighed and threw down his stylus rubbing his eyes with the heels of his hands.

"Problems?"

"Maybe. The biggest problem is that I can't really tell. It looks like the coffee prices have tanked. The market appears to be saturated with Sarabanda Dark and oddly, the wholesale price of Arabasti, which you can usually get for three creds a bucket is now twenty-two creds. If these prices are correct we can buy Sarabanda for less here than we just paid in Gugara. And there doesn't appear to be any Arabasti for sale in the whole system. It's crazy."

Cookie listened to our conversation and smiled. "I'm glad I laid in extra Arabasti in Darbat, then."

Pip laughed. "Good point." He consulted the pantry inventories and said, "Okay, we have sixty-eight full buckets of Arabasti. We paid an average of three creds each. Net on one of the Arabasti would be nineteen creds. We paid an average of eight creds a piece for a hundred and fifty buckets of Sarabanda. Net on the Sarabanda is a loss of three as we can buy it here for five."

This shocked me. "Wait, you're telling me we'll lose money if we sell the Sarabanda in Margary?"

Pip nodded. "Exactly. We've got that Sarabanda because we bought it to trade, not drink. How much Arabasti do we need to make St. Cloud?"

I considered the question. "We use about a bucket a day, more or less. How long is the Margary to St. Cloud run?"

Pip pulled up the schedule. "Eight days to jump, and twenty-eight on the back side. St. Cloud has a weak sun and the orbital is a long way down the well."

"Five weeks in roundish numbers. And we're a week out of Margary?"

He nodded. "About that."

"Call it six weeks. Between the rest of this run, the in port time, and the run to St. Cloud, we need forty-two, make it forty-five just to be safe. If we brew half Sarabanda, which the crew likes just fine, that means we only need twenty-two of each."

Cookie spoke up, "Might I suggest that we keep just two buckets of Arabasti and plan to sell the rest in Margary. If we shift to Sarabanda now, and only use the Arabasti for special occasions, we can sell sixty-six of the more expensive brand and turn a nice profit. That will give us capital to buy more Sarabanda and lower our average cost."

"Can we do that?"

Cookie shrugged. "Why not? The Sarabanda is actually a better quality coffee and the crew, as you so eloquently pointed out, young Ishmael, likes it just fine. Personally, I prefer it."

Pip started tapping again and nodding. "Yes, this will work. The prices are holding on St. Cloud. They might even be a little better."

Cookie nodded. "Very good, then. Yes, this is our best course. How are the mushroom prices looking?"

"They're good." Pip grinned. "Prices for fresh are holding steady but the dried have actually started dropping. Three varieties are available in commercial quantities and we can get two other artisan varieties in large enough bulk to make it worth stocking."

"Mushrooms?" I looked back and forth between the two.

Cookie nodded. "It's a kind of edible fungus."

I huffed. "I know what mushrooms are. We've never had them on ship before, have we?"

Cookie shook his head. "Not in some time. They are difficult to procure and expensive when they're available. Margary is one of the few sources in this end of the galaxy where they're commonly raised."

I rounded on Pip. "That's what you meant."

He nodded with a cat-ate-the-canary grin. "Yup. Most people don't know about the Margary mushrooms. Few consider them food so they get overlooked."

"Any insight on the empty container?"

"Depends on budget. Freeze dried mushrooms would be best. They're not very dense and they have a good upside potential. We can get container quantities of them but they'd cost upward of fifty kilocreds. The upside is that a container of good quality freeze dried mushrooms would net a hundred or hundred fifty on St. Cloud and even more at Dunsany Roads."

I whistled. "Not bad for spare mass. What else could we get?"

Pip browsed through his sources for a moment and said, "Well, there's no container sized lots, but there are several dozen pallets of minerals: quartz, beryl, jade, lapis, even some emeralds, and rubies. Those will be the bulk, industrial grade stuff, not the jewel grade. The prospectors and minors pick out the best pieces as they go. The minerals won't take up as much volume because they're a lot denser but the initial cost of the minerals is a lot higher and the profit potential on the other end isn't as high."

"What would you recommend to Mr. Maxwell if he were standing right behind you?" Cookie asked.

Pip blew out his breath noisily while he considered. "Sounds funny, but I'd leave the minerals and fill the container with mushrooms. While a kilo of mushrooms won't fetch the same price as a kilo of rubies, you can put a lot more mushrooms in a container for the same investment. It's not the mass that's the issue, six hundred tons is six hundred tons, but there is a big difference in cost. We could probably fill a container with a fifty kilocred investment. Profit on the mushrooms would be somewhere between one hundred and one hundred fifty. The prices for mushrooms on St. Cloud and Dunsany are quite high. A container of mixed gems would cost three hundred kilocredits, maybe more depending on what you got. You'd be lucky to get four hundred kilocredits on the other end. In both cases, you'd make about the same, but the initial investment is a lot higher on the minerals. Profit ratio on the mushrooms is likely to exceed two hundred percent while the ratio on a similar container of minerals would be maybe twenty-five or thirty."

From behind him Mr. Maxwell spoke, "Thank you, Mr. Carstairs, for that cogent and reasonable assessment. Please notify me if you identify any other opportunities."

Pip just closed his eyes and didn't appear to breathe for a long time.

CHAPTER TWENTY
MARGARY SYSTEM: 2352-JANUARY-05

The run into Margary station went quickly. The only interruption came in the middle of the night two days after the jump. The whoop-whoop of the environmental alarm woke me out of a sound sleep just before midnight. I scrambled out of my bunk and went to the suit locker as soon as I was able to find floor space for my feet. By the time I got there, Bev had the locker open and was handing out suits as people filed past her. I took one and kept walking until I found a clear spot on the deck. I remembered where to grab the suit and how to shake it to get it opened up to wear. I had it on and the helmet sealed before the drill announcement finished. This time I wasn't the last one by a long shot.

Everybody made it on time, and after the captain's congratulatory message, I stripped off my suit, set the used tag, and crawled back into bed.

❀　　❀　　❀

As we got closer to Margary, one question started to nag at me. Finally I decided to talk to Pip and approached him during the evening cleanup. "How are we going to sell the belts?"

"We talk to people who retail similar stuff... anybody who has a clothing store, that kind of thing."

I suppose I shouldn't have worried that much, after all, Pip didn't seem concerned and he'd been at it a lot longer. Being new to this whole thing, it still bothered me. His nebulous response left too much to chance for my comfort. Later, in the berthing area, I asked Bev about it. "How are you going to dispose of your belts?"

"I don't know. I usually just find somebody who wants what I have and I sell it."

"But how do you find them?"

"Me? I go to the flea market. Usually there's somebody there who sells something similar to whatever I've got and is willing to pay for new stock."

"Okay, that makes sense, but doesn't that eat into your profit? I mean, you wind up selling at wholesale, right?"

"Yeah, but that's the price of doing business."

"Why don't you rent a stall and sell retail?"

"It's not worth the hassle for just a few belts. Stall rental would probably eat the difference and I'd have to stay there until they sold. Doing it my way, somebody else does all the work."

"Sure, I can see that." I thought a moment. "But doesn't everybody have something to sell? What if we all got together, we could share the booth costs."

Bev blinked at me several times. It was rather disconcerting, to be truthful. "Out of the mouths of babes," she muttered.

Pip came in and crawled into his bunk just then. "Who you calling a babe?"

Bev just shook her head. "Not that kind of babe. But you're brilliant."

"Thanks," Pip said. "But what did I do now?"

Bev poked him playfully. "Not you, silly, I meant Ish. He's a genius, did you know that?" She jerked a thumb in my direction.

"What'd he say?"

"That we should all share a booth on Margary."

Pip turned all owly and blinky himself for a tick before saying, "Yup, I taught him everything he knows."

The next day Bev started circulating the idea around the ship looking for others who might want to go in on the booth. Not knowing what it would cost hampered the effort a bit, but several of the crew agreed, so long as they didn't have to hang around selling the whole time.

I mentioned it to Sandy Belterson when I ran into her on the track that evening.

"If you have any trade goods, Pip, Bev, and I are thinking about renting a booth at the flea market on Margary Station to sell our stuff. You're welcome to add yours if you like."

"Do you think it will work out?"

I shrugged. "I don't know but it seems worth a shot. We're trying to find out the costs now. That should give us an idea whether or not it's even possible. If it's too expensive, we won't do it. But since we're not going to be in port all that long we're trying to line up people before we hit the station. We'll give it a shot, assuming we can swing the price and we have enough stuff to put out."

We ran another whole lap while she thought about it. "That's a really intriguing idea, Ish. I've got a few things I'd be interested in moving. Let me know if it goes forward, okay?"

I nodded and we finished our laps together.

❀   ❀   ❀

The next afternoon we docked at Margary Station. Pip looked up the terms and conditions on the flea market. They charged ten creds a day for space rental and an extra cred if you wanted a table. They charged a one-day minimum fee. We looked at the tablet for a long time. Pip finally shook his head a muttered loud enough for me to hear, "It's too good. There has to be a catch."

I shrugged. "Well, I know who we can ask."

Pip looked at me with a raised eyebrow.

"Mr. Maxwell."

His eyes got big for a tick, but he nodded his agreement and we went in search of the first mate.

We found him in the ship's office, where he spent most of his port time. We knocked and went in.

Mr. Maxwell just sat observing us for a tick. "How can I help you gentlemen this fine day?"

Pip looked at me as if to say, *it was your idea.*

I took a deep breath and then rattled off the plan. I finished with the question we needed answered. "So what are we overlooking? Is there some hidden cost? Or some rule against crew renting tables?"

Mr. Maxwell pursed his lips and narrowed his eyes. I braced myself because I was pretty sure he was thinking really hard, or considering just how to kill me. Either way, I wanted to keep a low profile. "Just so I understand this, Mr. Wang. You're proposing to rent a booth at the flea market so that the crew members who have private trades have a place to sell their goods retail?"

"Yes, sar, that's the basic idea."

"Who's going to work the booth?"

"We'll need a couple volunteers from each watch section. Pip and I, of course, but I don't have any others yet because we're still trying to figure out if we can do it."

Mr. Maxwell swiveled his gaze to Pip. "You're in on this?"

"Yes, sar. Mr. Wang and I, being on opposite watches agreed that we can cover the booth so that it can stay open every day we're in port."

"Are you telling me you're giving up liberty so that your crew-mates have a place to make private trades?"

We both gulped. I shot a glance at Pip out of the corner of my eye before answering, "Yes, sar."

"Well, sar, it's only during business hours so it's not like we're giving up all our liberty," Pip added. "The flea market isn't open in the evening."

I thought Mr. Maxwell smiled at that, but it disappeared too quickly for me to be sure.

He let us stew in our own juices for about two solid ticks before answering, "Gentlemen, I have some good news and some bad news." Pip and I shot a glance to each other before Mr. Maxwell went on, "The crew is prohibited from engaging in any activity which might be considered competing with the trading mission of the ship. That's the bad news. The good news is that the ship is under no such restriction."

I was having trouble untangling that statement but Pip grinned.

Mr. Maxwell continued, "We frequently rent offices, warehouses, and other port-side facilities when they are required for legitimate ship's business. Ever since the incident at Darbat, the captain and I have been struggling with how to keep the crew safe without restricting their enthusiasm for private trading. You two seem to have hit upon a solution so obvious that we never would have thought of it. Let me run this idea past her and get back to you. I suspect you'll be able to set up shop tomorrow, but I'll let you know later this evening."

Pip spoke while I was still untangling my tongue. "Yes, sar, thank you, sar."

Mr. Maxwell nodded. "You're welcome. Dismissed."

We took the hint and headed back to the galley to start the evening meal. First night of liberty or not, neither of us wanted to leave the ship until we got the idea fully hashed out. As we expected, almost nobody came to the mess deck for dinner. We served the few watch standers left aboard and waited.

Near the end of dinner, a message from the captain pinged into our tablets simultaneously. It confirmed that the ship had rented booth four seventy-eight at Margary Station's flea market for four days beginning at 0800 the next day. She instructed us to pick up our authorization certificate from the market office no later than 0730 under the name of McKendrick Mercantile Cooperative.

Pip looked at me across the mess table. "Okay, I'll take the duty tomorrow. You get it set up."

"Me? You're the trading genius."

He grinned at me. "Your idea, so you have to do it."

I shook my head slowly. This trip just got stranger and stranger. I left Pip with cleanup duty and went in search of people to help me in the morning.

My first stop was the berthing area where I found Bev coming off watch and getting ready for liberty. "The captain approved the flea market."

She turned wide-eyed in my direction. "Wha—? How'd the captain get involved?"

"Pip and I wanted to make sure there wasn't any conflict so we went to Mr. Maxwell. As it turns out, only the ship can officially rent the space but can do it for the benefit of the crew. The only catch was he had to run it by the captain. We just got the confirmation a few ticks ago. They rented space in the name of McKendrick Mercantile Cooperative and anybody in the crew with trade goods will be free to use the space to sell their stuff."

"Sounds great. Will it be expensive?"

"That's the best part, the rental is only ten creds a day and it's a simple pay-as-you go plan."

Bev grinned. "I'll be switched. You actually did it."

"Yup. Only problem is that Pip has the duty tomorrow and I'm a little nervous about setting up by myself."

"I'm off tomorrow. I'll help ya. Besides, it'll give me a chance to check out the other booths." She grinned wolfishly. "Might find something else to spend my money on."

Relief washed over me. "Thanks, Bev. I really mean it."

"No worries. Besides." She paused and gave me a wink. "I can't have my boy toy wandering around unprotected now, can I?"

"Well, with Big Bad Beverly watching my back, there's nothing I'm gonna be worried about."

We both grinned and got on with our evening plans.

I found Sandy Belterson on the track and learned that Brill was off the ship already, but would be returning in the morning. I went down to the environmental section and found Francis and Diane at the watch station and filled them in on the plan. They each had some trade goods and were excited to join in. I asked them to pass the word and went to my bunk to rack out.

❀   ❀   ❀

When the messenger came for Pip the next morning, Beverly and I got up too. We put on shipsuits and headed to the galley for breakfast and to talk things over.

I made the coffee while Pip set up Cookie's omelet station. Bev accepted the first cup from the pot and let Pip practice his omelet skills on her while Cookie finished putting up the bread. In port mess duty seemed so laid back by this time that I found it ridiculous I had ever considered it difficult. The three of us had become a well-integrated machine, each doing the required tasks without the least interference from either of the others. Any one of us could probably have handled the breakfast alone, but Cookie spent his time preparing the signature breads, pastries, and desserts that were his pride and joy.

After the few crew members were served, Pip, Bev, and I gathered at a table to talk about how to proceed.

Pip started, "You two should go and take your belts. I can send the other crew up to find you later. Sell as many as you want and I'll take the big bundle up tomorrow. Bev, you have dibs, so I won't put mine out until you're done selling, okay?"

She grinned. "I'm only planning on taking four of the eight. If we do this on St. Cloud, too, we'll probably make a killing, and I want to have at least half of my belts available for that."

Pip sipped his coffee while he considered. "You're going to take yours up, aren't you, Ish?"

"Yeah, at the moment it's all I have to sell and I'd like to get something out there. I'll take the eight I bought with Bev. It won't matter if I sell them all, because we have that whole bundle. The big question is how much to charge?"

Bev finished her omelet and pushed the tray back. "I was thinking thirty creds. That's more than double what we paid for them."

Pip shook his head. "If it were me, I'd start at fifty and let 'em talk me down to thirty. These are top shelf goods. The leather is amazing and the tool work is exceptional. The rock jockeys and metal munchers will have money to spare and if you don't take it from them, they'll just drink it away instead."

"Point taken. We'll see what the market will bear and that'll help you move the large bundle later."

Pip nodded. It seemed like a logical plan to me.

I looked back and forth between the two of them. "Do you think any of the crew will come to sell in the booth?"

Bev nodded vigorously. "They will, but maybe not until they see how it works out."

Pip lifted his chin to get our attention. "I have one more question. How do we reimburse the ship?"

Bev and I looked at each other and then back at him. "Reimburse the ship?"

He nodded. "If Ish and I had taken this on, we'd have just absorbed the cost in the day's business, but this is ship's business. We can't expect the rest of the crew to absorb the expense, can we?"

Bev snorted. "We only need to cover ten creds a day, right?"

"Something like that." Pip shrugged. "The captain paid out forty creds for the rental."

"No table," I pointed out. "I wonder if I can add that at the office this morning."

"How much is one?" Bev asked.

"A cred a day."

"Whoa, can you afford it, big spender?"

Pip grinned. "I think that's the answer. Ish, you and I were going to cover this expense when we asked Mr. Maxwell so why don't we just do it."

"Do you need me to chip in?" Bev asked.

I shook my head. "No, we've got this. After all, you're only selling a few belts and we have that big bundle. We should make more than enough to cover it."

"Okay, well if you want me to, just let me know."

"Gimme twenty now and I'll add twenty and reimburse the ship while you're out setting up," Pip said before getting up to start another pot of coffee.

I pulled out my tablet and transferred the credits. "Done." While I was in my account I noted that I'd been paid again and that I was building up a respectable balance, even after having paid out the two hundred back on Gugara.

Bev stood up and grabbed her dirty dishes. "Okay, I need to get into some civvies and go get seriously commercial for a bit." She looked at me with a twinkle in her eye. "Wanna join me?"

We all laughed and started moving. We took the dishes to the galley and Bev and I headed to the berthing area to change while Pip returned to morning mess duty. As I slipped on my jacket, I couldn't help but remember that leather coat with the black silk lining on Gugara. I half wished I'd gotten it but the mass would have chewed into my trading. It only took a few ticks to change clothes and we headed for the lock with our belts in a duffel bag.

At the lock, Rhon Scham had the bow watch and gave us a bundle of blue cloth. "Compliments of the captain." She told us. We had no idea what it was, so we unfolded it. It turned out to be a banner, about two meters long, with shiny letters sewn onto it. When we got it fully stretched out, we could see that the silvery material spelled McKendrick Mercantile Cooperative.

"From the captain?" I asked.

"That's what the note says. She dropped it off just before mid-watch last night."

Beverly examined the fabric. "This is ancient. This banner has to be. . . maybe fifty years old."

Rhon and I both shrugged.

"What's the McKendrick Mercantile Cooperative?" I looked back and forth between them.

Bev shrugged. "I don't know, but I bet there's a good story behind this. Come on, we're gonna be late."

We refolded the banner and carefully tucked it in the duffel with the belts. Rhon keyed the lock and we bolted for the lift and headed up to the flea market office to check in.

The flea market manager seemed a nice enough guy. I suppose you have to be to coordinate the circus that constituted a major orbital flea market. He didn't even appear intimidated by Beverly. He wore a bright green vest that clashed horribly with everything else he had on, which probably was the point. He certainly stood out in the crowd. Across the back it said, "Margary Flea" in big yellow letters and on the left breast it said, "Fergus, Manager." He was happy to rent me a table for the four days and let me pick the one I wanted out of a battered collection stacked up in the storage area.

"You just bring it back tonight and it'll be safe until tomorrow." He handed me a plastic coated badge with all the pertinent information: dates, rates, services, along with a big four seventy-eight on its face. "Clip this to the drape at the back of your booth so that security knows you're registered and take it with you when you leave for the night. There's a magtag in it that will open the doors when you want to come back in the morning. It's good for the full four days. After 1700 on the last day it expires. You can just toss it. Your booth is over that way about forty meters. Follow the signs painted on the deck. Good luck with your sales."

Bev and I thanked him and headed off in the indicated direction to find our space. We had half a stan before the doors opened and let the public in. We joined the steady parade of merchants and the flea market felt like it was coming to life after a long night's sleep, which in truth, I suppose it was.

It took us five ticks to find the place but no time at all to set up. The table was a pull-the-legs-and-lock type, so it was easy. We pulled out the banner and debated where to put it. A pipe-scaffold ran along the back of the space with a drape on it. If we'd had some wire or string, we could have hung it up there. Some pins would have let us attach it to the drape, but, of course, we had none of them. Ultimately, we just laid it out like a tablecloth and put a selection of the belts for sale on it. We stashed the empty duffel under the table. The display looked completely amateurish, even to me.

Bev and I looked at each other.

I shrugged. "We're really not prepared, are we?"

She shook her head. "No. Not really." She grinned at my hang-dog look. "But it'll come. Live and learn, I always say."

More vendors filed in and set up around us. Across the aisle was a potter, a youngish looking guy with sandy hair and an artificial foot. He slid a grav pallet into his space, all set up with his displays. He just locked it down and was ready for business. Looking around, I saw that the grav pallet seemed to be the standard as there was a procession of them winding in from the lifts.

Bev and I looked at each other. "If this catches on..." we started to say at the same time and laughed.

An obviously married, older couple trundled up to the booth beside us and began unloading a simple cargo tote. The woman—a mousy, gray-haired matron in boots, a pair of jeans, a checked shirt, and a vest—began directing the man. He was nearly bald and wore a utility jumpsuit. Her voice carried over the rising noise level as she bossed him around.

"Not there, Virgil, I need that here." Her smooth alto carried a whip-crack undertone that made me instantly feel sorry for him.

"Come on, Virgil, the floor will be open soon and I need this set up now!"

She continued along this vein for quite some time. Poor Virgil had apparently done this chore many times but he just couldn't seem to do it to her satisfaction. They unpacked signs, display racks, and other paraphernalia from their little tote. With each new item, she'd give Virgil another order. Bev had to look the other way just to hide her amusement.

I joined her on the far side of our booth and elbowed her. "It's not funny. That poor guy."

Bev nodded. "I know, I know. It's just..."

Behind us we heard, "Virgil, I've told you a hundred times not that way. Set it up like this."

I had to bite my lip to keep from laughing and Beverly looked down with a hand on her brow to hide her face. Her shoulders were shaking as she tried to suppress her laughter.

Luckily, about that time, a loud pa-pong echoed from the ceiling speakers and the big entry doors at either end of the hall rolled open. A tide of people surged onto the trading floor. In a few ticks buyers began sauntering by and Virgil left the woman to tend the booth by herself.

Bev and I stood awkwardly behind the table and watched as people passed. Some stopped to eye the belts, but more were interested in Bev. She wore her black leather pants, jacket, and boots. Under the jacket she wore a cream-colored shirt with a stand-up collar. Even with the buzz-cut and piercings, the shirt softened the edge a bit in comparison to the aluminum pullover she'd worn on Gugara. I wore my only set of civvies and, compared to her, I was about as non-nondescript as Virgil had been.

"Lookie loos," Bev pitched her voice low enough to reach my ears without being overheard by those around us.

"What?"

"This first group." She indicated the crowd with a slight nod of her head. "They're the lookie loos. They have no intention of buying yet. Eventually they might, but for now..."

I nodded.

It didn't take long for the experience to get boring. I took out my tablet and started making a list.

"Whatcha you doing?"

I didn't look up. "Taking notes. Next time we need some clips so we can hang the banner on the drape, and Pip will need some kind of rack to be able to display that bundle of belts."

Bev nodded and stretched her back. "Stools would be good too. It's going to be a long day standing, I'm afraid."

I added that to the list, along with grav pallet followed by a question mark and thermos of coffee.

A couple stepped up to the table, so I put my tablet away. The next three stans eroded under the steady trickle of buyers through the booth. Bev did the actual haggling and I listened out of one ear while I explained to the next buyer that the belts came from Gugara and were hand-tooled by one of their master craftsmen. Most people who picked up one of them and could feel the texture and suppleness of the leather wanted to buy one, even if they weren't able to afford it. We set the price high and were in no hurry to drop it too quickly, something the hagglers caught on to right away. Nobody seemed too put out and Bev sold two at forty creds rather quickly.

About that time, Diane Ardele showed up with Francis in tow. He lugged a duffel stuffed with silk scarves, brocaded vests, and delicate china plates with oriental scenes painted on them. The plates were wrapped in sponge-foam and individually boxed. Bev and I moved the belts over to one end of the table and let Diane and Francis set up on the other. The booth looked more appealing with the brightly colored fabrics and shining glass. It also didn't hurt that Diane wore jeans that were one size larger than painted on and a deep, scoop-neck top. With her cheerful smile, she was soon attracting as much attention as Bev. Francis and I knew enough to stand back and let the experts work the table.

After a couple of stans there was a lull in the action and we all just stood around grinning at each other.

Diane had sold about half of her scarves and a couple of plates. Bev had taken the four belts she wanted to hold for St. Cloud and put them in the duffel but sold all the rest of hers and a couple of mine. At the rate they were going, we'd be out by midafternoon, but she'd made a profit already, and one more from my pile would put me in the black as well. Diane and Francis seemed pleased, too.

Bev announced, "I need to stretch my legs."

Diane volunteered to go with her. "You boys mind the store. We'll be back soon."

With that, they marched off toward the restrooms, heads together in some kind of feminine conference.

Francis and I were left staring at each other.

"So much for the window dressing." He shot me a wry grin.

"What? You don't think a little beef cake will work?" I pulled the leg of my jeans up to display the pale, hairy flesh beneath.

He grimaced and shook his head with a laugh.

A group of people came into the booth and Francis and I had our hands full for a few ticks. I managed to sell a belt at almost forty creds and Francis sold two of the plates and a rich, emerald green vest with gold threads. The woman who bought Francis' vest had red hair and eyes that matched the new garment perfectly. She was cute to begin with, but when she slipped on the vest, she was stunning. The redhead never took it off the whole time she was haggling and Francis got a hundred and twenty creds for it.

"Nice." I congratulated him as they left.

"Thanks. She was an easy sell. She wasn't going to leave without it."

I could still see her walking away through the crowd. "Yeah, I don't blame her."

Diane came back with a beverage carrier of coffees and a bag of sandwiches. "Bev's gone prowling. Was that one of the vests I just saw walking off?"

Francis smiled. "Yup, got a hundred and twenty for it."

Diane grinned and gave him a kiss on the cheek. "Thanks."

She smiled at me and winked. "Only paid twenty for that on Darbat."

The coffee tasted muddy and bitter, and the sandwiches soaked through the paper napkins, but I was hungry and ate every bite. The steady trickle of people continued and we took turns putting down our sandwiches to talk to them. I sold another belt before Bev got back.

She sashayed up to the booth pretending to be a customer. "What darling belts. Too bad they don't have buckles."

We all laughed until she produced a silvery chunk of metal inlaid with a blue stone and tossed it on the table with a thunk. The oblong metal block, about the size of my palm, tottered on a slight convex curve across the front. I didn't recognize it at first and then

I realized it was a buckle.

Francis scooped it up before I could reach it. "Is this turquoise?"

Bev shook her head. "That's what I thought when I saw it, but it's lapis."

Diane peered around Francis to look at it. "It's gorgeous, that's what it is."

Bev nodded and fished one of her reserve belts out of the duffel. It only took a tick for her to connect it to the buckle and hold it up for display.

We all just stared at it. "Oh—my," Diane summed up our collective reactions succinctly.

The combined product caught attention immediately. Several people stopped to admire it and Bev played the crowd. "Sorry, folks, this one's not for sale, but my friend here has more belts he'd be happy to sell you and you can get the buckles from booth two sixteen. The gentleman there has a nice collection available at very reasonable prices." About a third of the crowd headed off in that direction, another third stepped up to the table and began looking over the few belts I had left, and the rest wandered off.

When the group thinned out, I managed to get Bev to fill me in on the details.

"I was just wandering around after we hit the head and I ran across this booth. He has a big peg board of these buckles all about the same size and shape. Each is inlaid with different minerals. I don't know how he makes them, but the results are spectacular."

"No kidding." Diane grinned at her, fingering the buckle.

Bev pulled a small bundle out of the pocket of her jacket. "I got four of them, one for each of my remaining belts. He gave me a good price on the proviso that I not sell them on-station." She saw the look on my face and added, "I told him that you would be along shortly. He sold these to me for fifteen creds each. He's asking twenty-five to thirty-five depending on the stone."

Diane handed the buckle to Francis and he hefted it. "By the weight of this thing, the metal is probably worth that much."

Bev nodded in agreement. "Yeah, the mass is going to be a problem for taking too many of these with us. I need to weigh them but I bet they weigh at least a hundred grams each."

I did some quick math in my head. "Ten per kilo. I have mass for fifty and enough creds for about twenty."

Bev grinned at me. "Depending on how well the belts sell, you'll recover some of the mass, and a lot of the money."

Diane raised an eyebrow in my direction. "How many do you have?"

"Pip and I got a deal on eighty of them back on Gugara."

"Eighty? Whoa," Diane said with a whistle.

"You guys should pay me a finder's fee." Bev teased, much to Francis and Diane's amusement.

"Hey, I spotted the belts first."

"Kids, if you're gonna fight, please take it out of the booth, okay?" Francis grinned at us.

A new group of customers stepped up to the table and we had to behave, but I snapped a quick digital of the buckle with my tablet and flashed it over to Pip's tablet before I started answering questions.

Customers paraded through the booth in a more or less steady stream for the rest of the afternoon. Francis and Diane sold all the scarves, almost all of the plates, and three more of the brocade vests. Francis only put one out at a time and after each sale he rummaged in his duffel and pulled out another.

After he put out the third one, I shook my head in amazement. "How many of those do you have?"

"Three more." He grinned at me.

"Are you putting them out individually to make them seem more valuable? Like they are one of a kind or something?"

He shrugged. "They are one of a kind, just like the belts. I put them out that way so they're easier to keep track of."

I chuckled. "Never overlook the obvious."

Late in the afternoon, an attractive woman in a smartly tailored blouse and slacks stepped up to the table and looked it over. "How are things going?"

"Very well, Captain." Bev elbowed me discreetly.

I managed to suppress the gasp of recognition. "Yes, sar, very well. Thank you for setting this up for us."

She turned to Francis and Diane. "What do you two think of the idea?"

Francis spoke first, "It's been great. We've sold almost all our trade goods and it's been fun to boot."

Diane nodded as he spoke, "Yes, sar, I've been dragging those plates around for months. We've sold most of them and at good prices, too. My mass allotment will be wide open after today."

The captain smiled. "Excellent." She turned back to me and asked, "Is there anything you need?"

I shook my head. "We came in not knowing what to expect and the banner was a surprise. I've made some notes to myself to get some clips so we can hang it up on the drape behind us and to replace it with a tablecloth for tomorrow."

The captain's fingers strayed to the blue fabric and she stroked it gently. "Excellent plan, Mr. Wang. This has served as tablecloth more than once so you're carrying on a proud tradition. Is there anything else?"

Bev spoke up, "More trade goods, Captain. At this rate, we're going to run out. We need to let the rest of the crew know what we're doing so they can take advantage of the booth."

The captain nodded and smiled. "Mr. Carstairs has been recruiting all day. I think there will be enough to sell tomorrow." She scanned our faces. "Anything else?"

We looked at each other and I answered, "No, Captain. You've done a lot for us already, thank you."

"No, thank you, Mr. Wang. This is a good thing you and Mr. Carstairs are doing for the ship."

"Thank you, Captain."

She nodded to all of us and started on down the aisle after a few steps she turned back. "Oh, Mr. Wang, when you get aboard this evening, please collect Mr. Carstairs and report to my cabin? Around 2000 would be good. I'd like a status report."

"Aye, aye, Captain. My pleasure."

She smiled and, with a jaunty wave, disappeared into the crowd.

As soon as she was gone, Bev slugged me on the shoulder. "You didn't recognize the captain?"

"I've never seen her in civvies." I rubbed my arm. "How was I to know she'd be here?"

"You've seen her practically naked in the sauna and you can't spot her in civvies?" Diane laughed at me.

I looked to Francis for support but he shrugged in response.

"Well, if she'd come to the table in her towel, I might have."

Bev punched me again.

We proceeded to sell the table bare as the last crowd of buyers came through looking for end of day bargains.

Around 1645 the speakers gave a ping-ping-ping warning. The customers wrapped up whatever deals they were working on and began filing out. The big doors started slowly closing at 1700 and when the pa-pong tone sounded again, most of the vendors had already taken down the booths, and pulled their grav pallets and cargo totes toward the staff doors.

Diane and Francis helped by folding the banner neatly while I pulled the badge off the drape and Bev collapsed the table. We dropped it off at the office and headed down the lifts.

On the way down, Francis turned to Bev and me. "Diane and I are heading out to grab dinner. Either or both of you want to join us?"

I shook my head. "I need to get back to the ship. Pip is going to be chewing the bulkheads to find out how it went."

Bev declined as well. "I've got the duty in the morning and my legs are killing me. I just want to get back and into the sauna."

The banner and badge went into my duffel to pass off to Pip and we separated at level six. Bev and I headed for the ship while Diane and Frances went off to eat. We checked in with the officer of the watch and had our respective mass allowances adjusted. Mine went down but Bev's went up because of the buckles. They did indeed mass a lot for their size. Curiously, the banner didn't get charged to either of us, but instead was marked down to Lois McKendrick. I looked to Bev, but she didn't seem surprised so I didn't ask.

Back in the berthing area, Bev changed and headed for the sauna while I stowed my gear, took a quick shower, and jumped into a shipsuit before going to the mess deck to see Pip and Cookie.

It had been a long day.

Just after 1800 I stepped onto the mess deck and took advantage of mealtime by grabbing some pasta and bread from the buffet. Pip heard me and came out of the galley. Cookie followed right behind him.

Pip looked at me, anticipation radiating from his body. "Well? How'd it go?"

"Great. I sold everything I had, but I'm bushed. It's hard standing there all day."

Pip drew me a mug of coffee and delivered it to the table. "Okay, pleasantries over. Where'd you find that buckle?"

"I didn't." I swallowed a mouthful of pasta before continuing, "Bev did, booth two something. Two-eighteen, I think she said, or maybe it was two-sixteen. It shouldn't be too hard to find."

Cookie smiled and stepped back into the galley, but Pip nodded. "So? Tell me everything."

I ran through the day in roughly chronological order, starting with picking up the banner at the lock and ending with returning it. "In the morning, you need to take the badge to the office and get a table. It's already paid for. Somewhere we need to find some clips so you can hang the banner and you'll also need some kind of cloth to put down on the table to cover the top. They're in pretty rough shape."

Pip nodded.

"Now, it's your turn. The captain said you've been recruiting?"

He nodded again. "I've got a couple of people who are interested. Rhon Scham has a ton of stuff to sell and agreed to be my wingman for the day. She's good at buying but hasn't had a lot of success selling so she was really enthusiastic. Sean Grishan from the bridge crew and Biddy Murphy from cargo are coming along too."

"Sounds like it's going to be worthwhile again tomorrow. Oh, by the way, we have an appointment tonight at 2000."

"Yeah? Who with?"

"The captain. She wants a status report."

Pip chuckled nervously. "Well, at least we've got something to report."

I finished my dinner and took the dishes into the galley. Cookie smiled and waved to us as he left for his nightly card game. "You gentlemen don't need me under foot. Well done today—both of you." We waved to his back as he left. It was only a few ticks of work for us to clear away the dinner buffet, sweep, and swab.

We had a stan to spare before our meeting with the captain so we retired to the berthing area to compare notes. Bev was back from the sauna and got the packet of buckles out to show Pip. We spread them out on the berthing area's table and he looked them all over.

Pip considered the buckles as he asked Bev, "What did you think of the day?"

She grinned. "It was a kick. Between the selling and the ogling—"

"Ogling?" Pip shot me a glance. "You didn't say anything about that."

I shrugged and he turned back to Bev. "What is this ogling of which you speak?"

She laughed at his expression. "Well, between the ones who came to see the tough bitch in leather and the others who wanted to look down Diane's blouse, there was a lot of it. I might have even done a bit of it myself." She winked with a sly grin. "There were a lot of tight butts walking around there today." She looked at me. "Don't you think?"

I coughed in surprise. "Um, I didn't notice, actually. I was trying to figure out how the whole booth thing was going to work and then I got tied up in selling stuff and all."

She pulled a long face at me. "Oh, Ish, you were too busy watching the merchandise. If you want to be a real seller, you need to learn to watch the customers. That last belt you could have gotten another five credits for. That lady liked you."

"She was old enough to be my mother!"

"And your point is what?"

Pip rapped on the table. "Please, children, focus."

Bev sat up straight and folded her hands playfully in front of her before continuing, "Anyway, the initial set up was rough. We looked like the amateurs we are. If we hadn't had the banner, we would have been displaying the belts on that dinged up tabletop and that wouldn't have been pretty."

Pip nodded. "If we hang the banner, we'll need a cloth or something for the table. Anything else?"

"Several of the vendors had grav pallets with their booth already set up on it. They just towed the pallet into place, locked it down, and started selling."

Pip nodded. "Yeah, I told you about Drus' setup. She had something like that. I don't know how we'd manage that. We can't very well use one of the ship's and we can't afford the mass to buy one of our own." He shrugged.

Bev thought for a moment. "A thermos of coffee would have been good. There's a shop around the corner but the coffee was expensive."

I chimed in with my two creds, "And muddy. The only other thing I really missed was a place to sit between sales. My feet and legs are killing me."

Bev nodded. "Did you see those folding chairs what's her name had in her booth?"

"Oh, you mean Virgil's wife?"

Bev nodded. "Yeah. They had tubular frames with a mesh seat and back. They looked very light. When things got busy she just folded it up and stashed it under the table."

"Yeah, I saw that, but I don't know where to find them, or how we would stow them."

Pip pondered. "I wonder if we can rent them."

Bev and I both shrugged.

He turned his attention back to the buckles. "These are exquisite. What booth again?"

Bev spoke up, "Two sixteen. He's expecting to see you. His only concern is that we take them off-station to sell so he's not competing against himself in the flea market."

"That was the same thing that Drus Martin was worried about on Gugara." Pip turned to me. "How many of the belts should we try to fit with buckles and take to St. Cloud?"

I shrugged. "You know better than I do. We were selling the bare belts for thirty to forty creds each. The buckles should drive that up to fifty or sixty."

Bev shook her head strenuously. "Oh, no. More than that." She went to her locker and pulled out the belt she'd put the buckle on at the booth. "Look at this. It's worth at least a hundred creds."

She strapped it on around her waist and let it ride low on her hips. She only wore a ship's tee and boxers that made up the standard dress around the berthing area for men and women alike.

I found that I really didn't breathe right all of a sudden and Pip's voice came from a distance. "Well, if you model them like that, I think we can get a lot more."

Bev looked down and laughed. She took the belt off then and laid it on the table. "You get my meaning, wise ass."

Luckily, my tablet bipped to remind me that the captain was expecting us. Pip and I headed for officer country while Bev stowed the stuff back in her locker.

"Are you okay?" Pip looked at me as we headed down the passage.

"Yeah, why?"

He shrugged elaborately. "Oh, I don't know. You just seemed like you were having trouble breathing there for a tick."

I slugged him on the shoulder as we arrived at the captain's door and I knocked before he could say anything else.

The captain acknowledged our knock with a single word from the other side of the door. "Come."

When we entered the cabin, we found her seated at her desk. We stood in the approved handbook fashion and I did the honors. "Carstairs and Wang reporting as ordered, sar."

"Thank you for coming, gentlemen. Please, sit." She nodded toward two chairs. "Make yourselves comfortable and tell me how the enterprise is faring."

I gave my recap and Pip gave his. We tried to be brief and succinct. When we finished she looked back and forth between the two of us.

"You'll have enough to sell for the rest of our stay, then?" she asked.

Pip smiled. "It looks that way, Captain. Although it really depends if the pace can be repeated, and how many of the crew have goods to sell."

"Of course."

Pip grinned. "If we sell everything we have before we leave, I don't think I'll mind."

The captain chuckled. "No doubt." She turned serious. "Now, about this reimbursement to the ship?"

Pip glanced at me before going on. "Well, Captain, this isn't, strictly speaking, ship's business. . ."

She nodded. "Go on."

"While it's not a lot of creds in the grand scheme of things, it doesn't seem like a ship's expense."

I nodded. "Yes, Captain, I agree with him. I appreciate... we appreciate... the opportunity to sell our stuff and help the crew, but—"

Pip finished for me, "Well, actually, we had no idea what the right thing was, so we just split the cost to reimburse the ship."

"Who is we?" The captain looked back and forth between us.

"Pip and I, Captain."

"So you two are underwriting this, and the rest of the crew can just take advantage of you?"

Pip and I glanced at each other before he answered, "Well, I don't know that we thought of it that way, but fundamentally, yes, Captain."

She nodded. "Very altruistic of you— and also extremely short sighted."

Pip looked startled. "Captain?"

"If this little hobby of yours takes off, the crew will be selling hundreds, if not thousands of creds in your booth—the booth you two will be paying good creds for."

We shrugged almost in unison. Pip answered, "True, Captain, but we'll benefit as well. The overhead is low and fixed. The cost doesn't go up with more sales."

She nodded. "That's true, but I don't think you've thought this through. Are you going to use up your personal mass allotments for the materials needed in the booth? Are you planning to continue this beyond Margary? Will you both use up all your liberty time for every port we visit?"

Pip started to object, but I could see where the captain was heading so I spoke first, "You're right, sar, we haven't considered these things. With your permission, we'll finish Margary the way we've started, and we'll have five weeks to St. Cloud to figure out a better plan. Can we come back after we've had a chance to put our heads together in the Deep Dark?"

The captain nodded. "Not a bad approach at all, Mr. Wang. Permission granted. Any time you want to talk with me about this, please bip me for an appointment. Anything else?"

Pip and I shared a glance before we both said, "No, sar."

She smiled. "Very well then, gentlemen. Dismissed."

As we made our escape down the passage, Pip turned to me. "She never did say what she was going to do about the forty creds for the booth rental."

I shrugged. "It's probably coming out of petty cash. If regs say we can't rent the booth, then it will probably go on the books as a ship's expense."

He nodded as we continued down the passage. "Yeah, I can see that, but technically it's not rented by the ship."

I remembered then where the reservation confirmation had come from. "What is the McKendrick Mercantile Cooperative?"

He shrugged. "I thought I knew, but I'm not so sure now."

"I just remembered something else odd."

He looked over at me but we didn't stop walking.

"When we came back aboard and made our mass adjustments, the banner was pretty heavy. I wondered where it would be charged... you, me, or Bev."

"Where'd it come from?"

"Rhon had the watch this morning and said it came with the *captain's compliments*."

"So it was charged back to her?"

"No, it was charged to Lois McKendrick," I answered.

"You mean the ship?"

I shook my head. "No, ship's gear gets tagged as *ship* on the logs. This was the name, Lois McKendrick."

Pip thought for a tick before speaking, "But... she's dead, isn't she?"

I slugged him on the shoulder. "Dead or not, she's not a member of the crew, ya goof."

We didn't say any more until we'd made it to the gym for our nightly work out. I was in a fog from the exhaustion of the long day at the flea market and the confusing evening that followed. I wanted to run a few laps, steam my sore muscles in the sauna, and then take a cold shower to forget about how that belt had looked strapped low around Bev's hips.

When I got back to my bunk, I started thinking about Lois McKendrick again. I remembered the captain's comments about a proud tradition and the way her fingers had stroked the fabric of the banner under our trade goods. I took out my tablet and pulled up the ship's records. Sure enough, I found an entry on the history from the ship's origin. It was built in a Manchester yard over in the New Hebrides Quadrant. The ship itself wasn't all that old, nineteen stanyers—just one more than me. It explained that the ship was named for one Lois Marie McKendrick, a trade organizer.

The entry said that stanyers ago McKendrick had changed the face of company owned planets. Back in the bad old days, they completely controlled all dirt-side production. At that time *everything* an employee did belonged to the company. So if you gardened for a hobby, or your spouse knitted sweaters, or you made anything at all, it belonged to the company who ran the planet you lived on. I remembered reading about this in history, but my schoolbooks didn't really explain what happened to change the system. Mom often said the company texts didn't always reflect the unvarnished truth.

If this blurb was correct, Lois Marie McKendrick organized an opposition against the New Anglican Planetary Development Company on New Edinburgh. She and her group won the right for people to make things that the company didn't own. Her movement caught on and spread not just through the New Hebrides Quadrant, but throughout the organized galaxy. In many ways, she was responsible for the burst of trade that heralded the deployment of the big sailing freighters and prosperity of the trading houses that have grown ever since.

Apparently, Lois McKendrick died shortly before the ship was completed, but her great-granddaughter christened the vessel when it launched. The article featured a blurry digital of a young woman swinging a bottle of champagne against the airlock. I didn't recognize her until I read the caption, "Cargo Second Alys McKendrick Giggone christens Federated Freight's newest solar clipper, the forty-three thousand ton *Lois McKendrick*." Under that was another digital of a group of people standing in front of a familiar blue banner with silver letters that read McKendrick Mercantile Cooperative. Front and center, was a straight-backed woman with a warm smile holding the shoulders of a young girl standing just in front of her. On either side of her were a half dozen folks of various ages and the caption read: "Lois McKendrick (center) stands with the members of the McKendrick Mercantile Cooperative outside the courthouse at New Edinburgh." Judging from the looks, I guessed this was when the Galactic Circuit Court ruled in their favor. I also couldn't be sure, but I was willing to bet that I recognized that little girl.

Chapter Twenty-two
Margary Station: 2352-January-12

Next morning in the galley, Pip stopped by for breakfast before heading out to do his stint at the flea market and I shared the information I had found about Lois.

Pip nodded slowly. "Okay, that explains where the name and banner came from. But why did the captain give it to us to use?"

"I understand that part," I said. "It's probably been sitting around in storage for the last, I don't know how long, and when we started renting the booth, she broke it out."

Cookie tossed a tidbit of his own onto the table as he walked by. "The captain was in cargo before she went to the Academy to get her officer stripes. As I understand it, her whole family is involved with trading in one way or another."

I nodded. "See, that's all part and parcel. Very consistent. I mean this ship is named for her great-grandmother and if that's really her in this picture, then they were close."

Pip nodded with a shrug. "So? What part are you confused by?"

"Who is Lois McKendrick?"

"You just answered that."

I shook my head. "Not that Lois McKendrick. The one who has that banner registered on her mass allotment."

Cookie overheard and chuckled. "Oh, that's tradition, young Ishmael. Lois is the ship's pooka—a kind of spirit. There's always an honorary berth for the person that the ship is named for. It's an unpaid position, of course, and they don't appear on any duty roster, but that berth shares all the other benefits of being any other crew member. By tradition, a vessel's captain can use that berth as a kind of alter ego to do things for the benefit of the ship. Usually they are a kind of conduit for random acts of kindness."

"So over on the *Duchamp* there's actually a berth for Marcel Duchamp?" Pip asked.

Cookie nodded. "Exactly so. It gets peculiar on some vessels, especially those named for cities or animals, but the tradition is very common."

Pip just shook his head. "Live and learn." He rose to take his dishes to the galley and while he was gone, Cookie pulled out a package and placed it at the table where Pip had been sitting. He winked, held a finger to his lips, and then followed Pip into the galley.

When Pip got back and saw it, he turned to me. "What's this?" I just shrugged.

Looking inside, Pip pulled out some drapery clips and a dark blue tablecloth. "Oh, perfect. Where'd this come from?"

I shrugged. "Dunno. Must be from Lois." I could see Cookie peeking out from the galley.

Pip chuckled and called out as he left, "Thanks, Lois."

Some of the watch standers came in for breakfast, and I told Cookie to finish his coffee. Omelets, I could manage. It felt good, but before long, he was helping and eventually elbowed me off to make coffee and set bread. That man wasn't happy unless he was feeding somebody, so I left him to it and just filled in where I could. Beverly came in and I told her about the meeting with the captain and showed her the entry about Lois McKendrick with the picture of the banner.

"That's interesting. What do you suppose it all means?"

"Which part? The fact that she rented the space in the name of the cooperative, or that she gave Pip and me a short but blistering lecture on letting the rest of the crew take advantage of our booth? Or the strong sense I have that she's expecting Pip and me to do something, and that she'll support us if we do, but she wants us to figure it out on our own."

Bev shrugged. "I dunno. All of the above, I guess."

I sighed. "I have a lot to figure out."

"Well, I shouldn't take up any more of your time then. I need to get back to my duty station anyway." She left me and I went back to the galley to let the daily routine distract me from thinking any more about it. The routine felt good and I sank into it like a hot bath letting it carry me through the morning. I decided after lunch, I would go down to environmental.

❀　　❀　　❀

When I stepped through the hatch, Diane and Brill were there examining one of the oxygen scrubbers. I overheard them talking. "It looks like we're going to have to change out the matrix, I guess."

Diane nodded with a grimace. When she saw me, she grinned. "Just in time. You here to work or flirt?"

I chuckled. "Both if I can get away with it."

Brill smiled as well. "Well, you'll have to flirt with her. I've got quarterlies to finish."

"What's up?" I nodded toward the oxygen scrubber.

"This matrix is starting to die out and it needs to be replaced."

Brill sighed. "It really is a two person job, but I have *got* to finish this paperwork today or I won't be able to get off the ship tomorrow. Unfortunately, Diane is alone this watch."

"How long will it take?"

Diane shook her head. "Not long. Two stans if we work hard."

"I got two stans before I need to get back in the galley. Let's get cracking."

"Thanks, Ish." Brill chucked me on the arm. "You're a peach."

"Yeah, soft, fuzzy, with a hard wooden core, I know." I grinned at her then turned to Diane. "Okay, I'm at your disposal. Where do we start?"

The time whooshed past. Diane was as good with the scrubber as she had been in the booth the day before. The work consisted of stripping out the old algae matrix from the frames, washing them down, stringing up new material, and re-inoculating it. It would take about half a day before the algae settled in and started producing oxygen so it was important to do it as soon as one started to die off. Diane told me it was one of the least favored jobs in environmental, made worse by the fact that every scrubber had to be reworked about once a month.

The process wasn't difficult. A metal frame sandwiched the matrix foundation and held it taut. This film gave the algae something to adhere to. We pulled each one out of the scrubber, released the clips that held the front and back together, separated the halves, and rolled the old material out like a kind of slimy, brown jelly roll that was a meter long and half a meter thick. We had to wash the frame down and roll in fresh matrix material, then stretch and smooth it down before locking the halves together again. Diane used a sprayer to coat it with new algae. The completed assembly went back into the scrubber. While the process wasn't difficult, it was time-consuming with forty-eight units that needed to be replaced. We had to prevent cross-contamination, so we stripped and washed everything down before we started re-assembling and hanging the fresh frames. It was tedious, wet, and slimy work for the entire duration. When we were done, I was soaked, filthy, and exhausted. What's more, I needed to get back to the galley to help Cookie.

Diane and Brill both thanked me repeatedly for helping out, but I had to admit it was really kinda fun. Diane is what my mom would have called *good people* and had a wicked sense of humor that made even a boring exercise like changing out algae matrices enjoyable. Besides, she looked good in a mucky, wet shipsuit. Who could argue with that?

I was a little late but Cookie waved it off. "Brill called to explain you might be delayed, young Ishmael." He smiled in his understanding way. "If you can spend your free time helping out in another department, then I can forgive your being four ticks late to fix dinner. One thing, though—"

I finished for him, "Let me guess... we're out of coffee?"

He smiled beatifically. "Just so, young Ishmael, just so."

❈　　❈　　❈

Dinner consisted of a mushroom, ham, and spinach quiche with fresh crusty rolls and green beans. Cookie made one of his amazing granapple pies for dessert, which made a nice treat for the watch standers. About half past dinner, Pip came in, still in his civvies, looking tired but happy. He grabbed a wedge of quiche and some green beans and sat with us at a mess table to compare notes.

"Good?" I slid a cup of fresh coffee onto the table beside his tray.

He nodded. "But you were right about a long day standing there."

"How much did you sell?"

He strung me along a tick, pretending to be too hungry to answer but finally did, "Everything."

I looked at Cookie and back at Pip. "When you say everything, you mean what exactly?"

"Everything that we planned to sell and then some more. I left ten belts for St. Cloud here in my locker, but I probably could have sold those, too. The prices started going up as the pile dwindled. I don't even know what the final total is. I haven't had a chance to look."

"You're kidding."

He shook his head. "The banner looked really good hanging up and the tablecloth was exactly the right size and shape. The color showed off the belts perfectly. That Lois is really clever." He pulled out his tablet and opened the accounting function. "Okay, we took in three thousand five hundred and forty creds, less the three fifty it cost for the seventy belts. We made about three thousand one hundred and ninety creds today."

There was silence for at least a full tick before Cookie spoke, "Young Ishmael, you might want to close your mouth now."

I did so but immediately opened to ask the next question. "How did the others do?"

"Well, Rhon and Biddy did very well. Rhon had some very nice fabrics and a huge collection of entertainment cubes. Biddy had small wooden and stone carvings, mostly animals, that were very popular and expensive. They both sold out. I don't know how much they made. It seemed rude to ask, but they were both giggling like schoolgirls afterward. Sean Grishan had lace doilies and they evaporated off the table. He sold out by noon."

"Lace doilies? You mean like the little round things?"

Pip nodded. "He makes them, and by the looks, he's darn good at it, too."

"He makes them? Here? On the ship?"

Pip nodded. "Yeah. He knits, too. Claims sailors on the clipper ships used to do it to pass the time and he's been teaching himself for the last couple of stanyers. They sold well, so, to each his own, I guess."

"Excellent. What'd the belt buckle guy say?"

"He'll give us a good price, probably between ten and fifteen creds, depending on quantity, but of course we have to take them off-station. I explained we're leaving for St. Cloud in a couple days so that wasn't an issue. That was his biggest concern."

"What's the mass look like?" I pulled up my quota on my tablet. "I have about eight kilos."

Pip nodded. "I've got a little more, but about the same. The question is how many buckles do we buy?"

"We can't afford too many—" I started to say but then I noticed Pip's grin.

"Three thousand creds will buy a lot of buckles. How many do you think you can put in eight kilos of mass?"

Cookie interrupted us. "You gentlemen should think about this carefully, I think. Pip, you should either get off the ship, or change your clothing. Young Ishmael needs to clean up the galley and mess deck. Then you'll both be free for the entire evening to discuss this all you like."

He was right so we split up. I floated through the next stan or so of work.

Chapter Twenty-three
Margary Station: 2352-January-12

We picked up the conversation later in the sauna. "We're missing something."

"What's that?" Pip basked sleepily on one of the benches.

"The Mercantile Cooperative."

"Miss it? I was staring at it all day."

"I know, but I think I'm starting to see what the captain was talking about. What's going to happen to the booth for the next couple of days?"

"Nothing as far as I know. We don't have anything left to sell."

"Yeah, so we're out twenty creds rent for the time we paid for but won't use. It's a shame. There could be others on the ship who could benefit, but because they don't know about it, they're out of luck."

"With the margins we got today, that twenty creds is a rounding error. But I take your meaning about the rest of the crew. There's another thing too."

"What's that?"

"Time in port is limited and if you and I have to spend all day selling, we won't be able to buy anything."

That thought had been banging up against the inside of my skull already as well.

He sat up and looked at me. "Okay, some lessons learned. First, this was a last tick idea. Whatever we did here was really just testing the water."

I nodded in agreement. "Who'd have thought, huh?"

Pip grinned. "Obviously, the captain, because if I remember

correctly, she warned us of most of this."

"True."

"So, how does a mercantile cooperative work, anyway? We're thinking like traders but we need to act like businessmen. So what do we do?"

"I don't know, but there is someone who does."

Pip looked at me and we both said, "The captain."

"Okay, before we bother her..." I held up my hand and counted off with my fingers, "...we need to figure out what it's supposed to be, how it might work in our situation, and who we can get to help us."

Pip bobbed his head once. "The first should be easy. The second would be better discussed after we have an answer to the third."

"Makes sense, and I'm ready to get out of here."

We showered up and went out to find who else might be aboard. Turns out there weren't many.

"Hey, how's it going? Do you have a few minutes to talk?" I asked Francis when we found him in environmental.

"Sure, I just need to keep an eye on the gauges and fill out my logs. What's on your mind?"

Pip and I looked at each other and he nodded at me to start. "Well, we did pretty well in the flea market yesterday, don't ya think?"

"Oh yeah, that was not only fun, but profitable as well. I'm going back tomorrow afternoon and see what I can pick up to take to St. Cloud."

I nodded. "Yeah, that's what we wanted to talk about."

"You'll have another booth there, won't you?"

Pip chimed in, "That's what we're trying to determine. Margary was a spur of the moment thing and we weren't very organized."

Francis chuckled. "Yeah, that's true."

"We have five weeks to figure out how to do better on St. Cloud and we're trying to make this work for everybody without having Pip and me spend all our time at it." I summed the situation up for him.

"And we'd like to organize it so that the expenses are covered," Pip added. "Ish and I paid for the booth out of our own pocket, and it wasn't that much, but if we're going to do this all the time then we should share the expense. Plus, there are other things that we should get to make it easier."

"Like chairs?" Francis asked.

I nodded and grinned. "Yeah, chairs, food, signs, whatever we need to do a professional job out there."

Pip added, "I'd like to have a grav pallet set up like the regulars do so all we have to do is slide it out of the cargo lock and drag it up to the flea market."

"Whose mass would that come out of?" Francis asked.

"We don't know. That's just the point. Maybe we can get it assigned to Lois, but what we need now are people who are willing to form a co-op to do this on an ongoing basis. If we can get a core group who'll be responsible for organizing this between ports, then we should be able to make out better from here on out."

He pursed his lips and nodded. "Makes sense to me. When are we doing this?"

Pip shrugged. "I don't know. We're just testing the waters to see who is interested at this point."

Francis didn't even pause. "I'm in. I had a ball out there and I'd love to do it again. Hell, just watching Diane and Beverly play the crowd was worth the price of admission. If you want me to contribute to the rental fund, just let me know."

I shook my head. "We're good for now. The captain actually paid the rental from ship's funds and we'll pay the ship back. We just need to think this through more."

"Okay. Look, it's time for my rounds," Francis said, "but count me in. I made more creds yesterday than I did all of last stanyer. If we can do that all the time, that would be great."

Pip and I both nodded. "Thanks, Francis. Spread the word if you can. Let us know about anybody else who is interested. We'll try to set up a meeting for just after pull out."

We headed back to the berthing area and I turned to Pip. "Do you have a handle on stores trades for St. Cloud?"

He shrugged. "Between the Sarabanda and the mushrooms, we're in good shape. We're bound for Dunsany Roads after that and there's a lot of similarities between the two. To get a good margin, it's better if there is more of a difference."

"How about the empty container?"

He shrugged again. "I met with Mr. Maxwell while you were in the booth. The beefalo robes were popular but the rugs didn't sell. We're taking them to St. Cloud. Having a planet under you and room to spread out might make them more viable. I should have considered that."

"Did you make any profit?"

He grinned. "Yeah, between the robes and the odd pallets of stuff I had on that manifest, we cleared fifty kilocreds. That's on what we've sold so far, so basically the rugs still left are free."

"Wait. You cleared fifty kilocreds on a ten kilocred investment?"

Pip nodded smugly.

"Nice. What did Mr. Maxwell say?"

Pip stopped and swiveled his head in imitation. "Very good, Mr. Carstairs. I shall expect a similar report for the market on St. Cloud when we get there."

I chuckled. "You know, that's a little scary that you do him so well. What are we taking to St. Cloud?"

"Mushrooms, of course. What else?"

"Oh yeah, I forgot. How many you planning on?"

"Every kilo we can stuff in there. I really think they're going to do great."

I whistled. "That's a lot of mushrooms."

He nodded. We continued down to berthing and hit the rack.

❀　❀　❀

Bev came to wake us in the morning. She had the watch until 0600. "Well, what have you two been up to overnight?"

"Planning. I think we want to make the McKendrick Mercantile Cooperative a formal entity, or at least more organized by the time we get to St. Cloud."

She nodded once. "Good. Count me in. How'd you do yesterday, Pip?"

He grinned. "I managed to hold on to ten of those belts."

She whistled. "How many did you sell?"

"All of the rest." His grin broadened. "Seventy in all."

"We softened 'em up for ya." she teased him.

"No doubt. No doubt."

Pip headed for the galley while I considered my options.

"What's on for today, Ish?" Bev asked.

"Shopping. We did pretty well in Gugara. Fancy a look around later?"

She gave me a thumbs up. "Sure, but I've been up since midnight. I'm gonna rack it until noon but I'm up for it after that."

"Better deals in the afternoon," I said with a grin.

She chuckled as she went back to her watch station. "You're practically a veteran now, Ish."

I felt bleary-eyed and foggy. Pip and I had stayed up later than normal and my feet were sore from the day at the flea market. I still couldn't believe we'd made over three kilocreds on the belts.

I pulled out my tablet and brought up the sections explaining various economic organizations. "Co-operative" brought up several entries. The crux of the situation explained that a co-op was a group of people who banded together and worked toward the common good of their group. It wasn't much to go on, but I started thinking about Lois McKendrick, and all the people on New Edinburgh who got together to break the stranglehold that the company held on their lives. I decided I had to see the captain again. I wanted to

170

know more about Great-grandmother McKendrick and her co-op. But first things first, I was awake, needed to pee, and I wanted my coffee.

It felt odd to step onto the mess deck just as breakfast was being served, probably because there weren't that many times in the last four months when I'd not been serving said breakfast. I took a mug from the rack, filled it with fresh Sarabanda Dark, and stood in line with a tray, grinning. Diane was in front of me.

She glanced over her shoulder to see who was behind her and laughed. "I'm not used to seeing you on this side of the line."

"I'm not used to it, myself."

"Thanks for helping with the scrubbers, Ish. That really made a difference."

"My pleasure. We're all in the same boat, as it were."

"True, but not everybody would help with a slimy job like that one if they didn't have to."

I just shrugged and changed the subject. "You sold all your stuff the other day, right?"

She nodded but the line had moved and Pip interrupted loudly, "Excuse me, I'm trying to serve breakfast here."

Diane turned around with a giggle. "Oh, sorry." She held out her plate for Pip to slide the omelet on it. "Thank you so much."

"And you, sir, how may I serve you this morning?" He laid it on with a trowel and grinned the whole time.

"Two egg omelet, some of those excellent mushrooms, a bit of onion, some crumbled bacon, and a bit of grated cheese, if you please. Moist in the middle, my good man. Mind you don't dry it out."

"How about I just hit you with the pan and toss your carcass out an airlock?"

I laughed. "Okay, okay, I get your point."

Cookie must have been helping him with his skills as well, because he slid a perfect omelet onto my plate in just a couple of ticks. "Thanks, Pip. Looks great."

He waved his spatula at me with a pleased nod of his head. "Enjoy."

I looked around and spotted Diane sitting alone at a table. She nodded to the chair across from her.

As I settled into the seat, she braced me without preamble. "So, Francis says you guys visited him on watch last night?"

I nodded. "That's why I was asking about whether or not you sold all your stuff. Pip sold everything we had yesterday. By all measures, this was an amazing success."

She sipped her coffee and nodded. "It was for me. I sold stuff that I've been dragging around for months. And it was much easier than trying to find some buyer and haggling with them and safer then deals made in shady bars. I turned a nice profit, so I've got both mass and cred to spend today."

"Yeah, me, too." There wasn't anybody in the mess line just then so I motioned Pip over. "What we were talking to Francis about was the possibility of getting organized before we hit St. Cloud."

Pip joined us. "Yeah, next time around we should be better prepared. I suspect that there are people aboard who could have used the space and didn't know we were doing it because the whole thing was so slapdash."

"We've been thinking that we should actually form the McKendrick Mercantile Cooperative," I put in. "You know, like on the banner? We thought we'd ask the other traders on the crew to join. Together, we can coordinate coverage on the booth and expenses. With a little investment we could put together a booth that looks like we know what we were doing."

Diane laughed. "I'm being double-teamed here, but I think you're right. What will it take?"

I shrugged. "Even if all we do is get the word out to the entire crew, that's more than we had going on in Margary."

"Good point," she agreed.

Pip plunked down beside me. "I'm trying to think of this like a business. I don't want to share everybody's profits because that's not right. But there's a lot of things we can pool that would help everybody."

"Like what?" Diane looked at him.

I snickered. "Like chairs. My feet are still recovering."

"Mine, too." Diane grimaced.

Pip nodded. "Exactly. So, the co-op invests in things like chairs, but the expense should be shared by all the members somehow."

Diane cut off a piece of her omelet and chewed it for a moment before speaking, "That makes sense, but whose mass allotment takes the hit?"

Pip and I glanced at each other before I answered her, "I'm thinking we ask Lois."

Pip grinned. "I was thinking the same thing."

Diane looked confused. "Lois who?"

"Lois McKendrick, of course." I smiled at her confusion.

She blinked at me a couple times, maybe trying to decide if I was kidding. "Let me know how that works out for you."

Pip smirked. "Oh, I think we'll convince her."

Diane looked doubtful. "Well, if we do this, we'll need creds for expenses: booth rental, chairs, signs, cargo totes—"

"Grav pallet?" I suggested.

Her face lit up at the thought. "Ooh, that would be excellent, but maybe a bit of a stretch all things considered."

I nodded. "True, but we're on the right track. I'm willing to toss a few creds in the pot as seed money, but how do we replenish the pot?"

Diane ate some more of her omelet while she considered. Finally she nodded once as if she'd made up her mind. "Okay, I see three ways: dues, buy in, or fees."

I grimaced. "I thought of dues, but that's a problem because it limits who can participate. If you don't pay your dues then you can't sell, but if you want to drop out halfway through the period, how can we give a refund?"

Pip nodded his head in agreement. "How would the buy-in idea work? You pay a fee to set up in the booth at the next port?"

Diane nodded.

"Down side is that you have to pay before you have the income. If you don't sell anything it would be tough," Pip said.

We sat there looking at each other for a couple of ticks. Finally, I broke the silence. "It sounds like we go with fees then. How are you thinking this would work?"

Diane gestured with her fork. "If you sell in the booth you should pay some nominal amount. Like one percent. We could cap it at some amount, say ten creds, and the trader would pay whichever is smaller. That way somebody who doesn't sell a lot can still get in. People who sell more won't get smacked too hard."

Pip nodded slowly. "Rental here in Margary is ten a day, the table cost an extra cred. With that arrangement just one person would cover that easily."

Diane pointed out the obvious. "If we'd been operating under that rule during this past exercise, all four of us would have paid ten creds for that first day."

I shook my head. "No, ten creds is one percent of a thousand. Bev and I only made about a hundred each, but that big bundle of belts would have covered it easily."

Diane shrugged. "Well, I made almost a kilocred on all my stuff, so I'd have made up the difference."

Pip nodded his agreement. "And yesterday, Rhon Scham, Biddy Murphy, and I would have also."

Diane looked back and forth between us. "That seems fair to me. I'd gladly have kicked in ten creds for what I got out of it."

Francis came in looking for breakfast so Pip went to get him an omelet.

"Thanks, Diane. That was kinda what I was thinking, but you really solidified it for me."

She speared the last bite of her omelet. "My pleasure, Ish. Count me in on whatever you've got going forward, okay?"

I nodded and paused for a moment. "Hey, do you know anything about mushroom farming?"

"Huh?" She blinked at me for a few heartbeats and a wry smile twisted her lips. "Do you know what the phrase smooth change of subject means?"

I laughed. "Sorry, my brain is hopping around this morning. Did you know that Margary is the mushroom capital of the galaxy or something?"

"You're kidding."

I shook my head. "They have plenty of dark tunnels here to grow them in. I thought I'd try to find out more about what it takes besides dark and space. It has got to take some kind of growing medium, but what do they have out here in the Deep Dark?"

She looked me straight in the eye and grinned at the realization. "Sludge."

"That's my thought, too. Fancy a little exploration?"

"Ten minutes. Main lock."

"I'll be there."

I waved at Pip and Francis as I bussed my tray and headed to change into my civvies.

Fifteen minutes later, Diane met me on the docks. She gave a half shrug. "So, how do we find a mushroom farm?"

"Look for someplace dark?"

"That's most places here, I would think."

I smacked myself on the forehead. "I'm so stupid," I said as I grabbed my tablet and pulled up the ship's stores records. The invoice for what looked like a huge amount of mushrooms was on file along with the name of the supplier and their information. Their office was on deck twelve and there was a contact number.

Diane smiled when she saw what I was doing. "Hmm, there's a comm-link right over there. Think we can get an appointment?"

"All they can say is no."

We crossed the deck and I keyed the contact number from the invoice. "Margary Mushrooms, Helen speaking. How can I help you?" The woman answered on the first ring. She looked like a typical front door greeter on the screen.

"Hi. My name is Wang. I work in the galley on the freighter *Lois McKendrick*. You sold us a quantity of mushrooms day before yesterday...?"

"Yes, Mr. Wang, is there a problem?"

"No, they're excellent, but my colleague and I are interested in how they're grown out here in the Deep Dark. It must be fascinating. We were wondering if we could talk to someone about it?"

"Let me connect you with Mr. Cameron. He's in charge of our field operations."

A moment later a red, pudgy face filled the screen. "Cameron, here. How can I help you?"

"Hello, Mr. Cameron, My name is Wang and I'm from the freighter *Lois McKendrick*. Your company has sold us some mushrooms and my colleague and I would like to learn more about how they're grown out here."

"Well, Mr. Wang, we grow them in tunnels in the mined-out asteroids. Thank you for your interest."

"Is there a chance we might visit one of these asteroids this morning?

"I'm really sorry, kid, but we're terribly busy here, and I don't know how we'd find the time..."

Diane, who had been off camera for the conversation, sighed and shook her head. She unbuttoned the top of her blouse and elbowed me out of the way. She practically cooed into the comm, "Mr. Cameron, is it? I'm Diane Ardele. We're sorry to be such a bother but we'll be leaving tomorrow and this is our last chance to come and see your excellent operation up close." She leaned into the pickup so the breathy voice she used would carry clearly. "Don't you think you could find some errand boy to take us on a tour of just one little mushroom farm?"

I thought he was going to turn purple as Diane idly stroked one finger up and down the edge of her collar. "Well, yes, that is, I think my next meeting was just canceled. Let me check. Yes, I'm free after all. I could take you, Ms. Ardele—"

"Oh, please call me Diane," she interrupted, breathily.

"D-Diane, yes. I could take you over to see a farm. Oh, and Mr. Wang, too, of course. Could you meet me at lock forty-two on the dock level in say, twenty ticks?"

Diane squealed convincingly. "Ooh, that would be just *so perfect*. Thank you ever so much, Mr. Cameron. I'll look forward to meeting you."

"Likewise Ms. Ardele...I mean D-Diane."

"Toodles until then." Diane waved her fingers in the direction of the pickup before cutting the connection.

I just stood there staring at her. "You know, you're shameless."

She gave me a smug little grin. "Yes, and thank you for noticing. The nice thing about clichés is that they only can become one if

enough people recognize them. Trust me, Ish, that man is a cliché."
She shook her head and sighed.

Fifteen ticks later, the very busy Mr. Cameron was shaking our
hands outside a private shuttle dock halfway around the station
from the *Lois*. He wasted no time getting us into the ship and we
boosted away from the station. It took less than half a stan for us
to cruise to a nearby asteroid. We watched the approach through
the shuttle's ports.

Diane dropped the cutie-pie routine when we settled on the shuttle. Mr. Cameron was too intent on her cleavage to notice, but he
played the tour guide role well.

"This is one of the larger residential rocks in the system."

"I thought we were going to visit a farm?" Diane turned from
looking out of the port.

"We are." He beamed a self-satisfied smile. "Our farms are all
in the residential areas."

"Really? Is it because you need labor?" She kept her face
straight and I gained a new level of respect for her acting skills at
that moment.

Again, he made with the condescending smile. "Oh, no." He
reached over and patted her hand. "We need their—" He stopped
in mid sentence, apparently realizing what he was about to say and
casting about for some other way to say it.

"Sludge?" I suggested.

He seemed to notice for the first time that I was aboard. "Yes,"
he said at last, "the...ah...sludge."

The shuttle docked in a fully enclosed landing bay and we walked
into a processing area. It was all automated but Cameron pointed
out the salient parts. "This is where we harvest the mushrooms
and freeze dry them for transport. We keep a few for fresh product,
but the real money is in dried. Less mass, you know."

Diane nodded. "Oh really? How interesting."

He showed us to the next room, a large chamber with several
noisy machines. Cameron shouted so we could hear him over the
racket. "We get the growing medium in big cakes from the environmental sections. We run it through these mills to break it up
to make it easier for the mushroom's roots to grow." He beckoned
us through the next door and the noise level dropped. He showed
us piles of flaked sludge being mixed with some kind of wet, green
plant material. "We mix the by-products from our hydroponics
with the flaked medium here and form it into what we call logs."
He pointed out where a machine extruded the mixture into loose
net tubes like sausages a quarter meter in diameter and a meter
long. I could see Diane biting her lip to keep from laughing. The

environmental crew had a rather literal view of their work. That view colored their perception of the world and tended to make them laugh at common euphemistic digressions.

Cameron pointed to where a small diameter tube stuck each log before being clipped onto an overhead track and trundled down a long dark tunnel. "Here we inoculate the log with mushroom spawn. It takes about a month for the roots to spread through the log. After that the roots start pushing through the surface and forming mushrooms which we harvest."

Like some magician, he flung open a nearby door and showed us a nearly identical track bearing logs now studded with fresh mushrooms. The track ran into a large machine. "We strip off the netting, shake out the medium, and separate the mushrooms from their roots."

"Mycelium." Diane corrected him with a wry smile.

"I beg your pardon?" Her comment took Cameron off guard.

She gazed at him for a moment. "They're not *roots* but *mycelium*, or probably more correctly, hyphae. Do you use the same growing medium for all your varieties?"

Cameron blinked rapidly, trying to catch up with where he had been derailed. "Yes, basically. Some require temperature variations and other get different nutrient baths but I couldn't tell you which gets what."

Diane nodded and held out her hand. "Thank you ever so much, Mr. Cameron." She cooed and dropped smoothly into cutie-pie mode and let him get back on his internal script. "Do you think we could go back to the station now? All this excitement has made me a little dizzy." She fanned herself with her free hand.

Cameron became immediately solicitous. "Of course, my dear, of course. Please, right this way..."

It took less than a stan for us to get back to Margary and bid our fond adieus to Mr. Cameron. The hard part was not laughing ourselves silly before we got out of sight and earshot.

After the worst of the giggles tapered off, I turned to Diane. "So, what do you think?"

"I think sludge just got a lot more interesting."

"Yeah, me too. If we were going to grow mushrooms on the *Lois*, what would we need?"

"So that's your game. I knew you were up to something. Changing the whole trading culture isn't enough?"

I just chuckled and shrugged. "What can I say, I'm frugal. My mom raised me not to waste anything and when I heard we were giving away sludge cakes as terraforming base, I got this wild idea that there must be something better we could do with it."

Diane laughed. "You want to make money on sewage?"

I shrugged. "The more money the ship makes, the more money I make. I don't care what it starts life as, so long as it ends as a cred in my account."

She looked me up and down before speaking, "Ishmael Wang, I like the way you think."

Chapter Twenty-four
Margary Station: 2352-January-12

When we got to the *Lois'* lock, I turned to Diane. "Come on, I'll buy ya a coffee."

"Coffee's free, ya cheapskate."

"Okay, then you buy."

We went to the mess deck and found Pip setting up for lunch. He looked up when we entered. "Where have you two been?"

"We took a tour of a mushroom farm," I told Pip.

Diane nodded. "Yeah, it actually was quite interesting."

We settled into a table just as Brill and Francis came in for lunch. Diane waved them over. "You'll never guess where we've been."

Francis looked at her for a heartbeat. "Mushroom farm."

Diane started to say, "How—"

Brill interrupted her, "We heard you as we were coming up the passage. I recognize the symptoms so you better spill your beans before your head explodes."

Diane tried to look innocent. "I don't know what you're referring to."

It didn't work. Brill and Francis just looked at her.

She shrugged. "Okay, we've been thinking about sludge."

"Sludge?" Francis repeated.

"Yeah."

Brill looked at me. "Let's try you. Do you know what she's talking about?"

I nodded. "Yeah, it's just like Diane said...sludge."

Brill and Francis started chuckling. Brill looked back and forth between the two of us. "Can you give us a bit more of a clue?"

I took pity on them. "Ever since I heard that we were giving away sludge cakes I've had this idea that we might be able to use it in some way. When I learned that Margary is a huge producer of mushrooms it occurred to me that the only thing they have out here is tunnels, dark, and sludge."

Diane nodded with a rueful grimace on her face. "Ain't that the truth."

"So I called up the supplier who sold us the mushrooms for the galley and asked if we could see the facilities. He was nice enough to run us over in his shuttle this morning and we saw a mushroom farm."

Francis looked at Diane. "And you just went along for the ride?"

She shrugged. "Mr. Cameron was a sweet man who was more than happy to show lil' ol' me his great big logs," she said in her cutie-pie voice.

Brill almost snorted coffee out of her nose laughing. "I wish you would warn me before you do that."

Francis ignored the performance and prompted me, "I still don't get it."

"All their farms are in the residential asteroids. They get the sludge from their environmental sections and use it as the base for a growing medium for the mushrooms."

Brill frowned. "But it's sterile."

I nodded. "That's actually a good thing. There are plenty of nutrients left in the waste and they're concentrated. What it is, is dense. They run the sludge cakes through a chipper and then mix it with hydroponics leftovers to add moisture and texture. That keeps the flakes from clumping up tight again. Cameron seemed to indicate it was for nutrients for the mushrooms, but he had a lot of misconceptions."

Francis and Brill both looked at Diane then.

"What? Why are you lookin' at lil' ol' me?"

Francis snorted. "Yeah. Right."

I continued without letting them get me off track, "Anyway, they extrude this chipped sludge mixture into loose netting. It looks like sausages only a lot bigger. They inoculate them with... what did he call it, Diane? Not spores."

"Spawn."

"Yeah, that's right. Then they send them into the tunnels to grow. When ready for harvest, the logs are brought back and run through a shaker to separate the mushrooms from the dross. Finally, they freeze dry the results."

Brill nodded and looked back and forth between Diane and me.

"Okay, sounds interesting. But I still don't see what that has to do with our sludge."

I shrugged and looked into my coffee mug. "I don't know. But I just keep thinking there's something we could do with it. Make it into compost and grow something. I don't know."

Francis snorted a laugh. "Really? What would you compost it with? You need plant material, don't you?"

Diane and I looked at each other before Diane looked back at Francis. "Used algae matrix."

Brill sat her coffee cup down gently. I could see her and Francis lock eyes across the table and they were both nodding slowly, apparently following the same logic path.

Finally Francis spoke, "That's brilliant."

Despite my initial enthusiasm, I was shocked. "You mean it could work?"

Francis shrugged. "I don't know. We'd have to play with it to find the right mixture, but I can't imagine why not. All the chemicals are there. The question is structure."

Brill said what we were all thinking, "Holy crap."

We all nodded.

My tablet bipped to remind me about my plans for the flea market. "I'm going shopping with Bev. Anybody want to join us?"

Brill shook her head. "Other plans."

Francis nodded. "You bet."

Diane popped up from her seat. "Count me in."

I followed her lead and stood. "Okay, let me see if Bev is ready. Meet you at the lock in what...fifteen ticks?"

They all nodded, and I left them there talking about sludge and algae while I headed for deck berthing.

❀   ❀   ❀

Bev was just buckling into her leathers when I got to the berthing area. "Hey, where have you been all morning?"

"Checking out a mushroom farm."

"You're kidding, right?" She shook her head and answered her own question. "No, you're not. I'm getting to know you well enough by now."

"Right. I'm not kidding, but I'm ready to go shopping. Is it okay if some others join us."

She shrugged. "Sure, the more the merrier."

"Francis and Diane will meet us at the lock. They wanna stock up for St. Cloud."

She chuckled. "Let's hope we have as good of luck here as we did in Gugara, eh?" She slammed her locker and we headed for the lock.

The flea market was in full swing and the four of us caravanned through the aisles. There were a lot of stone and metal goods. It didn't surprise me given the nature of the system. The trick would be to find stuff with low enough mass that we'd be able to get it aboard. As we strolled along, I really began to appreciate Pip's idea of filling the empty container with freeze-dried mushrooms.

We hadn't been there long when we came to booth two-sixteen. I recognized the workmanship on display before I realized where we were. Bev introduced us to Ingo Reihtman the guy who made them. He had shocking red hair, redder even than Diane's and a slight limp. There was no question he was a master of the belt buckle. The majority of them were the size and shape that Beverly had showed us but the variation in use of stone, polish, and pattern were amazing.

I stepped up to him and shook his hand. "Mr. Reihtman, my friend, Philip Carstairs will be around tomorrow—"

He nodded impatiently. "Yes, yes, Pip. I talked with him yesterday and I understand you have mass requirements that need to be satisfied. I look forward to doing business with you. This is a good opportunity for my work to get exposure beyond this system. I am quite excited."

As we talked one particular buckle caught my eye. It was cast in a gold colored metal with a rough, knobby finish. The stone was shaped into a black dragon's head in silhouette with a red inlaid eye.

"Well, I have a souvenir of my last port. I picked up an exquisite hand tooled leather belt and I need a buckle for it. Would you sell me one of yours?"

"Mr. Wang, do you think I'm sitting here for my health? Please, save the haggling preparation. Do you see the buckle you wish?"

I nodded.

"Fifteen creds."

"A very generous price."

"In that case. . ." He took the dragon's head buckle down from the wall without my pointing it out. He had a small smile on his face. "Would you like me to wrap it for you?"

As we left the booth Beverly said, "I had to jaw him down from forty for mine."

"Well, Pip and I will be buying a bunch of them tomorrow. Maybe he thought he was priming the pump for the deal."

"Maybe. I thought you sold all your belts the other day."

"All but one that I left in my locker. Drus made it specially for me."

"Can I see it?"

I realized suddenly that I had just painted myself into a corner and tried to change the subject. "We still need to find some trade goods to take to St. Cloud. So, keep your eyes open, okay?"

She chuckled.

Diane pointed out a display of ceramics at a booth coming up and we descended on the seller as a group. The goods were nice, but expensive. Clay had to be imported which drove up the price. I passed on it, but Francis bought a couple of small pieces.

We continued through the flea market, eventually passing by slot four seventy-eight, empty since we hadn't set up, and walked by Virgil's wife with a nod, a smile, and a wave. Bev and I did our best not to crack up but we did admire her chair.

A few booths farther down a display of necklaces caught my eye. The seller had pinned them to a fabric backing for display. Each was unique. Bev saw me looking and said, "I gotta give you credit, Ish. You've got one hell of an eye." She turned back to look for Diane and Francis and nodded discreetly at the necklaces. I could see Diane's eyes widen from where I was standing but she and Francis sauntered over nonchalantly. We all wandered over to the display.

The fellow behind the counter introduced himself as we approached, "Good day, gentle people. My name is Franz Neubert. These fine necklaces were created by my wife, Nerile, from only the finest local materials. May I show you anything in particular?"

The pieces consisted of small, highly polished beads with an accent stone or pendant hanging from each. Franz pointed out that they were strung on a slightly elastic thread that helped prevent breakage. He spent some time pointing out the durability of the workmanship. There was an excellent variety. Some were strung in monochromatic patterns while others were brilliant explosions of color.

Diane saw the one I was focusing on and shook her head slightly. "It's pretty, but you would have to be wearing just white or black."

I reconsidered the necklace and had to agree. Diane had style. If she said it was a problem, I wasn't going to argue. There were enough other pieces in blacks, whites, blues, and soft yellows.

I was standing there considering another one when I realized that I was being crazy. The prices were good, but I tried to think about selling these in a flea market on St. Cloud. The necklace I was focusing on was made of dozens of small black beads with a gold colored vein running through it. The accent bead was a natural nugget of a gold colored mineral that I assumed was iron pyrite. The price on the display said five hundred creds. Even assuming that I could talk Franz down to something like three hundred, I had a hard time imagining that I would find a flea market buyer on St. Cloud who'd pay the kind of money it would take for a decent margin. I sighed and put the necklace down.

I bowed slightly to Franz and slipped from the booth to see what else I might be able to find. Beverly, Diane, and Francis followed. "What's the matter?" Bev looked at me curiously when we had stepped out of earshot. Franz was busy with another set of customers at any rate.

I shook my head. "Those were beautiful, no question. The prices were good and the mass was ok."

Francis raised an eyebrow. "I hear a but coming."

"But I can't afford to buy more than one or two of them. At the prices I'd have to charge on St. Cloud, I'm not sure I would make a good profit."

We stood there, silent for a full tick. Diane finally spoke, "Yeah, you're probably right."

Bev sighed and shook her head. "Pity. He has some beautiful pieces."

Francis nodded. "I knew I heard a but in there."

We continued our shopping trip, eventually wandering to the loose gem dealers at the back of the hall. Francis, Diane, and Bev all bought a few things here and there.

Soon we heard the signal for the end of day and we joined the throng leaving the market.

On the way down in the lift, Francis asked, "You didn't buy anything but the buckle?"

I shrugged. "I didn't see anything else I wanted. It wasn't like the belts on Gugara. Pip's handling the buckle deal and we're probably going to buy ten, one each to go with the ones we have left."

Diane nodded. "Some days are like that. You walk through and don't see anything."

Bev smiled at me. "Keep shopping. You've got good instincts." The others nodded. "When you find something you like, let me know. I wanna buy some, too."

We all had a good laugh. I looked around at them. "Can we find some dinner? I'm starved."

Francis stopped the lift at level eight and led us to a nice place that specialized in pasta dishes. We spent the next two stans getting stuffed and just slightly tipsy on one too many bottles of wine. By the time we got back to the ship, the heavy food and unaccustomed alcohol took its toll on me and I had to call it a night.

Pip was going over some cargo data in his bunk when Bev and I wandered into the berthing area. "How was it?"

I shrugged. "Good, but I didn't buy anything. The mass or the price—"

Bev cut in, "Or both."

I nodded my agreement. "Or both, were too high. I didn't see anything that grabbed me. There were some gem dealers but I don't know anything about gems. I think they're supposed to be clear and everything I saw was kinda cloudy and inconsistent."

Bev finished for me, "So we went out to dinner and came home to sleep it off."

I headed for my locker. "How's by you?"

He gave a half shrug. "Quiet night. Got my manifest exercise in order. We've lined up some fresh produce on St. Cloud to swap the mushrooms for."

By then I had slipped out of my civvies and into my ship-tee and boxers. I went to hang up my jacket and the buckle fell out. "Oh yeah, I almost forgot this." I showed it to Pip. "I met Ingo and bought a buckle for my belt."

He grinned. "The one Drus made for you?"

I nodded and pulled it out of my locker. I fumbled with it for a bit but finally got the thing attached. The ivy pattern and the knobbly gold colored finish of the buckle looked like they were made for each other. I strapped it on to see how it fit, just as Bev came out of the san. She froze and stared. I realized that I was standing there with my belt riding low around my hips wearing nothing but my ship-tee and boxers, just as she had been. I blushed furiously, I'm sure, and scrabbled the belt off.

Bev raised an eyebrow. "So that's the one you were talking about?"

I nodded and she held out a hand. "Lemme see."

I gave it to her, knowing I was going to regret it, but helpless to stop myself.

She ran it through her hands and fingered the ivy vines and leaves. She flexed it a couple of time and then handed it back. "Yeah, Drus knows her leather. That's a real keepsake, Ish."

I took it back from her and hung it in my locker. Pip was smirking behind his tablet, peeking out every so often to see my red face. Beverly, for her part, likewise in ship-tee and boxers crawled into her bunk with a groan. "Oh gods, duty tomorrow."

Pip contributed a cheerful, "Ha-ha, I'm off."

Bev and I both chuckled.

I reached up and clicked off my reading light. "I've got breakfast duty in the morning. Good night."

"Night, Ish. Sleep well." Pip's voice had that distracted voice that he got when he was on the trail of a deal.

From below, I heard Bev mumble, "Sleep well... boy toy." It was followed by a sleepy giggle.

Chapter Twenty-five
Margary Station: 2352-January-13

Pip got up with me in the morning and helped set up for breakfast. We still had the issue of how many buckles to buy and we needed something else to take to St. Cloud for trade goods.

Cookie smiled when I stepped into the galley. "Good morning, young Ishmael. Your day off went well, I presume? I heard you visited the mushroom caves?"

"Morning, Cookie. Yes, very well, thank you. And, the caves were quite interesting."

"Well, you'll find today's menu on your tablet. Can I trust you to handle breakfast solo this morning? I have some business ashore myself."

Pip and I looked at each other. *Cookie was leaving the ship?*

I nodded. "No problem, my pleasure."

"Thank you, young Ishmael, I've set the bread to rise but if you could get the biscuits and pie crusts?"

"Of course, of course."

He gave me an odd little bow and left the galley. Pip and I looked at each other. "Solo?" Pip raised an eyebrow.

I shrugged. "Not like there's anything on this menu I haven't done a hundred times already."

"True. And in port it's slow, especially in the morning."

"To tell ya the truth, it makes me feel better that he's going ashore."

Pip looked at me quizzically.

"Well, I'm not sure he hasn't gone ashore in the evening, because he doesn't talk about what he does. But I bet it has been ages since he's gotten off this ship. I think his card game takes up a lot of his spare time."

Pip nodded. "Yeah, me, too."

"The never-going-ashore thing makes him seem a little. . . I don't know. . . unnatural. This is better especially since we really don't have enough to keep both of us busy."

"Amen, brother. So, can I get an omelet? Lots of mushrooms and extra cheese, please."

I chucked a towel at him. "Yeah, sure, if you'll make the coffee for a change."

A few ticks later we settled on the mess deck to eat. I had the biscuits baking and was ready to make omelets for anybody who wanted one. It was early yet and I had time to enjoy the fruits of my omelet pan.

"So, how many buckles?" I asked Pip.

He shrugged. "We have ten belts, we should take at least that many to match. Should we pick up some extras?"

"They're excellent work, and not that much mass. If you get them for ten creds each, and they're all in the two hundred gram range, that's five per kilo. We'd burn two kilos for the first ten. What if we doubled it, how much would that be?"

Pip answered instantly, "Two hundred to three hundred depending on the price."

"We've got three kilocreds." We looked at each other and grinned in disbelief. "But I don't want to tie up all the cash if we don't have a good cargo."

"We only have about twelve kilos of available mass allotment between us, I think, maybe as many as fifteen. With twenty buckles, we're down to around eight with some room for anything we might spot that's small. We could get maybe forty additional buckles," Pip rattled off in quick succession.

"But we'd be betting the farm in terms of mass," I pointed out.

"Two things—no, three things left to consider."

I raised my eyebrows in question.

He ticked them off on his fingers. "First, we're almost certain to clear the first two kilos and the weight of the belts because those ten will evaporate on St. Cloud. Second, we don't have a line on any other cargo. Third, the mass is only a problem if we find something we really want to buy."

"Good points. What about St. Cloud?"

"Nice place." Pip got the dreamy look and went into his recitation mode. "It's one of the more established systems in the sector, owned jointly by a farming and a fishing company. The surface is about sixty percent ocean and the landmass is mostly divided into three continents. One is almost a continuous flat plain, one is mountainous, and the smallest island is near the southern pole. We're picking up containers of grain, fish, mutton, and wool. We're dropping machine parts and communications equipment."

"Farmers, fishermen, and shepherds," I summed up.

Pip blinked until his eyes focused on me again. "Yeah, sounds about right."

"What's with the wool? Is it raw or textiles?"

He pulled up the manifests on his tablet. "Bales. It could be either."

"What's the value?"

He grinned. "You're good. Looks like bulk wool. I shoulda caught that."

"You're rubbing off on me. If you were living up in the mountains with a bunch of sheep, what would you do with your spare time? Besides the obvious."

"Try to keep warm. I'd spin wool. You think the companies would let the herders keep some of it?"

"I'm pretty sure they would find ways to keep at least the odds and ends, perhaps buy it back from the company at wholesale, that kind of thing. Just like I bet they eat a lot of mutton and fish."

Pip smiled. "Does that suggest anything to you?"

"Yeah. Let's see if you can find a good deal on powdered dye."

"Really?"

I nodded. "Primary colors like red, blue, yellow, maybe even black."

"Why dye?" Pip asked, frowning in puzzlement.

"Well, sheep are almost always white. It just makes sense that a bit of color would make their goods sell better."

"You think on a crooked path, my friend. I like that."

"Doesn't mean I'm right. I feel like I'm missing something."

"What?"

"I dunno. But something."

The entire environmental crew came in for breakfast and I had to get back to work. Pip waved as he left and I slipped into serving mode. Anyway, I had to get the biscuits out of the oven.

As expected, the pace on the mess deck was slow and spotty. I got the bread punched down around midmorning and set it to second proof. Cleanup was easy and I even got a nice mushroom-barley soup going. Mr. Maxwell stopped by for coffee a couple of times and nodded to me without speaking. I found some unbaked cobblers in the walk-in and slid them into the ovens so they'd be ready for lunch. Even though I didn't get a morning break, I confess it felt kinda nice pottering about the galley. I could see what Cookie enjoyed about it.

Around 1100, just as I was setting up the lunch buffet, Cookie bipped me to let me know he'd be there by noon and I felt a little disappointed. I was beginning to anticipate doing lunch solo as well and the idea appealed to me for some odd reason.

I had a lot of time to think about St. Cloud, too, in the back of my brain. I was having second thoughts about the dye idea. I was coming to the conclusion that we should just go ahead and buy up buckles for about half of the available remaining mass. That would leave some wiggle room in case they didn't move, and give us something to sell beyond just the ten buckled belts. Something wasn't quite right, but I just let it percolate.

The lunch set up went off without a hitch and Cookie breezed in just before noon. "Thank you, young Ishmael. Sometimes you just have to get out and about. I feel much better and you've done an excellent job." He patted me on the shoulder.

"My pleasure, Cookie. It was fun." I brought him up to speed on the lunch status.

Just before lunch prep was over, Pip breezed into the galley with a smug look. "I found the dyes."

"Did you buy any?"

He shook his head and helped himself to a bowl of soup. "I found that thing you were missing."

"What was it?"

"The dyes I found here came from the Erehwon Dyeworks on St. Cloud."

We laughed. "That's what I was missing. I bet they have roots and berries and such to dye their own wool."

Pip shook his head. "Snails."

"Seriously?"

"Yeah, apparently when processed they yield a really rich purple. There's also a red and a black version. That's in addition to the plant-based dyes."

"So, what do we take?"

Pip shrugged. "We play it safe or we play it out. We're out of here tomorrow afternoon. Whatever we get, we have to buy it today. Safe, we go with just the ten buckles, or maybe just a few more. Or we can fill up the mass with buckles and hope they like them as much there as we do here."

I sighed. "You know, neither of those really appeals to me. What we need is something small that we can buy a lot of cheaply here that we can sell there at twice the price without costing an arm and a leg."

Pip got a funny look then and fished in his pocket. "Like these?"

He tossed three smooth stones onto the table. There were both flattened and round stones in natural looking, circular shapes. One looked like quartz with a silvery mineral threaded delicately through it. The second one was a rich blue that looked like the stone on Beverly's belt buckle so it was probably lapis. The last one was a lustrous black with a fine texture showing through the polish. None of them was more than three centimeters across. Each had a hole bored widthwise through the top. They looked like the accent stones on Neubert's necklaces. I picked up one and didn't want to put it down. The stone slid smoothly under my fingers as I rubbed it.

"Where'd you find these?"

"A guy back in the gem aisle had a booth. Just him and a couple of buckets full. They were three for a cred and I liked the way they felt."

"How many of them do you think it would take to mass a kilo?"

Pip grinned. "A lot. These three averaged ten grams each."

"Can you find him again? Because I think you found something here."

"Yeah, how many do we want?"

"Let's go with the ten buckles for the belts, twenty buckles extra. That leaves us, what? About six kilos?"

Pip nodded. "Something like that."

"Two kilos of these would work out to about two hundred of them. The actual income isn't very large but the margin is potentially pretty big."

Pip shrugged. "Let's go all six kilos. It's not going to take that many creds so if we get stuck and need the mass we can just toss 'em."

"Sounds like a plan," I said excitedly. "Let's do it."

Pip nodded and headed back out to finish the trading.

With Cookie back in the galley and lunch all ready, there wasn't much for me to do and I had the afternoon cleanup done almost as soon as lunch ended. Cookie planned a spicy beefalo dish for dinner and he began humming as he puttered around the galley. I pulled up a stool and watched for a time but he waved me off. "Go, young Ishmael. You didn't get a break this morning, and I can certainly handle making a small batch of this by myself." He smiled at me, his eyes crinkling at the corners. "Thank you again for doing such an excellent job with the morning duty."

"My pleasure, Cookie. I'm glad you got some time in port. Any time I can help like that, you know I'm always willing."

"You're a good shipmate, young Ishmael. Lois is happy to have you aboard."

I chuckled. "I'm going for a run and a sauna then."

He pursed his lips in question. "No environmental this after-noon?"

I shook my head. "I've taken enough of their time lately."

Cookie chuckled. "I heard—sludge duty."

"And algae! Don't forget the algae."

He laughed and waved as I left him humming over his sizzling beefalo.

I ran three extra laps beyond my normal workout. My wind had gotten much better and the extra exertion felt good. The showers sluiced off the grime and I had the sauna to myself. It felt odd. I enjoyed not having to share, but it seemed empty without the good-natured banter that usually filled the room along with the steam. Afterward I stretched out in my bunk and went back to reading up on being a steward. The quarterly exams were just a few weeks off.

❀   ❀   ❀

At 1600 I went back to the mess deck to help Cookie set up the dinner buffet. I could smell the spiced beefalo all the way from the berthing area and it made me drool. I suspected the dinner turnout would be better than usual. I was right. About halfway through, Pip showed up wearing his shipsuit and a big grin. We didn't have time to talk until we'd secured from dinner, but he came to help me clean up after.

Cookie eyed his jaunty grin. "Judging from your smile, your trading went well."

Pip grinned even wider. "Very well, indeed." He turned to me. "Ingo gave us thirty buckles all at ten, so three hundred creds and just under six kilos. There's some serious upside potential there. The rock guy was surprised that we'd want to buy them by the kilo, but he had a ton of them so he was happy to unload some. He gave me as many as I wanted for five creds a kilo. I bought the six we agreed to."

I blinked, trying to do the math in my head. "You got about six hundred of them for thirty creds?"

He nodded. "Twenty per cred. The total upside is nothing to write home about, but even at a cred a piece on St. Cloud, the margins are huge."

"I'll take six hundred creds. That's more than the salary and share I got for the Margary leg."

"Yeah, but you have to split it with me. Even so it's really good."

Chapter Twenty-six
Margary System: 2352-January-15

We pulled out of Margary right on time. The captain scheduled it
for just after dinner, so we didn't have to make bento-boxes. Always
thinking, Cookie called the captain and offered to distribute coffee
and cookies at 2100. That was about halfway through the evolution
and a lot of bleary-eyed spacers who'd celebrated port-side until the
last possible tick appreciated the pick-me-up.

Around 2230 we set the normal watch and I could almost hear
Lois sigh as we settled into the familiar routine of sailing between
the stars. It didn't often strike me, this romantic notion that we
were out here in our little ship spreading our sails to catch the solar
wind, but when it did I remembered a snatch of ancient poetry that
my mother used to recite to me. It was a kind of lullaby she used
when tucking me in. "I must go down to the seas again, to the
lonely sea and the sky. And all I ask is a tall ship and a star to
steer her by," I mumbled to myself as I drifted off to sleep.

❀ ❀ ❀

Pip and I convened what we called a steering committee on the
first day out of Margary and invited Beverly, Diane, Francis, Rhon,
and Biddy. We agreed that the finances should come as part of a
sales fee, and most liked the one-percent capped at ten creds. Biddy
wanted the cap at twenty and Francis wanted five because he only
wanted to cover expenses, and not build up reserves. In the end,
we decided on ten because it provided some contingency funding
and we didn't really know how much we'd need as startup. Diane
provided the deciding argument. "You'll have less opposition if you

decide to reduce the rate than if you try to raise it." Nobody had anything to dispute that so we left it at ten.

Over the next few days we kept having meetings figuring our way through all the various problems that could arise. The stickiest issue was the idea of consignment. Beverly brought the idea up about two days out of Margary. "What if somebody has stuff to sell, but doesn't want to sit around the booth? If we're going to be there anyway, could we have an arrangement to sell for them? Maybe take a flat percentage for doing it?"

Rhon objected, "But we're doing the work and they're getting the benefit."

We threw different ideas around including reduced fees for working the booth or an hourly stipend. That last idea wasn't popular because it increased overhead without assuring revenue. We still had a lot to work out.

It seemed we'd barely got underway when suddenly we were at the St. Cloud jump point. We were still stymied over consignments, but we all agreed that we probably should find some kind of solution. I knew from my brief experience on Margary that we needed some kind of system of coverage so the booth would be available the whole time. It was important that this obligation should carry some benefit to those doing the work. My time selling had been fun, but if we were going to do this as a regular thing, I didn't want to be stuck doing it all the time and I didn't think anybody else would want that either.

We'd no sooner secured from navigation stations in the afternoon when my tablet bipped with a request from the captain to meet with her, "at your earliest convenience." I had been on the ship long enough to learn that the phrase was officer-speak for, "get your butt over here." Pip had a similar message so we hustled to her cabin.

When we entered we found the captain, Mr. Maxwell, and Mr. Cotton seated around her small conference table. The captain indicated empty seats. "Sit, gentlemen. It's time we talked."

For my part, I was a bit nervous. I'd been eager to talk over our plans with her. I felt like we were on the right course but wanted to get the captain's opinion. Seeing the first mate and cargo chief made me think I was about to find out more than I'd bargained for. Out of the corner of my eye, I could see Pip licking his dry lips and he kept wiping his palms on the sides of his shipsuit.

We took the indicated chairs and waited.

The captain started right in. "So, gentlemen, how was the flea market?"

I glanced at Pip. He nodded so I started first. "Well, Captain.

You saw our first day's efforts and, in spite of being somewhat unprepared—" Pip snorted quietly, but I ignored him and continued, "we did really well. We traveled in pairs and the people who participated that first day were very satisfied."

Pip picked up the story. "I took the second day along with three other crew and we all sold out of our trade goods. Ms. Sham and Ms. Murphy both indicated that they were pleased with the outcomes."

The captain nodded. "And the third and fourth day?"

Pip motioned for me to answer that one. "We didn't have any more goods to sell and since we weren't aware of any other crew members who needed the booth, it went empty those days. Instead we used the time to research and purchase items for St. Cloud."

Mr. Maxwell spoke quietly, "That included visiting a mushroom processing facility?"

I tried to keep my voice flat when I replied, "Yes, sar."

The captain ignored the comment and continued, "And what have you learned about running the booth?"

Pip answered her with a rueful grin, "That it's not as easy as it looks, Captain, and if we're going to do this regularly, then we need to get better organized."

The captain nodded with a small smile. "I see, and I concur. You've formed a steering committee to start this process rolling. Is that right?"

I nodded. "Yes, Captain. I can give you the names..."

She shook her head. "No, that's not necessary. I'm more interested in what you've decided so far."

I took a deep breath and let it out before continuing, "We realize that to be successful we need to be professional and systematic. Part of that is maintaining economic viability. We need to pay our own freight, as it were."

Mr. Cotton spoke for the first time, "How do you propose to accomplish that, eh?"

Pip answered him, "By taking a commission, one percent of sales, capped at ten creds. You can sell as much as you like, but you owe the co-op one percent of what you get up to ten creds then after that you keep it all."

"I'm familiar with the concept, Mr. Carstairs, ya." A small smile played around Mr. Cotton's mouth.

Pip blushed. "Of course, sar. Sorry, sar."

The captain looked like she was suppressing a grin and addressed the next question to me. "And what have you decided about booth coverage and consignment sales?"

"Well, Captain, we know we need to split the days up. Our

normal port stay is about four days. If we have four people as designated booth managers, we could either assign one of them each day or split the duty so no one gets too tired. We have four people but we need to check watch schedules against the volunteers to make sure we're distributed properly among the watches."

She nodded. "And consignments?"

Pip stepped in on that one. "We're deadlocked on that one just now, Captain. We're thinking an increase in commission, but the notion of we-work-and-they-profit is getting in the way. The problem is that the commission goes to the co-op but the people doing the work aren't getting anything from it."

She nodded. "So you're not paying the booth managers?"

Pip and I both shrugged but Pip answered her, "That came up at the last meeting, Captain, but we didn't come to any definitive answer."

"How would your great-grandmother have done it, Captain?" The question just popped out of my mouth before I really considered what I was saying.

The captain smiled though and answered in a gentle voice, "She would have split the commission between the booth and the managers."

It was so obvious. As soon as the words left her mouth I knew it was the right answer, and I suspect Pip was kicking himself as hard as I was.

Mr. Maxwell broke in at that point, "What will you spend the money on?"

Pip handled that while I untied my tongue. "We need to cover booth rental. They won't always be as straight forward as Margary, I suspect. We also need some booth fixtures to keep from looking like complete rubes."

The captain appeared to sneeze quietly at that point and covered her mouth and nose with her hand.

Mr. Maxwell arched an eyebrow. "Rubes, Mr. Carstairs?"

"Yes, sar. Most booth vendors have display racks, signage, chairs, and such. The pros have them all set up on a grav pallet and all they have to do is float it in, lock it down, and begin selling. That first day we wouldn't have even had a tablecloth if not for the banner—"

The captain interrupted, "So you're planning on purchasing all this with the proceeds from the booth?"

I sighed. "That's our problem, captain. The creds we can cover. We probably can't afford a grav pallet right away but the other stuff is relatively easy to come by except for the mass."

"The mass?"

Pip nodded. "Yes, Captain. All that stuff has mass and some-body needs to book it onto the ship. None of us have a mass allotment high enough to cover it all."

Mr. Maxell swiveled his gaze back and forth between us. "How are you going to deal with that?"

I shrugged. "Well, sar, short term, we'll make signs on station and leave them there. Boards and markers are cheap and dispos-able. Chairs we'll rent as well as the tables. It'll add to the over-head, but it'll be worth it. We have a tablecloth now in addition to the banner and clips, so we're good there."

Pip added, "We're planning on buying a couple of extra duffel bags for transportation when we get to St. Cloud. But we don't have spare mass for even a couple of cargo totes, let alone a grav pallet."

The captain nodded and pursed her lips. "What about renting a grav pallet as well?"

Pip nodded. "We looked at that, Captain. They're expensive compared to the booth rental, but if this works out perhaps we can do that later."

"Mr. Cotton," the captain said, "does the ship have a grav pallet they might rent?"

"I'm sorry, Captain, no, in port we need every pallet we can find, ya." He pulled up his tablet and consulted his inventory. "But... we do, have one that is scheduled for scrap, ya. Ach, it was supposed to have remained on Margary, in fact."

She nodded slowly, and I had the odd feeling that she had known all along. "What's the mass on a grav pallet, Mr. Cotton?"

"Ya, fifty kilos, Captain."

She turned to the first mate. "Mr. Maxwell, does Lois have sufficient mass in her allotment to cover fifty kilos?"

"Yes, Captain, she does."

"Well, then I think we have the grav pallet problem solved." She gave us all a little self-satisfied shrug. "I'm very pleased with the progress you gentlemen and your group have made. A captain likes to keep the crew happy—busy, but happy." She looked around, first at Mr. Maxwell and then Mr. Cotton. "Is there any other business for these two spacers, gentlemen?"

"No, Captain," they answered in near unison.

"Very well." She turned to us. "Thank you for coming, gentle-men. I appreciate your diligence."

We stood and started out but at the door the captain stopped us with a final question. "Oh, what are you calling this enterprise of yours?"

Pip and I glanced at each other, and I told her. "The McKendrick Mercantile Cooperative, of course. I understand it has a proud tradition, Captain."

The captain grinned. "Yes, Mr. Wang, it does indeed. Thank you, again, gentlemen."

We beat a hasty retreat from officer country and the whole way back Pip kept shaking his head and making little tsk'ing sounds.

When we entered the galley, I finally broke down and asked, "What's the matter?"

"Split the commission. How stupid can we be?"

I chuckled. "I don't know about you, but I have a proud history of being pretty stupid."

"Hmm. Maybe it's contagious and I'm catching it from you, then."

Cookie was icing a cake for dinner and looked up at Pip. "No, Mr. Carstairs, you've always had a very healthy amount of your own," he said with a wicked grin. He turned back to his icing. "And if you're finished lazing about, number one coffee urn is out again."

CHAPTER TWENTY-SEVEN
MARGARY SYSTEM: 2352-JANUARY-15

After evening cleanup, I settled on the mess deck with my handbook and a cup of coffee. The quarterly exams were only a few days away and, while I was pretty confident about the food handler test, I had barely looked at ordinary spacer.

It was huge.

Everything that didn't appear on one of the other exams was on the Deck Division test—ship configurations, basic communications, and standing orders for: watches, helm, and gangway duty. My brain froze and shut down. Sandy found me half a stan later just sitting there staring into my tablet.

She waved a hand in front of my face. "Ish? Ish? You okay?"

"Oh yeah, thanks, Sandy. I just realized how much is on this deck exam. It flipped me out for a bit. The test is in ten days and I'm planning on taking this one and the food handler exam."

She chuckled. "You are a glutton for punishment, aren't ya? Didn't you take cargo and engineering last cycle?"

I nodded.

She looked over my shoulder at the tablet. "This isn't so bad. I'm finally taking my Astrogation II exam this round. Once you start specializing it gets a lot harder. Look." She pointed at the port-starboard diagram. "If you don't know that by now, you're just so much congealed saltwater."

I chuckled. "True."

"And tell me you haven't absorbed the watch stander schedule. What watch are we on now?"

"Evening, but..."

"See, this isn't hard. You still have plenty of time. What haven't you gotten to?"

"Standing orders. Look at how many there are. How am I supposed to memorize all that?"

She punched the button and brought up the first set. There were ten of them, but each was just common sense. She'd brought up the gangway watch orders and it started with, "Watch standers will report to duty stations fifteen ticks before the change of watch to assure a smooth transition of duty."

"Hmm. This doesn't look all that hard."

"You've been hanging around with Pip too much. Maybe you should spend more time with Beverly."

I'm pretty sure I blushed.

She patted me on the shoulder. "Look, you know how to eat an elephant?"

I nodded. "One bite at a time."

"Yup. Dig in. I bet you can finish this one in a couple of days."

I flipped back and forth a couple of times and began to realize she was right. The list was long, but the individual items were small. A lot of it I knew already having lived aboard for—gods could it really have been almost five months? "You're right," I said. "I don't know what happened there. My brain just kinda seized up."

She looked at me with a frown. "Hmm, you've been up since 0500 and worked all day?"

I nodded.

"You've got a lot on your plate. I heard you had a meeting with the captain this afternoon. It seems like the co-op is shaping up."

I nodded again.

"Well, let me ask you this. Don't you think you should get some sleep? It's almost time for the midwatch."

I chuckled. "Which would make it nearly midnight and I've got to get up at oh-dark-thirty."

She laughed then. "It's all dark out here, but yeah. I'm off watch myself in a few minutes and I better not find you on the track."

"Okay, okay, sheesh." I laughed and stood. "Thanks, Sandy."

"No problem, Ish." She waved and headed out of the mess. "Sleep well."

When I got to the berthing area, Pip and Bev were both already asleep. As I settled into my own bunk, I heard the little snorty-snores through the partition and thought, *One bite at a time.*

❀   ❀   ❀

For the next couple of days I focused on my exams and let Pip worry about the steering committee. He kept me filled in while we worked the serving line or during cleanups. The group liked the idea of splitting the commissions but were hung up on whether to split all of them or only consignment sales. Eventually they agreed to split them all and to put a ten percent no-cap commission on consignments. That seemed about right to me. Beverly and Rhon wanted more, but Diane and Francis wanted less so it was a good compromise. Personally, I liked the idea of splitting them all. Of course, we'd already decided that booth manager wasn't subject to the one percent sales commission. It was a way to get more people to volunteer to be booth managers. Adding the commission split between manager and co-op, we developed a nice economic model that gave a little extra to anybody who worked for the common good.

I got through all the ordinary spacer material in just a couple of days and took a practice test with a seventy-five score. Good, but not enough to pass. I took a break and ran quickly through the food handler again, just to refresh myself and tested at ninety-four. By the end of the second day after transition, I was passing both tests consistently and I messaged Mr. von Ickles to let him know I'd be taking both deck and steward tests.

Sandy caught me after cleanup a couple of nights after that. "How're you doing? You still have a few days to study. You need help on the deck exam?"

"I think I'm good. Of course, I won't know until I take the test next week."

"Too true." She gave me a sympathetic chuckle.

"How are you doing?" I asked. "You've been studying astrogation stuff ever since I came aboard."

She smiled at me. "That's normal. I had just made third before we got to Neris. After you make full share, you have to pick a specialty and work up through that ranking system."

I grimaced but nodded my agreement. "Yeah, I saw that in *The Handbook*, but there's nothing that says I have to go beyond full share."

"Well, the extra mass is nice, and I suspect you'll be full share before you know it. Look what happened with Pip."

"Very true. Well, if you have a couple minutes, would you drill me on the deck stuff and see if I'm ready?"

"Sure, I'd be happy to." She reached over and took my tablet. For the next twenty ticks, she asked me questions and I gave her answers. It was fun. She had that same dry wit that Diane had and a take-no-prisoners attitude that reminded me of Beverly. When we were done, she handed the tablet back. "Okay, you just qualified for able spacer. I think you can pass the ordinary test."

We laughed and I thought she was joking until I got my tablet back from her and looked to see the testing pool she'd been drilling me from. That made me feel a lot better.

❀   ❀   ❀

On test day, I reported to Mr. von Ickles at the appointed time. He grinned when he saw me. "Do you have your frequent testing card? I can give you a discount."

I chuckled. "Sorry, sar. I musta left it in my other shipsuit."

"You sure you want to do this?"

"What's the worst that can happen, sar?"

"You might not pass."

"And?"

"Yeah." He grinned. "I know, but I have to ask. If you're ready...?"

Some indeterminate time later, from my perspective, I heard him say, "Time." I put my stylus down and looked up at him.

He stared at me intently. "Are you some kind of machine? I've never seen anybody disappear into a test like you do. Let me ask what test did you just take?"

I hadn't quite re-surfaced into reality. "Um, ordinary spacer, sar?"

He laughed. "You don't sound too sure for somebody who's been answering questions for almost a full stan."

"Wasn't it, sar?" His comment made me nervous.

He nodded. "Yeah, it was and that's probably the hardest test. How'd you do?"

"You tell me, sar. I'm not even sure what test I took." We both laughed at that.

He pulled up his display and showed me, ninety-six.

"Congratulations, Mr. Wang. You are now rated ordinary spacer and I will add a note in your jacket this afternoon," he rattled off the formula.

I grinned. "Thank you, sar. Steward tomorrow."

"You'll have collected the full set. Do you have the commemorative binder?"

"Wha—?"

"Sorry." He grinned sheepishly. "Joke."

I laughed. "I get it. It just took me a tick to process what you said, sar. I'm still a little groggy from the test, I think."

Mr. von Ickles smiled. "Well, I mean it. I've seen many people take these tests and you slide into some kind of zone, a world unto yourself. You didn't even see Mr. Maxwell come in, did you?"

I shook my head. "No, sar. I didn't."

"Or the captain?"

I looked up in alarm.

"Just kidding. The captain didn't come in."

I laughed. "Thank you, sar. I'll see you tomorrow."

The rest of the day went by in one of those strange fogs where you get to the end and you know you did something but can't remember what it was. I knew about the test, but nothing else seemed to stick. I had a vague memory about helping Pip and Cookie with lunch and cleanup. I'd used the afternoon break for a run and sauna instead of studying. After dinner I made one last pass through the food handler test and hit the rack early.

❀   ❀   ❀

For breakfast Cookie made pancakes and waffles with hot fruit compotes in several flavors along with the usual selection of pork products. Myself, I would have preferred a nice cheese omelet with some mushrooms, but I enjoyed the waffles with granapple topping. Cleanup went smoothly and Pip and I were trading off on coffee duty. We had it down to a science. After finding the proper grind and proportion—we had standardized that early on—the rest was just keeping the urns clean and the brew water cold. We had to make some adjustments when we switched from the Arabasti but less than I would have thought. When it came right down to it, the two weren't that different except for the expense.

At the appointed time I presented myself to Mr. von Ickles, "Ah, the machine. Are you ready?"

I surfaced about a stan later.

Mr. von Ickles offered me his hand and I shook it. "You now have the full set of half share ratings, congratulations."

I thanked him, and went back to the galley.

Cookie and Pip both congratulated me but I really didn't feel like it was much of an accomplishment. My duties remained the same as they were before taking all the tests. Sure, I could move up, if something became available, but one of the reasons for doing all this was to determine what I liked best, and in the end I still didn't know. All I really had was a collection of entries in my personnel jacket.

After lunch and cleanup, Pip convened a meeting of the steering committee on the mess deck so we could map out our strategy for St. Cloud. In my absence, they started a list of crew who wanted to be booth managers: Rhon, Biddy, Diane, and Francis. I felt a little miffed that I wasn't listed, but that would let me come and go as I pleased. I'd owe the ten creds, which they had decided should be per-person for the entire port stay instead of a per-day fee. That made sense for somebody selling a little something each day who might not sell a thousand creds in one session.

They also started compiling a list of crew who wanted to sell something, along with a catalog of goods for sale. They had a short discussion on scheduling times so everybody didn't show up at once, but soon chucked that out as too restrictive. The watch schedules would sort out some of it in any case.

After the discussion ranged for a bit, I started getting concerned about the level of detail. "How many people are we talking about here?"

Pip looked at me and answered with a completely flat expression, "Seventeen."

I almost choked on my coffee. "Seventeen? That's almost half the crew! Do they know they have to chip in to the co-op?"

Rhon nodded. "Oh yeah, in fact most of them wanted to before I told them. When they heard it was one percent or ten creds, most of them were willing to pay right then. I had to explain that we would collect after they were done selling."

Biddy piped up, "Yeah, you have no idea what it's like to try to find buyers for this stuff without a table. The things I sold the other day I had dragged through three systems without even a nibble. This is just such an obvious idea, I can't imagine why nobody ever thought of it before."

Pip shrugged. "Well, I know why it never occurred to me." We all looked at him. "Lone wolf syndrome. I thought I was a wheeler-dealer. Then I got mugged... man, that was stupid and less profitable. I made more in the last booth than I've made in my whole career."

Rhon nodded and grinned. "Yeah, and it beats the sneakers off trying to use other people's booths. Selling wholesale really takes a bite and it's not always easy to find someone who will carry the stuff you have. Even the successful traders like Bev and Tabitha are switching to this model."

Pip pointed at me and grinned. "Well, we owe it all to Ish."

I groaned. "Oh, come on. Save the kissing up until this actually works. We've got a lot of things to figure out yet."

Francis snorted a laugh. "Like what?"

"Well, does everybody know how to move the grav pallet? Are we all clear on how to set up the booth? Have we established who'll handle the money? If we're going to take a percentage we should have a cashier, and maybe that's the manager. I don't know. Where do we stow the pallet when the market is closed? Do we know where to rent chairs on St. Cloud? Has anybody looked at the rental agreements there?" I ran through the issues rather quickly off the top of my head. The group sat staring at me.

Pip shook himself out of a daze and pulled out his tablet. "Could you run through that list again?" he asked, holding his stylus.

Everybody laughed and we got on with the process of organizing the co-op. I wanted Lois to be proud of us.

Unfortunately, we were interrupted by the pingity-pingity-pingity of the abandon ship alarm. We bolted for the boat dock and arrived at the gym just as the announcement came for the drill. We split up to attend to the ship's business.

❀   ❀   ❀

Two days later, after the evening cleanup, the steering committee convened in the main cargo lock where we practiced locking, unlocking, loading, and unloading the grav pallet. There wasn't a lot to it, but if you had never done it before it could be intimidating. The secret was in the tow handle and Biddy had us all maneuvering pallets around like pros in less than a stan. She also arranged with Mr. Cotton to be able to bring our pallet back from the flea market each night and park it in the ship's cargo lock. There was a kind of vestibule where we could leave the pallet without it being in the way. We'd have to stow it with the rest when transporting but that was only to be expected.

Three days out of St. Cloud we gathered for one last planning session in the mess. We identified sources for tables, chairs, card stock, and markers. We worked out a rough plan to display all the various items that the crew had to sell. The group determined that we'd need two tables but we only had one cloth. Pip suggested a standard ship's blanket, but Cookie, who had been lurking in the background, tossed a covering matching the original. Officially, the cloths stayed as part of the galley's stores so we were probably violating some rule, but we trusted Lois wouldn't mind. Drawing up the final schedule for booth shifts, we split the days in half so nobody had to stay the whole time if they didn't want to. Last we created a list of the people who'd be moving their goods up first and another for those who would be bringing theirs along later.

I was amazed, frankly. What had started with the innocent concept of let's rent a booth had become a paramilitary operation complete with scheduled supply runs as Cookie volunteered to pack bento-boxes and fill thermoses.

A day out of St. Cloud, Mr. Maxwell called Pip and me to the office so we could sign the legal agreements to formally form the ship's cooperative. This made it possible to have accounts in the ship's ledger to keep the money straight. As a recognized sub-entity of the ship, we also stayed within the regulations on use of rental spaces. While we were there setting up the accounting and going through the procedures, the captain joined us.

"Gentlemen, I don't want to interrupt, but I thought I would stop by and thank you for what you're doing for the crew."

Pip and I looked at each other. "Us, Captain?"

Mr. Maxwell added his two creds worth with a dramatic sigh. "Yes, you. The polite response would have been to say, 'Thank you, Captain,' but I suppose that would be too much to ask."

"Thank you, Captain," Pip and I spoke together.

The captain smiled at us. "I'll be frank. When I first heard about this idea, and that you two scalawags were involved, I had my doubts. But already it has improved morale aboard the ship. You boys are doing a good thing and even if it all comes crashing down when we get to St. Cloud, the progress you've already made in breaking barriers between our various divisions is astonishing. So, I've come to thank you on behalf of the ship. Good trading, gentlemen."

"Thank you, Captain," we replied in unison again.

She nodded to Mr. Maxwell and left.

After she had gone Mr. Maxwell turned his attention back to us. "Well, lads, I think that about sums it up. You're in business. If you'll tell me how many of the days we're in port you'll be using, I'll have Mr. von Ickles message the orbital on behalf of the co-op. Then you'll be off and running."

Pip had the numbers all ready. "We're due to dock tomorrow afternoon and the schedule says we're pulling out in the morning five days later so we'd like the four full days we have in port, please."

Mr. Maxwell nodded. "Easily done. You probably already know the St. Cloud Orbital has the same rental agreement as you found in Margary. I believe it's the same subcontractor operating both markets actually."

Pip nodded. "Yes, sar, and the same company has Dunsany Roads' Orbital as well."

I added the specifics of what we'd need to the list. "Sar, could you request the booth, two standard tables, and two chairs? The rental agreements listed those options and it should come to sixteen creds per day for a total of sixty-four creds."

He nodded. "Of course, Mr. Wang. Will that be the standard configuration?"

I nodded and Pip answered, "Yes, sar, We have a total of seventeen crew planning on using the booth over the four days and at least three consignments which should cover that amount and then some."

I had one more piece of business. "We took a collection and have a hundred creds as seed money to open the accounts with."

Mr. Maxwell smiled and shook his head. "That's not necessary. You already have a hundred and forty creds in your balance."

Pip asked before I could. "Where did that come from, sar?"

He smiled and, I'm not sure if I was just getting used to his grin, but for once it wasn't frightening. "Forty came from you, Mr. Carstairs, back on Margary. The other hundred came from Lois."

Chapter Twenty-eight
St. Cloud Orbital: 2352-February-17

We docked at the St. Cloud Orbital right on schedule and the captain declared liberty almost immediately. By prior arrangement, Pip took Biddy and Rhon to scope out the flea market and rent a locker so we could have secure storage nearby.

Cookie and I made a pasta bake and garlic bread for the evening buffet. We suspected that few people would be aboard for dinner except the few who had to be. Everything was ready by 1600.

"Cookie? When was the last time you went out for dinner?"

He stopped wiping down the counter and thought for a long time. "I confess it has been a while, young Ishmael. Why do you ask?"

"Because tonight would be a good opportunity for you to go. Dinner is all prepared and just needs to be put out. The dessert is already warming in the oven. You deserve a night out. You should go. I can solo one dinner service especially on a first night in port."

Cookie cocked his head to one side as he considered the proposition. After a couple of ticks he smiled. "You are correct, young Ishmael, and there is an old friend who has a restaurant here. I'll do it," he said enthusiastically with a little nod of his head. "This is very thoughtful. Thank you." With that, he strolled out of the galley and left me alone with the pasta.

About then Bev stuck her head in the galley door. "Hey, Ish? You know you ran out of coffee out here, don't ya?"

I laughed and went to the mess to start a fresh urn of Sarabanda Dark, while we still had it.

When I finished I went back to the galley. It felt good to be there on my own and I took a few minutes to check out the stores Cookie and Pip had reserved for trade on St. Cloud. Almost all of the Sarabanda Dark was on the block as were about half of the mushrooms. In return we were restocking Arabasti and some root crops which stored well in any cool, dark space as well as a lot of fresh greens. They decided to fill the extra freezer with lamb and a local fish called munta. It was sort of a cross between a salmon and a sea bass in flavor. The lamb would give us a welcome break from the beefalo, and had the added benefit of being Cookie's favorite meat. He was sure to have many recipes that would feature it prominently.

Pip had calculated that after all the trades cleared and the ship was restocked we would break even with consumption, basically eating free since Margary. Cookie thought we were actually down about a kilocred. Either way, their trading turned out to be a marvelously effective way to feed the crew well, while still reducing overall costs.

The ship's container turned out even better. Pip's assessment had been right on the mark. Mr. Maxwell stocked up on four different mushroom varieties, not just one. The value of almost a full container netted the ship more than two hundred kilocreds. They even sold the beefalo rugs for another ten. I wondered if the crew knew that Pip almost single-handedly threw an extra two hundred ten kilocreds into the profit pool. Not all of that would be distributed to share, but still, everyone would benefit from Pip's astute trading skills.

Just then, the timer beeped and I started setting out dinner on the buffet. Comforting feelings washed over me carried by the warmth of the pasta and the wonderful smell of the garlic bread. Cheerful greetings from the crew who came for dinner added to my good mood—I could sure do worse.

Right near the end of dinner Pip came in, wearing a shipsuit that had seen better days. He grabbed some food and sat down with me.

I eyed him with a frown. "What did you get into?"

"Wet paint," he said between bites. Holding up his hands he showed me black splotches and dirty fingernails. "It'll be dry by morning, though."

"So, how does the flea market look?"

He slurped a little coffee before answering, "Excellent. Just perfect. There's a lot of fleece items but also some very nice leathers—goat as well as sheep—and a good supply of carved wood. I didn't see any stonemasons or metal workers so the buckles and gems should sell well. The clientele seems to be pretty upscale, but I guess that's because shepherds can't afford the ticket up on the shuttle."

"Sounds about like we anticipated."

He nodded again and sat back with his drink in hand. "Cookie has his stores lined up and they should be coming in over the next couple of days. The empty container may stay that way leaving here. We really can't make much on raw wool and there are no commercial quantities of textiles available." He shrugged. "Sometimes winning involves just getting to the next port."

Dinner mess ended and Pip helped me clean up. I brewed a fresh half urn of coffee before we headed for the gym. I had a good work out, but it occurred to me that I hadn't seen Sandy since just before the deck exam, and she wasn't on the track. Pip and I had the sauna to ourselves as well. First nights in port really made the *Lois* feel large and empty.

❀　　❀　　❀

The next morning I got up when I heard Pip heading for the galley. I didn't need to leave for the flea market quite that early, but I wanted to go with the first group. Pip and I had packed all our goods into a duffel the night before. We had permission from the co-op to pool our sales for the purposes of the cap since neither of us had individual items. It's not like the bag weighed much, but I had planned to use the grav pallet just because it would feel posh.

I headed down to the galley and while Pip set up the omelet station I made fresh coffee and put some biscuits in to bake. When Cookie showed up, he was smiling broadly. "Good morning, gentlemen. You do my old heart good by coming in and setting up perfectly without being told." He sighed happily. "It's been a long time since the galley has been such a well-oiled machine."

"Did you have a nice evening out?" I asked.

"Yes, young Ishmael, it was lovely. I visited one of my countrymen who has an establishment on level five. We had grilled lamb, couscous, and strong tea. We talked until the early morning. I feel tired but am glad that I went. Did all go well here?"

I nodded. "Oh yeah, dinner was easy. No problems."

"And today is the official commencement of your new trading empire?"

Pip and I laughed. I shook my head. "Well, perhaps not a trading empire, but we're at least going to try to turn a little profit."

Pip made me an omelet and I poured coffee for everybody. I still had a few minutes before the mess deck opened officially so I settled down with my breakfast. It would probably be a while before I would have another chance to eat.

By the time I'd finished a few of the crew had lined up at Pip's station. I took my plate and cup out to the dishwasher and stacked them there.

Cookie called to me as I was leaving, "Best of luck."

Pip looked over his shoulder and saluted with his spatula. "Keep me posted."

I was still chuckling as I reached the berthing area and changed into my civvies. My clothes were getting—not worn exactly—but certainly tired. My good boots weren't anything compared to some of the footwear I'd seen in the last six months. My jacket was little more than an outdated windbreaker. My pants weren't special either, what my mother called, "good, solid trousers."

I put them on because that's all I had, but I started to realize why people dressed up when changing into their own civvies. As nicely made and practical as shipsuits were, months of wearing them on a daily basis made putting on anything else kinda special. If I got new clothes I'd have to get rid of these, or take a hit to my mass allotment. I understood now why so many people did exactly that.

I saw the boy toy belt hanging in the back of the locker and, with a sudden burst of daring, stripped off my old, perfectly adequate belt and buckled on the supple leather with its gold metal and black dragon. I looked at myself in the mirror, and if I were being perfectly honest, the new belt looked out of place. It didn't go with the rest of the outfit at all. It did, however, go with me. So I kept it on.

I scooped up the duffel, slammed my locker, and headed for the cargo lock. I got there just after 0700 and found a crowd had gathered. I walked up to see what they were looking at and burst out laughing.

When we first received the grav pallet from Mr. Cotton, I could see why it had been slated for salvage. It had been pretty torn up and would only lift about half its rated capacity. Not that it would matter for our purposes, since its normal load was mea-sured in kilotons and we only needed it to carry a few dozen ki-los. Freshly painted a rich, matte black, the pallet looked almost new. A uniform layer of pristine, gray skid-grid covered the top, which had been scarred by dropped loads and untold cargo calami-ties. It was the same nubby, rubbery matting used in cargo entries and engineering spaces where good footing was important. Along the skirting on all four sides, somebody had stenciled McKendrick Mercantile Cooperative in gray paint that matched the skid-grid. Judging from the smudges on Biddy Murphy's cheek, I could guess who'd done that. The black told me where Pip had found wet paint the day before. A stack of gear already waited on the pallet, including a basket with the banner and table coverings. I added my duffel to the pile and we all stood there looking at it for a few ticks before Rhon, the morning's booth manager, took the tow handle and pushed the pallet out the lock.

I stood there watching them go and really didn't know what I felt. This crazy group of people headed out on an adventure that was no more exotic than a yard sale. The gray-haired members of our merry band seemed to be having as much fun as the younger ones. The scene felt all the more surreal when I considered that in their real life, when not selling trinkets at a flea market, they sailed a deep space leviathan between the stars. It sounded romantic, but it wasn't exciting. It was just their job.

"You'd better hurry, Ishmael, or they'll leave you behind."

I turned to see the captain standing there watching the parade streaming out of her ship and across the orbital's dock. "Aye, aye, Captain. By your leave?" I saluted for what might have been my first time since signing The Articles.

The captain grinned and returned the salute. "Carry on, Mr. Wang. Carry on."

As I stepped through the lock, I swore I heard Lois laughing.

The Golden Age of the Solar Clipper

Quarter Share

Half Share

Full Share

Double Share

Captains Share

Owners Share

South Coast

Tanyth Fairport Adventures

Ravenwood

Zypherias Call

Awards

2011 Parsec Award Winner for Best Speculative Fiction
(Long Form) for *Owners Share*

2010 Parsec Award Winner for Best Speculative Fiction
(Long Form) for *Captains Share*

2009 Podiobooks Founders Choice Award for Captains Share

2009 Parsec Award Finalist for Best Speculative Fiction
(Long Form) for *Double Share*

2008 Podiobooks Founders Choice Award for *Double Share*

2008 Parsec Award Finalist for Best Speculative Fiction
(Long Form) for *Full Share*

2008 Parsec Award Finalist for Best Speculative Fiction
(Long Form) for *South Coast*

Contact

Website: nathanlowell.com
Twitter: twitter.com/nlowell
Email: nathan.lowell@gmail.com

About The Author

Nathan Lowell first entered the literary world by podcasting his novels. The Golden Age of the Solar Clipper grew from his life-long fascination with space opera and his own experiences shipboard in the United States Coast Guard. Unlike most works which focus on a larger-than-life hero, Nathan centers on the people behind the scenes—ordinary men and women trying to make a living in the depths of interstellar space. In his novels, there are no bug-eyed monsters, or galactic space battles, instead he paints a richly vivid and realistic world where the hero uses hard work and his own innate talents to improve his station and the lives of those of his community.

Dr. Nathan Lowell holds a Ph.D. in Educational Technology with specializations in Distance Education and Instructional Design. He also holds an M.A. in Educational Technology and a BS in Business Administration. He grew up on the south coast of Maine and is strongly rooted in the maritime heritage of the sea-farer. He served in the USCG from 1970 to 1975, seeing duty aboard a cutter on hurricane patrol in the North Atlantic and at a communications station in Kodiak, Alaska. He currently lives in the plains east of the Rocky Mountains with his wife and two daughters.